Praise for
I, in the Shadows

"Bovalino has reeled me in once again with her loving and nuanced character work—two flawed, emotionally complex teenagers trying to make sense of the strange tangle of life, death, and love. She deftly folded all-too-real topics like addiction and complex family dynamics into the otherworldly elements, offering readers a story that is engaging, funny, and bittersweet."

Erica Waters, author of *The River Has Teeth* and *All That Consumes Us*

"*I, In the Shadows* made me feel so much! Drew, Liam and Hannah are charming and complicated, and their story is haunting, healing, and imbued with deep emotional truths."

Vanessa Len, author of the Only a Monster series

"*I, in the Shadows* is a deeply moving exploration of grief and love in all its forms – and I swallowed it whole! Drew and Liam are heartbreakingly compelling, as they try to grapple with the messy aftermath of death. It's gloriously haunting and human, all at once."

Georgia Summers, #1 *Sunday Times*-bestselling author of *The City of Stardust*

"A haunting meditation on loss, guilt, and the ghosts we create from our own desperation."

Kirkus

"[I]n this pensive horror novel by Bovalino [...][,] charged romantic chemistry and [...] sparkling banter brighten a sometimes somber narrative that thoughtfully and sensitively addresses issues of grief and loss."

Publishers Weekly

Praise for
My Throat an Open Grave

"Raw, brutal and heartbreaking in turn, Bovalino
masterfully weaves deliciously sinister horror with
unflinching, complex themes. I am in awe."

Kat Dunn, author of *Bitterthorn*

"A deliciously creepy, haunting exploration of love,
hate, and what it means to forgive yourself."

Kate Dylan, author of *Mindwalker*

"Whimsical, dark, and acutely painful. This is a story that will
reach into your soul, pull taut, and make itself at home there."

M. K. Lobb, author of the Seven
Faceless Saints duology

"Propulsive, original, and deeply compelling, *My Throat an
Open Grave* whisked me straight into the dark and mysterious
realm of the Lord of the Wood, where nothing was quite what
I expected. A fascinating blend of folk horror and fairytale,
just as I've come to expect from the talented Bovalino."

Erica Waters, author of *The River Has Teeth*

"Sweet as honey and brutal as a knife—Bovalino has
crafted a parable of self-forgiveness and community
power fearsome enough to drive men and gods, alike,
to their knees. If only all vengeance could be so lush."

GennaRose Nethercott, author of *Thistlefoot*

Praise for
Not Good for Maidens

"With equal measures of terror and tenderness, Tori Bovalino crafts a vivid story as alluring as the taste of goblin fruit."

Lyndall Clipstone, author of *Lakesedge* and *Forestfall*

"A spellbinding dark fantasy of generational magic and mischief. With haunting prose, this riveting tale will hold you captive like the call of the Goblin Market itself."

Rosiee Thor, author of *Fire Becomes Her* and *Tarnished are the Stars*

"Even though I know the Goblin Market is full of human body parts, I still wanna visit! *Not Good for Maidens* was a compelling read and I would love another book set in this world."

Erica Waters, author of *The River Has Teeth* and *The Restless Dark*

"A beautifully imagined examination of the bonds that tie sisters, friends, families, and lovers [...] A violent and voluptuous adventure."

Kirkus

"Bovalino constantly keeps you wanting more, drawing you into this blood-drenched world where every action has consequences and everything has its price. Her writing is stunning in every way."

The Nerd Daily

"*Not Good for Maidens* is a violent and magical coming of age tale."

Paste Magazine

Praise for
The Devil Makes Three

"Bovalino delivers an ink-splattered love letter to old books
and dark academia. Wicked and sharp as a pen stroke,
this is a delight for library goths—me included."

A. J. Hackwith, author of *The Library of the Unwritten*

"A glorious, darkly atmospheric journey into the disturbing
power of books, ink and the horrors that live inside them."

Tasha Suri, author of *The Jasmine Throne*

"A spine-tingling, entrancing read. *The Devil Makes Three* is
the perfect blend of supernatural horror and contemporary
gothic, with each page as heart-pounding as the next.
Tori Bovalino is an absolute master at atmosphere."

Chloe Gong, *New York Times* bestselling
author of *These Violent Delights*

"A perfect blend of gothic terror, slow-burn romance,
and irreverent humor—this novel is a must-read.
I loved every page and paragraph of it."

Joshua Phillip Johnson, author of *The Forever Sea*

"Grimoires, demons, and a creepy school library
make this dark academia sure to keep readers up
at night. I couldn't put this book down."

Kristen Ciccarelli, internationally
bestselling author of *The Last Namsara*

"Bovalino's debut crackles. Dripping with dark atmosphere,
The Devil Makes Three is perfect for fans of Leigh Bardugo's
Ninth House. Make sure to read this with the lights on!"

Erin A. Craig, *New York Times* bestselling
author of *House of Salt and Sorrows*

I, IN THE SHADOWS

*Also by Tori Bovalino
and available from Titan Books*

The Devil Makes Three
Not Good for Maidens
My Throat an Open Grave

I, IN THE SHADOWS

TORI BOVALINO

TITAN BOOKS

I, in the Shadows
Print edition ISBN: 9781835416495
E-book edition ISBN: 9781835416518

Published by Titan Books
A division of Titan Publishing Group Ltd
144 Southwark Street, London SE1 0UP
www.titanbooks.com

First edition: January 2026
10 9 8 7 6 5 4 3 2 1

This is a work of fiction. All of the characters, organizations, and events portrayed in this novel are either products of the author's imagination or are used fictitiously. Any resemblance to actual persons, living or dead (except for satirical purposes), is entirely coincidental.

© Tori Bovalino 2026
Published by arrangement with Page Street Publishing Co.

Tori Bovalino asserts the moral right to be
identified as the author of this work.

No part of this publication may be reproduced, stored in a retrieval system, or transmitted, in any form or by any means without the prior written permission of the publisher, nor be otherwise circulated in any form of binding or cover other than that in which it is published and without a similar condition being imposed on the subsequent purchaser.

Not for sale within the United States of America,
the Republic of the Philippines and Canada.

A CIP catalogue record for this title is available from the British Library.

EU RP (for authorities only)
eucomply OÜ, Pärnu mnt. 139b-14, 11317 Tallinn, Estonia
hello@eucompliancepartner.com, +3375690241

Designed and typeset in Adobe Garamond Pro by Richard Mason.

Printed and bound by CPI Group (UK) Ltd, Croydon CR0 4YY.

For Becca
In honor of the impossible projects
May they never find us again <3

CHAPTER 1

"The exorcism didn't work," I say into the phone, held not-so-securely between my cheek and shoulder as I fumble with my key with one hand and try not to drop the stack of library books teetering in the other. The stack is a mix of things: books on ghosts and ESP, a Bible, a Quran, a Torah, and a beat-up library copy of *The Grapes of Wrath*.

I'm covering my bases here. And to be clear: The Steinbeck is for English class, not exorcisms. I don't think this is a problem I can solve with breast milk.

Finding the house key is a problem, but it's a problem of my own making. My key ring is cluttered with keys to our old house (which probably no longer work); one to my best friend Andie's house (definitely works, but is approximately eighty miles away); my car key (works, accessible, rarely used); Dad's office (works, stolen); and Bee's bakery (works, also stolen).

On the other end of the line, Reece snorts. "I told you it wouldn't," they say. I hear a rustle of pages—they're probably studying. I'm probably interrupting. The last thing they probably want to talk about is ghosts.

"You're the one who told me to handle it myself," I grumble.

"Bro, have you ever seen *me* do an exorcism?"

I drop my keys, groan, and kneel to retrieve them, tipping over the stack of books in the process. At this point, I think it's brave of me that I don't curl up on the front porch and give up. It's one of those days.

"Oh," Reece says, ignorant to my suffering. "How was the Stats test?"

"NOPE!" I gather up my books, my keys, and finally find the right one. The door creaks ominously as it opens, but that's not much of an omen when I already know the place is haunted. And possibly cursed.

The sound would tip off Bee and Dad that I'm home, but neither of them are here. If they were, I would not be talking about exorcisms so openly. I would also, unfortunately for all involved, be answering way more questions about the Stats test.

"But the ghost," I say, redirecting with all my might as I drop my backpack and leave the stack of books on the table in the hall. "Do you know of anything else that will help? That will *work*?"

"Not an exorcism."

"Thanks. Genius advice."

Reece is quiet for a moment. Usually, they're the one who . . . well, *does* anything about ghosts. We can both see them. We've both always been able to see them. But I prefer to ignore them, whereas Reece has always taken a more hands-on approach.

Unfortunately, due to proximity, there's no avoiding this particular ghost—and if he does degrade in the way ghosts do, it could lead to a dangerous situation for me if I leave him alone. It's one of those moments where I feel Reece's absence keenly.

My sibling has a much stronger understanding of ghosts than I do, and also a much better moral code. Even after . . . well, my entire life, I'm not sure if I've mastered the compass points just yet.

I hang my keys on the strip of hooks by the door and make my way to the kitchen, the wooden floorboards creaking with every step. The house itself is really not *that* old. Our last place was an early nineteenth-century farmhouse. This house is bright, airy, and open-concept downstairs with big rooms and good closets upstairs. It's everything Bee and Dad always wanted.

We've only been here for about a month, so I'm in that weird phase in which everything about it is pseudo-familiar: the creaking of the floors in every room, worst on the stairs; the scratching of the trees against the windows at night; the far-off whistle of the trains as they pass through, headed for Ohio or across Pennsylvania.

Oh, yeah. And the fucking *ghost*.

He's not here as I pull down a box of cereal, hop up on the counter, and eat it dry by the handful, as Reece still sighs and mutters on the line.

The ghost tends to prefer my bedroom (it's very inconvenient for both of us), which leads me to believe that it was once *his* bedroom.

(You don't have to tell me I'm a genius. When it comes to ghostbusting, I am a top student.)

(I can't say the same for real school.)

But back to the bedroom thing. To be clear, he's not a creeper ghost, from what I can tell. He doesn't watch me change, or leer, or do anything else that one would suspect of a semi-visible teenage boy now sharing a bedroom with a fully visible teenage girl. Who knows. Maybe he's queer too. Maybe he likes running. Maybe he also is kind of bad at school. Maybe, if we were living in the same timeline, any of those things would be in the center of our little Venn diagram.

Maybe we would even be friends.

Finally, Reece sighs. "I wouldn't usually recommend this," they say, their tone taking on a hint of dubiousness, "but have you tried *talking* to him?"

Now, it's my turn to snort. Unfortunately, I do it around a mouthful of dry Cheerios, which leads to a lot of coughing and sputtering, which lessens the effect when I say, "Isn't that breaking, like, Reece Tarpin's Rule Number One of Ghost Management?"

"Drew—" Reece starts.

"Maybe Rule One is 'do not bang a ghost,'" I speculate, this time with less choking on Cheerios.

"*Drew*—"

"Or 'no kissing ghosts?' But I'm pretty sure you broke that one with—"

"*ANDREA PENELOPE TARPIN*," Reece shouts. "DO YOU WANT MY HELP OR NOT?"

I press my lips together. Stop swinging my feet. Set the cereal box down. ". . . Yes."

Reece sighs, and I can just imagine them pinching the bridge of their nose, eyes closed, trying to tamp down the frustration. I cause this expression a lot, so the image of it comes easily—along with that fierce ache of missing them. Reece is a freshman in college at Boston University, and they moved at the end of the summer, a couple of weeks before Dad and Bee and me relocated here. I'm still not used to the emptiness of my life without Reece's constant presence—and Reece's constant willingness to step in and take the lead on anything ghostly.

But let's get one thing straight: I am not asking for Reece's help because I'm *afraid* of this ghost, okay? Fear has nothing to do with it. I just don't like him, and I don't want him in my room, and I am a growing girl, and I should be allowed my space and privacy.

Plus, he's very judgmental, which I can tell because he makes weird faces at me at night when I'm doing my ab routine. I find it very disruptive.

And when Reece is in charge, they just . . . usually go away on their own. Or with gentle convincing from light rituals. They are not usually this persistent.

Enter: Reece.

"I'm video-calling you," Reece says, resigned. "Switch over."

I pull the phone from my face and accept the video request. Reece's face floats up, too close for a moment, their nose and septum piercing and top lip swimming on my screen before they back up. I scan over their freckles and shorn red hair—the shock of copper is the only thing we share between us that Dad does not also have—before focusing in on their brown eyes, still a bit tired.

"Take me to the ghost."

"You won't be able to—"

"Just do it, mmkay? You're the one who wanted my help."

I sigh, but I take Reece with me upstairs. I also nearly die on the way when I trip over my backpack, discarded on the first step, and I am annoyed to find that, for a brief moment, I understand why Dad is always getting on my case to hang it up or put it in my room.

It's the worst kind of self-betrayal to find that I agree with my parents' nagging, even for a second.

Reece doesn't say anything until we're in my room with the door shut behind us. Then, they shout, scaring me out of my skin: *"HEY GHOSTIE. IT'S DREW'S BIG SIBLING. SQUARE UP."*

"*Reece*," I say, aghast.

But *something* in it works. My eyes snap to a corner, where the bed is pushed against the wall: For the barest moment, the air shimmers, and then the boy appears.

He's sitting on the bed, back against the wall, one knee tented, arm thrown over it. He died wearing jeans and a short-sleeved top with three buttons at the throat, all open. He's white, I think, with dark hair and brown eyes and a beaky nose keeping up his glasses. He looks a little nerdy but also kind of nice—not the sort of kid you'd think of dying at seventeen or eighteen or whatever age he was when he kicked it.

He also looks mega bored. I would probably feel the same, if I were dead for an indeterminate amount of time and unable to communicate with the living.

I turn the phone around. I'm not sure if Reece can see him over the video call, but it doesn't much matter. Reece is good at playing things off, and they know the ghost is there. If I can see it, of course it's there.

The thing is, I *did* want to solve this on my own. All our lives, Reece has been the one who cared more about ghosts (see: when the going gets tough, I get avoiding) and knew how to deal with them. And when they lived with us, it was easy to let that be their thing, to let every little issue fall under Reece's remit. But Reece is in Massachusetts, and I doubt they'll be coming back—in the last few weeks, I've watched them talk about home less and less as they've made new friends and gotten used to Boston.

I can't even blame them. The world is a bit shit right now—I'm proud they're finding what space they can, carving safety and protection into it.

Either way, I thought that working through the ghost issue would make us closer. Bridge that gap that's been building between us since Reece left. But they told me to figure it out, and I—well. I reached for the exorcism when I probably shouldn't have.

But in my defense, it's actually very creepy to share space with a ghost. They don't really knock when they want to come in—right now, the ghost and I can't communicate at all, which means he spends his sentient hours staring at me from the corner like I kicked his puppy.

Reece is good at making them go away, solving their problems and cutting their ties to the mortal world before sending them peacefully into the afterlife. Fixing the mess before well-mannered ghosts degrade into angry husks. I am patently not, and that's what's getting me into trouble. And yes, maybe I did go straight for an exorcism on purpose—because if I failed, I knew that Reece would have no choice but to help me. Selfish? Possibly.

I just . . . I really miss them. This might be a shitty bonding experience, but it's better than *nothing*.

"Ready to do this, Dree?" Reece asks me.

I press my lips together, glaring at the ghost so he doesn't get any ideas. Reece is the only one who calls me Dree (and the only one who is allowed)—a shortening for Andrea, which annoys me. Everyone else calls me Drew, because my best friend, another Andrea, took Andie first.

"Ready as I'll ever be," I grumble.

The ghost cocks an eyebrow. He doesn't look pleased, either, but that might have something to do with the failed exorcism that happened last time I saw him.

Yeah, I doubt he's forgiven me for that yet.

"Look," I say, trying to soften my voice a bit. "I'm sorry about . . . the whole holy water thing. I am just trying to help you move on, okay?"

He frowns, unconvinced.

"Just do it," Reece mutters on the line.

I stick out a hand. If he comes forward, touches me, then I can bring him back into corporeality. Meld my spirit to his, even temporarily. And I'll be able to hear him properly, to know what he wants.

Reece is really good at it. They can listen to a ghost, figure out what they want, and get them moving on in record speed. It would never take my sibling three weeks to deal with a ghost.

But I hate the squidginess of it, the vulnerability. Reece taught me how to do this when I was ten, and I've only done it a couple of times since then.

When you open yourself to a ghost, you always take a bit of them, too—and I hate knowing those deaths, feeling the shattered fractals of their memories, and not being able to put them down. Not being able to forget them, when the ghosts do move on.

Sure, they don't become husks, the angry remnants of a soul left behind. But I keep the other half of memories no one else will ever share: the sweet bite of an apple in springtime eighty years ago, and the first kiss with someone's wife, and the feeling of dirt in my hand as someone buried their mother, and the taste of blood in my mouth as someone wrecked a car. It's all there, still mine, even though they were never really my memories to begin with.

He regards the hand, then looks up at me. I know his name—when I moved in, small town that this is, everyone was stepping over themselves to tell me about the dead kid who lived here before—but I don't want to think it now, when he could be in my brain soon.

"It will help," I say. "I'll stop trying to get rid of you."

He tilts his head, a question there. He stopped trying to talk to me after the first week, when it was clear I couldn't hear.

That doesn't mean I've stopped talking *at* him. Small things—announcing my presence when I come in, or reminding him that I can't hear him, or apologizing for failing at exorcisms.

"And if she can't," Reece says, "I might be able to."

He looks doubtful, but he shifts forward. Gets off the bed. He doesn't need to walk, one foot in front of the other, but he does. He could just float, or appear wherever he needs to go, but I learned early on that he's not very good at being a ghost.

"I won't hurt you," I say.

He rolls his eyes. Takes my hand. I take a deep breath, reaching for not just his hand, but the shadow of his soul still here on this mortal plane.

It's like surfacing from underwater, bringing him back into being. Like tasting every second of his seventeen years, two months, twenty-two days, eight hours, seventeen minutes, and eight seconds on my tongue, all those vague reminders of who he is hitting all at once—and I can't hold back his name anymore.

"You *can't* hurt me," the ghost of Liam Orville says. "I'm already dead."

WELCOME TO THE AFTERLIFE, PLAYER ONE
PLEASE ENTER YOUR NAME

                                                          Liam Orville

WHAT ARE YOU AFRAID OF?

                                                              ... death?

HA! TOO LATE FOR THAT!

                                          What is this, actually?

GAME LOADING...
        Should I understand what's happening right now?

WHAT ARE YOU AFRAID OF, Liam Orville?

                                                                  I don't know

WHAT ARE YOU AFRAID OF, Liam Orville?

                                                              I don't know!

WHAT ARE YOU AFRAID OF, Liam Orville?
        Ceasing. Stopping. Ending. I don't know, seriously.

SURVEY SAYS: THAT'S A LIE!
                                What is this? What am I doing?

WHAT ARE YOU AFRAID OF, Liam Orville?
                Being forgotten. Being left behind. By my family.
                        Friends. By her. By everyone.

SUCCESS!
LEVEL 2 LOADING...

CHAPTER 2

The first thing that comes to me is not his death—that happens more often than not, which is part of the reason I really, *really* didn't want to do this—or his most treasured memory. For a half-second, I'm Liam, sitting back in a desk chair in this room, and I feel . . . well, alive, for one thing. And happy. I lean back in my chair, feet resting on the edge of the bed, and I feel that all-too-familiar scrape of the chair back on the wall as I turn to face *you* and—

He was in this room, back when it was his room. My gaze trips to that scuff on the wall, a black mark against the cream paint, and I can physically feel the routine of Liam leaning back in his desk chair. How he changed the topography of this room with his physicality: the scuff on the wall, yes, but also the sections of lighter paint, where pictures and posters hung on the wall, and the circle of a water spot on the windowsill where he must've once left a glass or watered a plant, warping the paint. Dead or not, Liam is in every bit of this room.

It's probably why he's still here. That, and his age when he died. It's easier for younger ones to stick around—more vitality there. More tragedy. More meat to chew on that can convert easily to a restless spirit.

I cut the memory off as soon as I can, taking back control. It doesn't stop the physical reaction; I'm breathing hard. My heart races in my chest. Gooseflesh pebbles over my arms, and I drop his hand.

It's okay. I don't need the contact now that I've let him in.

I set Reece up against the desk so they can see us (if they can see Liam at all, that is). Reece takes over, because if I had my way, I'd banish all ghosts without a conversation. Easier that way—less fraught.

It doesn't leave space for camaraderie, either, or getting to know them, or having any affection for them whatsoever. All of that—all things involving ghosts, really—is firmly in Reece's wheelhouse.

"Right," Reece says, all business. It's clear why they're studying to become a lawyer—they've always been assertive, confident, good at laying down the law, with a brain that rivals Dad's. For a second, I feel that odd, unfounded ache of jealousy. "Let's figure out why you're still here."

Liam raises an eyebrow. "It's *my* house."

"Not anymore," I mutter. Reece ignores me. My specialty in Reece's usual investigations, unfortunately, has never been helping ghosts—I've always been best at antagonizing them.

"But you can't stay here," Reece says.

"I don't see why not," Liam answers. "Considering I was here first."

"Yean, *not* how this works," I say, earning another look from my sibling. But for all of the antagonizing I'm doing, Reece isn't pushing it far enough.

Liam crosses his hands over his chest. "Well, I'm not leaving."

I mirror his posture. Liam is taller than me by a few inches, but there's no beating around the bush: That boy has not worked out a day in his life, and when I cross my arms, his gaze flicks to my biceps for the briefest moment. There's that look again, the one he has when he appears and finds me doing pull-ups in the doorframe, and he looks like he has the worst luck in the world.

"You don't get to call the shots anymore," I say. "You're dead."

"Drew—" Reece starts. Reminding a ghost of their own inexistence is usually a bad call, because it can piss them off, and a pissed-off ghost can lead to a few things: poltergeist-like behavior, flickering lights, and broken vases and windows. They only bring so much energy with them into this liminal area; let's face it, they're already a dying ember. So causing Liam to feel anything too powerful could speed up his degradation into a husk, and a husk is unfortunately a much bigger problem than a ghost.

And, yeah, that bad energy? It gives off a kind of call, and sometimes whatever comes seeking that bad energy is a whole lot worse than the ghost we started out with.

"I'm well aware," Liam says sharply. I draw a breath, feeling the crackling of energy in the air—but nothing breaks. Nothing shatters. And besides a few lengthening shadows, nothing else comes.

I make an effort to calm myself as Reece says, "Look. I know the situation is not ideal. But hanging around here is not going to fix anything, nor is it going to make you feel better. How about you think about what could possibly be keeping you here, and what would help you move on, and we can reconvene? Drew has done this before. She's good at helping spirits move on."

He eyes me dubiously. Perhaps I shouldn't blame him for that. I try to make my expression plaintive, open.

Reece is also lying. Liam doesn't need to know that.

"I'll think about it," Liam says finally. "But in the meantime, can we come to an agreement on one thing?"

"Yeah?" Reece says.

"No more exorcisms."

I sigh. My sibling sighs louder. I know, after we hang up, they'll text me with a big, well-deserved *I told you so*.

There's no point just telling Reece they should've helped me in the first place. They want me to fight my own battles, which I know is a part of growing up. Unfortunately, for most kids, "fighting your own battles" doesn't mean "putting up with your own ghosts."

"Yeah," I say. "We can try this without any more exorcisms."

Liam nods. "Then I'll think about it," he says, "and I'll let you know."

It's shockingly reasonable—reasonable enough for Reece to agree, and for Liam to disappear. When he's gone, they give me a long, level look.

"I thought you said you'd handle it," Reece says.

I roll my eyes, flopping back onto my ghost-free bed. "I said I'd *try*. But I told you at the beginning—I want nothing to do with it. Ghosts aren't my thing."

"You can't just decide if they're your *thing* or not, Dree. Ghosts are a fact of life—and you are one of very few people who can make a difference."

I roll my eyes. It's an argument we've had so many times that it's worn-in, like the steps of a dance I don't even need to think about anymore.

"If you would've just helped in the first place—"

"What did you want me to do? Drive ten hours? Not happening. Not when I *know* you know what to do."

"I don't!" I insist.

"Bullshit," Reece says. When I glance over at the phone, they're not even looking at me anymore.

"But I don't want to," I say.

"Yeah, and I'm sure Liam Orville doesn't *want* to be dead," they snap. It's a diversion from the dance, a stumble. They sigh and set their pen down, then rub their eyes.

"Okay," Reece says. "Let's talk through it, then. What do you need to do?"

I'm quiet for a long time, staring up at the ceiling. Maybe because I know that Reece is right, and it's my job to help Liam move on, even if it's the last thing I want to do. Maybe I'm waiting for the sound of the front door, for Bee or Dad to come home (though the likelihood of either coming home at 3:00 p.m. is slim to none) so I can hang up the phone with an excuse; Reece would never talk to me about ghosts if they were home.

"Dree," Reece prompts, soft and weary.

"Start from the end," I say. "Find out how he died. If there's trauma left, or unfinished business. If I can wrap that up, it will be easy."

And if not? Well.

"And his family?" Reece asks.

I sigh. "Tell no one what I'm doing. If I tell anyone about the ghost, that will only make it worse. Right?"

"Exposure to grief speeds up degradation," Reece says, like they're reciting from a textbook. "No friends. No family."

"Right."

"Great," Reece says. There's a long, weighted pause between us, like they're waiting for me to say something else. I just keep staring at the ceiling, watching the revolutions of the fan. Finally, "It's just, there's not much I can do from here, you know. I'm far—"

"I've got it," I say, probably a bit too sternly. "Thanks for the help." Before Reece can protest further, I hang up the call, then toss my phone across the room, onto the pile of not-dirty-enough-for-laundry-not-clean-enough-for-drawers pile in the corner.

The fan keeps spinning. My thoughts won't quiet. And above all, more than anything: I don't want to do this. I want nothing to do with ghosts, or Liam, or this whole help-him-move-on business. The sooner I can make him disappear, the better.

Dad and Bee are both home by six, and Bee orders pizza for dinner. "We've got to find new takeout," she laments, sorting through the flyers and junk mail that keep clogging up our mailbox. When the pizza comes, Dad tips the driver with a wrinkled twenty and the three of us sit on the couch in the living room, eating straight from the boxes. We still don't have a perfect routine for this house yet, partially because the kitchen table is still covered in boxes we're all ignoring, and partially because, before we moved out here, there were four of us and not three and none of us really know how to correct a routine in Reece's absence. There's a large gap between Dad and me on the couch even now, the sagging cushion where they used to sit, a space held for Reece even as they're hundreds of miles away.

"How was school?" Dad asks, wiping grease off his hands on a paper towel. This is the first time we're trying this pizza place, and I can see him frowning every time he dips back into the box. He hates grease on pizza, but Bee loves it, and it will be a thrilling adventure to see if this place makes it onto the auto-buy shortlist for future evenings: Will Dad's love of Bee outweigh his pizza preferences? It remains to be seen.

"Fine," I say. "I went to talk to the track coach. There's no track in the fall, and it's too late to join the cross-country team, but there's a club that does conditioning runs after school some days. I think I'll join that or something."

I don't tell them that, actually, it's *not* too late to join the cross-country team, and really, I have no intention to join track in the spring when it does pick up. When we moved here, I made a secret promise to myself to just be a person, to letting those things go. I can't really handle another year of Dad hoping I do well enough to get a scholarship to somewhere that overlooks academics—and I don't really want to deal with the rigid system of enforced practice and needing to be places.

I'll cool my heels for a year. There's no reason to get too involved with anything. And this club seems casual and non-competitive, and it'll maybe scratch some itch for socialization if I can work up the nerve to talk to anyone.

"Oh, that sounds great," Bee says, smiling in that easy, comforting way she does. She reaches for another slice of pizza, completely ignorant to the way Dad sighs as he reaches for another paper towel. "Oh, hey—your room."

I nearly choke on my pizza, certain for a second that she found the Bible and holy water I stashed in the bottom drawer of my desk. My parents don't actually know anything about what Reece and I can do—we discovered early on that ghosts fit into the List of Things We Should Not Tell Dad.

"What about it?"

"Do you want to paint or anything?"

The relief is sweet, and I take a bite of pizza to cover my hiccup. But then I'm thinking of that scuff on the wall, that streak of black. It was one of the first things I noticed, when I went inside the first time. There's something about it—I saw it, nearly a month ago, and I crossed the room to touch it, and I was hit with this overwhelming wall of sadness. Then I turned around and saw him. The boy. The ghost.

"Maybe," I say, but I don't think I can cover that little scuff, one of the last reminders that Liam Orville once lived in this house.

Damn—one dead kid in my bedroom, and I'm losing my edge.

"I could do a mural, if you want," Bee says. She reaches for another slice of pizza. The pepperoni has curled up at the edges, making little bowls for the grease.

"Ah, that would be cool," I say, and she smiles—but we both know I'm too indecisive for that. She offered to do a mural in my last room, too: It was one of the first things she offered when she moved in, when I was six and Reece was seven and a half. Reece took her up on it immediately, requesting a jungle. Their room quickly became a home for rich green leaves and stalking tigers and brightly colored birds, half-hidden in the painted foliage.

And mine? Well, that was almost nine years ago now, and I just never made up my mind.

After we're done with our pizza, we settle into our usual routine: Dad goes into his office to handle anything that has come up for his cases that needs to be handled urgently. Bee turns on whatever reality show she's in the middle of with the volume up loud—usually someone is getting married to someone they've never met, or engaged to someone they've never seen, or working on a yacht—and she and I head into the kitchen to tackle one of the table boxes.

Alone in the kitchen, she says, "The Stats test?"

I sigh, setting down the box of videos I just opened—I don't know why we brought them with us. We don't have anything to play them on anymore. If it were up to me, I'd just donate them all.

"Yeah. It was not great."

"How not great are we talking?"

I wince. "D+?"

"Ah."

I step away from the boxes and the table and glance over at Bee. "I'm trying," I tell her. "I'll figure it out. I'll fix it. Can you just . . . not tell Dad?"

Bee chews on her lip. "For now," she agrees. She leans back against the counter and opens her arms, and even though I'm taller than she is now, I walk into the circle of her arms and bury my head in her shoulder. Her arms wrap around me, carving out a safe haven that smells like vanilla and flour and sugar and the lemon-scented cleaner she uses at Bakerbee. Her curls tickle my nose.

Bee isn't my mom. Our mom left when we were little kids. We saw her a couple of times, but I barely remember her—the memories come more in flashes and glimpses of things she might've said and done. In TV shows and movies, it always is such a big thing: the mother who isn't there, the absence she's left behind, the unfillable ache. But Dad has always been so good that it's not like I felt the absence, or maybe I just never knew differently, and then he started bringing Bee around, and it was like our little family made even more sense.

For me, at least. I know Reece loves Bee, but I can't be certain they feel the same. It does help, though, that Dad put us through lots and lots of therapy.

"It's an adjustment," she murmurs, her hands stroking down my back. "You've done so well, and given up so much—your dad and I are both proud of you and grateful for the person you are. You'll figure it out, and we're here to help."

"I know," I say, but that's not really how it works for me. It's not like I'll just suddenly "figure out" Stats or Gov or English. I can't just "figure out" school. It's a necessity, and knowing Dad, so is college, even though I can't imagine putting myself through even more learning after this whole hell of high school is over.

There were a lot of reasons why we moved, and all of them are boring. Dad has worked for a big firm in Pittsburgh for years, pretty much since he and Bee have been married, which meant an almost two-hour commute for him. But in the spring, a bakery space here in Pine Hollow opened up, and it only made sense for Bee to take it, for us to relocate. Now, Bakerbee is just five minutes down the road, and Dad's job is a thirty-minute drive, even with traffic, and Reece was already going to Boston anyway.

The only variable was me and my senior year—and it's not like moving would make me less close with Andie. Plus, pretty much every school around here has a track team. It was an obvious decision on my part to push for the move.

Bee pulls back, kisses my forehead. "I'm proud of you, you know," she says.

I snort. "Why?"

"For existing," she says, "or something sappy like that."

I poke her hard in the ribs, and she laughs, and then we go back to the box. We hide the videotapes in the basement. (One would think the basement is the creepiest and most haunted place in the house, but I have never seen Liam down here, so the weirdest thing is the "Pittsburgh toilet" (a freestanding toilet in the basement, just there, by itself, which I have been assured is a regional staple. Jury's out.)

When we're done, I go upstairs and do my pull-ups and crunches and push-ups and squats. Liam doesn't appear to judge me or speak to me, which is fine. For one night, I can pretend to be normal.

It's the last night the illusion can last for a long, long time.

CHAPTER 3

There's a line of cars when we pull up in the morning, but Dad is already running late, and I don't want to keep him. I get out before he turns into the school drive so he can turn around on the road and avoid the traffic.

It's early September in Pennsylvania, and honestly, those autumnal candles have nothing on this: The air is just starting to turn crisp, cool humidity from a late-night rainstorm lingering on the breeze. The woods behind the school are a tapestry of greens and oranges and golds.

Unlike the forest, Pine Hollow High School is nothing to look at. It's gray and pretty much windowless unless you're in the exterior classrooms, which I can and will use as an excuse for my inability to focus in class.

The bell for homeroom is in ten minutes, so the courtyard is packed. School has only been going for two weeks, so I don't really know that many people—I keep my head down and weave through, making a beeline for the cafeteria, where there are fewer people and it's easier to fade into the background.

It's odd, changing a routine I've had for most of my life. Before we moved, back at Fairhope Creek, I would get to school early and meet Andie in the gym. Coach Bruna wouldn't mind if we used the fitness room until the bell for first period rang, so we would get a workout in before class and still have time to rinse off before school. I don't know any of the coaches here well enough, and I still don't know my way around the gym, so there's not much I can do in terms of escapism.

There's the library, which is boring but offers the refuge of *being* boring, and Rin from down the street always retreats to the band room, but I don't think either place is the kind of area where I'd normally hang out. I think, tentatively, that Rin is a friend, but we're in that awkward stage of friendship where I'm never really sure if I can text them without a reason. It's nothing like the easy friendships I left behind with Andie and our other group, with people I've known since I was in preschool. I never needed a reason to text them other than boredom—I knew them before texting was even a thing for me, after all.

I think about messaging Andie, but she says texting makes her miss me more. Instead, we pour our long-distance friendship into phone calls every Thursday and video calls over the weekend. Except, if I think about that, then I have to think about the fact that she skipped last Thursday's call and the video call the weekend before that.

Is it lonely? Yes. But it's one year, and . . . it'll be fine. I'm sure. It *has* to be. Because it's worth it to see Bee and Dad so much happier.

I *like* making them happy.

So I go to the corner of the cafeteria, away from the noise, and I pull out my notebook for some doodling. There's a group in front of me, and I know a couple of them from my English class—

And then *she* walks in.

She walks in, and it's like the whole cafeteria goes quiet (it does not, actually, but bear with me).

I've seen her a few times before, when I turned a corner while heading to the guidance office during sixth period last week, or waiting for Rin in the parking lot. But it doesn't matter how many times I've seen her, and I don't think it'll matter how many times I keep seeing her. Every time I do, it takes my breath away.

She's laughing, twisting her straight brown hair up on the back of her head before she secures it with a clip. She seems to glow from the inside, light shining through her olive skin and brown eyes—though if I got close, I think her eyes would be that type of brown that is so deep, rich, and shining, like Reece's collection of agate from museum trips when we were kids.

I finally caved at the end of last week and asked Rin who their friend was, and they laughed at me so long they turned red and had a coughing fit. I guess she has that effect on people.

Hannah. Hannah Sullivan.

Top of our class, APs across the board, set to be the valedictorian (she was second in the class last year, but by all accounts, no one has surpassed her since Liam Orville kicked it). She's in choir and plays soccer and was the lead in the musical last year and plays the marimba in the marching band—which would be very nerdy if it weren't so endearing.

And she is so beautiful that it makes my chest ache every time I look at her.

Reader, listen: I know. Yes, we all hate love at first sight. But hear me out: I know myself. This is infatuation, right? It has to be. Because there's no way that Hannah Sullivan actually lives up to my idea of her. And it's weird and voyeuristic for me to be sitting here in the corner, heart pounding, pretending to doodle as she walks up to some guy, and he reaches to brush the hair from her cheek—

I scan him over. I'm pretty sure I don't know him (yeah, big surprise, I know), and if I track down Rin in the band hallway, they will probably laugh themselves into an asthmatic fit yet again.

For an annoying half-second, I wish I had someone with me who grew up here. Who just *gets* the history between all of these people in the way those who grow up in small towns do. Who understands the layers of Pine Hollow like I know Fairhope.

Tabling that—back to Hannah.

So he brushed the hair out of her face. No big deal, and my heart should stop racing, because it's not like I've ever spoken a word to her. I don't even know if she likes girls, and it's a pretty big leap to make that she does, let alone that she'd have the time of day for *me*.

But I'm still thinking of her when the bell rings and the cafeteria starts to empty out. I scramble to put my notebook in my bag and, in my frazzled state, somehow manage to knock my pen case off the table.

Pens, highlighters, erasers, and pencils go skidding across the polished linoleum.

"Ah, shit," I mutter.

I duck down, blushing hard as a bunch of people look at me like it's my first day having hands. As I scrabble for the still-rolling pencils, I *feel* the weight of the stares on me, like some of them are clocking that there's a new girl for the first time, even though I've already been here (and mostly invisible) for a month. In this moment I wish for Andie or Reece like I never have before—

"Here, let me help."

I glance up and—tendrils of brown hair frame her face; she reaches out, and her hands are small and trim, nails unpainted; and when she meets my gaze, she smiles. She's wearing a white eyelet top and shorts, showing off the compact muscles of her thighs, her calves. Her Converse are scuffed with grass stains. A dainty gold chain hangs around her neck, the pendant disappearing beneath her shirt.

There is not a single word in my brain. *Say something*, my ego urges, but every single one of my brain cells is busy dying or spiraling out of control, because *Hannah Sullivan is looking at me*.

I have had crushes before, okay? And even a couple of hookups, exploratory friends with benefits that might've become something more.

I just don't know how to convey that she is, hands down, not just the most beautiful person I've ever seen—but the most beautiful person that could exist *to me*.

And I don't recover. Hannah's smile falls a little, but she holds out a handful of my pens and highlighters. I take them, still silent, probably still looking at her like a fool—and she smiles once more, then gets up, and goes. I sit back on my heels, my heart thudding in my chest.

There are . . . better ways I could have played that.

THAT afternoon, when I get home, I change into my favorite running shoes and a comfy pair of clothes and run until I should only be thinking about the pounding of my feet and the pattern of my breath—but I'm not. Even though I run until I get through my favorite crying-inside-indie playlist twice, I'm still thinking of her.

I shouldn't be. There are loads of other things I should be worrying about instead: telling Dad about my Stats test and getting ready for the next one, studying for the English quiz on Friday, contemplating my hideous lack of meaningful connections in this town, or even poking the problem of Liam Orville. But it's nice for a while, to pretend. To daydream.

And I'm still thinking of her when I go up to my room and do my post-run stretches and sit-ups to find Liam Orville haunting my corner.

It comes with that shock of surprise that always hits when I see one of them—no matter how many times I've seen a ghost, there's no way to acclimate your body, truly, to the idea of death and the presence of it—then a rush of annoyance, recalling my conversation with Reece yesterday.

This would be so much easier if they could just handle it.

Liam nods in greeting when he sees that I've noticed him.

"I can probably still hear you," I grumble, reaching for my water bottle. "The connection doesn't sever until I break it."

"Good to know," Liam says. He clears his throat, which brings up a lot of questions for me in terms of biology and ghosthood. "I came here to talk to you. I've been thinking about what you said, and I think we just . . . got off on the wrong foot."

Right. I don't know if "I'm haunting your room against your will" can be considered getting off on the wrong foot.

He looks at me for a moment, expectant, and I realize this is probably my time to apologize.

I sip my water, considering. "Sorry about the exorcism." I can admit that, at least, was not my finest moment.

But I panicked, okay? It was really the first time I had to actually tackle a ghost alone, without Reece—and I've seen what they can do. What a husk can do to a person, and what a ghost can, and I honestly want nothing to do with them. Reece can pretend all they want that we're witches or some shit, prepared to deal with the worst the universe has to offer—but I'm not deluding myself here. If I'm in a fight against a ghost, the ghost is winning. The best I can do, at any point, is make them go away as quickly as possible.

Liam must read some of this on my face. "And I'm sorry about . . . well, I guess I can't really apologize for being here," Liam says, thinking through it. "But I'm sure it's not an ideal situation for you."

I shrug. It's not really something either of us can fix easily, as we have already discovered.

"I've been thinking about what you and your . . . sibling?"

I nod.

"Said yesterday," he finishes. "About helping me to move on."

I sit back, leaning against the wall. *What would Reece do?*

Reece would be nice to him. Reece would talk through it. Reece would find a way to encourage him to leave without resorting to the kind of tomfoolery I am currently cooking up.

Reece would fix this—but Reece is a lot more patient than I am. I think I need to embody that, unfortunately.

"It'll make things easier for you," I say, searching for every word. "It's not . . . good to remain here, to hang around forever. Ghosts deteriorate over time."

He's looking at me shrewdly, like it's possible I'm lying to him for my own benefit. Considering our history, I'm not sure I can blame him. "How do you mean?"

I hesitate. I've never had to explain husks to an actual ghost before. "You're not really meant to stick around, you know? I don't know what the science is—I don't know if there *is* a science to it—but whatever is left of you can't stay like this forever. Over time, you'll lose all the things that make you *you*. When that happens, it just leaves the bad stuff behind, the sadness and the anger. Reece and I call those husks; they're still kind of sentient, floating through the world, but they search out other husks and drain energy from ghosts." I chew on a hangnail, worried for a second that I'm droning on, but Liam looks cautiously interested—and a little bit sick. "You haven't attracted any yet, I'm guessing?"

"How would I know?"

"You'd know."

"Then . . . no."

I nod. That's good, at least. Husks would make this a lot less appealing of a job, and I would actually need to call in Reece; with no tethers left to the living world, no memories or cares, husks are a lot harder to get rid of. "I know being here might feel easier than moving on, but trust me—you don't want to stick around. It's scary, the not knowing, but it's even scarier becoming something you don't recognize."

He takes a shuddering breath, and I'm pretty sure it's just muscle memory; ghosts don't need to breathe. "You're probably right," he says, like it pains him. Liam sits back on the bed cross-legged, so I shift up to the desk chair. "So where do we start?"

I'd love to start with a shower, but there's no guarantee he'll be so forthcoming when I come back. Besides, now that I've accepted this is something I have to do, I know Reece is right—he's been dead since sometime last school year, judging by the gossip, and even though he hasn't attracted any husks yet, it's only a matter of time before one finds him. The sooner we wrap this up, the better.

"Let's start with the end," I say. "How did you die?" I have some suspicions about this (thanks a lot, small town rumor mill), but it's better hearing it from him.

Liam wrinkles his nose. "I don't really . . . know."

"You don't *know*?" This is an odd one. Usually, for ghosts, that's the source of pain: Interrupted lives have unfinished business. In most cases, the ghost knows what that business *is*.

"I don't remember," Liam says. He takes a breath. "I know it was last year, October maybe? But I just don't remember anything leading up to it. The last memory I have is of leaving for the Homecoming game."

I'm not sure if it's better coming from me or not. But there's not much of a choice, is there? "You don't remember a car accident?"

He frowns. "No. Not at all."

I can't be sure when it was, though—maybe it was after that Homecoming game he remembers, or maybe a little bit later. I pull out my laptop. Liam stretches out so he can read the screen from the corner of my bed as I type in *liam orville obituary pennsylvania*.

Behind me, Liam draws a breath through his teeth.

"This will be unpleasant. You don't have to read it," I mutter, clicking on the first news article: *One Dead, One Injured in Tragic Accident*.

"You were right," he says. "A car accident."

I hesitate before scrolling further. "I'd heard . . . rumors."

His head snaps so he can look at me. If he were living, the speed would've given him whiplash. "From who?"

I shrug. "A few people, when I said where I'd moved. It's a small town. You know how it is."

He swallows hard. I imagine he does know. I imagine he's watched the spinning rumor mill of this town churning out things about his classmates, his neighbors. I wonder if he'd ever been the top story before himself—and I doubt it.

"A car accident," he says again, slower, coming to terms with it. "That's . . ."

"Yep."

"Mundane."

"Yup."

"Random."

"Mmhmm." I scroll down, skimming the article.

"*Fuck*," he mutters behind me, and there's a raw edge of tears in his voice. I don't dare look behind me, because that might make things worse—and I really, really don't see the benefit of making Liam angry or upset, knowing what he could attract if he does.

The only way out is through. It's something our birth mom used to say all the time when she was handling this kind of thing—when she was handling ghosts. I grit my teeth, because I don't like reminding myself of her when I don't need to—and I like it even less when memories like that come rising from the depths of my brain without me calling on them first.

"November first," I say. "Ring a bell?"

There's a pause behind me. I glance over my shoulder, in case he decided it was all too much for him and disappeared. But Liam is still there, chewing his lip. "No," Liam says. "I don't know the exact date, but Homecoming was a week before. Maybe two."

I nod. Despite my better judgment, I dig a notebook out of my top desk drawer. It's a Moleskine, one of Reece's hundred of them, but not one of their top fifty, so they left it here. I open to a blank page.

"Okay. So we know you died in a car accident on the first day of November." I glance back at the article. "Someone else lived, but they're not named, because they were a minor. Any ideas?"

He thinks for a minute, then shakes his head. "My first guess would be my sister, Ella, but I . . ." He looks away. Swallows hard. "I heard my parents telling her I was dead."

I try to move forward clinically, to not linger on any of the details. I make a new column for *Friends/Family* and write *Ella*. "Okay. So not Ella. Anyone else?"

Something flickers on his face; he shakes his head. "There are dozens of people it could be. I got my license early-ish, for my friend group, and I didn't drink at parties. I drove a lot of people around."

For some reason, this sticks out, so I write *responsible* on the other page. It's a weird list that doesn't make much logical sense. "Then maybe that's the first thing we do. We find out who was with you, and what really happened. Maybe that will help us figure out why you're still here."

"Drew."

I glance back at him. He's got a strange look on his face, like he doesn't quite trust all of this—or maybe it's relief. I'm pretty sure this is the first time he's said my name.

"What's up?"

"Why are you doing this?"

I blink at him. I thought it was pretty clear. "I'd actually really like my room back?"

He shakes his head. "You tried to exorcise me," he said. "Clearly, you have other tricks up your sleeve that don't involve my cooperation."

I'm pretty sure he A) watched too many *Ghostbusters* movies, B) read too many fantasy books, or C) is overestimating me, or maybe it's a mix of all three. It's kind of flattering, actually, because my bag of tricks is actually empty right now.

"I'd rather help you before you become something else, if I can," I say, which is close enough to the truth. It's definitely more personable than *I don't want you to become a black hole poltergeist sucking all of the joy from my life and forcing my family to move.*

Liam nods. "And is there anything I can do to repay you?"

It's an odd thing to ask—and annoyingly fortuitous. Because, actually, yeah, there are a few things I could use his help with. I chew on my hangnail for a moment while I get over my own measly pride. "There's one thing," I hedge.

"Yeah?"

"Can you help me with Stats?"

"AP Stats? I can't, I didn't take it—"

I snort. "No, regular. I, um." He's looking at me oddly, reconsidering, in that way that booksmart people do when they are recalculating how they think of you, and it makes me bristle.

I set down my pencil and turn to face him head-on. "Let me guess," I say. "You were in AP everything, and probably lined up for some incredible school and some wonderful future."

Now, he looks like I've caught him off guard. "I never got to apply," he says.

Of course. Because he died as a junior. Now, it's my turn to feel a bit shitty.

And maybe because I think I owe him some explanation for my prickliness, I say, "I just . . . I've never been good at school. Never liked it, and never done super well. C-average student to my core." *And I'm kind of struggling, even though we're less than a month in, even though you think it's easy.*

"Oh," Liam says, but the furrow between his brows doesn't clear. He moves back, sitting on the bed, and pulls one of his legs up to his chest. "I'm sorry. That *was* dickish of me, wasn't it?"

"Yeah," I say. "And I heard you were good at school, so it would be . . . helpful."

"I was," Liam says quietly. He chews his lip, and I wonder if he can feel it, or if he's just going through the motions. "I want you to take me to school. I don't know why I'm still here, nor why the thing . . ." He cuts off sharply, glances over my shoulder. I turn, following his gaze, but there's nothing there. "But if I'm with you, at school, when you're investigating, then I might remember more or figure something out, and I can help you with your classes. Stats, and whatever else is worrying you."

I'm actually not fully sure I can take him out of the house. Reece had a way around it, but their success rate with time/space/ghost manipulation has always been higher than mine. I decide that is a problem for later, because Liam is looking at me with this eager expression on his face.

"Okay," I say. I know I should make this harder for him, but what's the point? I take a breath. Let it out. I have more to gain from this situation than he does, right?

I hate it, but this one is for Dad, and it will make him stop looking at me like I'm his sad puppy. "If you do this, then yeah,

I want your help studying. Especially since you'll be going to classes with me."

"But no cheating," he says.

"No cheating," I agree.

He looks at me for a moment, and I can't read a single thing in his expression. But then he sticks out his hand. After a second, I lay my hand over his. We shake.

"Consider it done," Liam says.

Question 1: Object 1 (car) is traveling at 62 miles per hour. Object 2 (a tree) is at rest. Object 1 collides with object 2. How quickly does Liam Orville die at the scene?

Question 2: Object 1

(a car you can only half remember, but it's blue. You remember the press of your keys in your palm on your sixteenth birthday. Too much for a birthday present, you thought at first, but it's a hand-me-down from Aunt Linda. Your mother's smile, tearful, as she reminds you to drive safe—moot, because you won't have your license for six more months. In the background, the sun streams through the kitchen window. It smells like the Funfetti pancakes she makes for you every birthday. After breakfast, you put the keys on a CMU lanyard, a present from Ella. She doesn't know you saw her buying it last week when you took the bus downtown to go see CMU's museum, when you walked through the campus and pretended to be years older, when you watched her self-consciously push her hair behind her ears. You remember the weight of the keys in your pocket every day, the red-and-black lanyard hanging out of your pocket, how lanyards were a thing when you were a sophomore as everyone started getting their keys. The car was blue, and the interior was beige, and it smelled like the faintest hint of Aunt Linda's tobacco underneath the cleaner your mom used to get the smell out)

is traveling at 62 miles per hour. Object 2

(a tree? Really? It could be any tree. You don't actually know what road it was on, but this part of Pennsylvania is *all* trees. Conifers and deciduous trees, rippled over the Appalachian foothills. This area is all hills and trees, their leaves going gold and orange and red in a riot of colors in autumn, spreading over the mountains like a sunset flag of autumn's dying breath. You like trees. Actually, you like trees a lot, and it pisses you off that one killed you)

is at rest. Object 1 collides

(Rain. The screech of tires. A scream—maybe two. You can't remember it, can't dredge this dying moment out of the scene. You don't remember the crunch of your own bones or the iron tang of your own blood in the air. You don't remember your dying breath. "Instantaneous," one of the reports reads, but what does that mean? One second you were there, and one second you weren't, and in the breath between those two moments you . . . what? Your heart stopped? Your brain stopped? What went first and what came next and who was there and who witnessed it? What happened to your body? Did flesh cave in, did bone break through? Did the parts that made you Liam Orville suddenly vibrate apart, become meat, become bone and cartilage and flesh and blood, become a clean-up project rather than a boy? Did you look like you? Did you know? Did you feel it? Did you feel anything at all?)

with Object 2. How quickly does Liam Orville die?
Were you there?
Did you know?
Did it—
Did you—
Are you—
Did it hurt?

CHAPTER 4

"I have good news," I announce that evening when I call Reece—after dinner, when I'm sure Liam's not lurking in any corners. I would like him to be somewhat confident in my abilities, which probably won't work if I keep running back to Reece.

There's a heavy sigh on the other line, which I'm not sure I fully deserve. "What did you do now?"

"I've figured out how my ghost died," I tell them, "*and* I have a new Stats tutor."

"I am really hoping those two points aren't related."

I flop back on the bed, pulling the towel from my head, letting my wet hair fan out over the edge of the bed. "And what if they are?" I hedge.

"Drew . . ."

Immediately, I dislike the tone of their voice. I know Reece's voice, all the inflections and changes of it—and I know, without a doubt, that they're disappointed in me.

"You make exchanges with ghosts all the time," I say, chewing on the cuticle of my left thumb, jumping immediately to the defensive. "Like that time the ghost on Evergreen told you about the secret, easy parking lot downtown. And the time that older woman you helped while we were on vacation gave you that curry recipe."

"Drew," Reece says again, differently. "Those were all *thank-yous*. Things after-the-fact. Not *payment* for my time."

I chew on the inside of my lip—I knew this conversation was going to be a mistake. I don't even really know why I called Reece in the first place. If I wanted to prove that I was actually helping Liam . . . well, Reece doesn't need to have a play-by-play.

"I thought you'd be happy for me," I say. "That I'm making progress."

Reece snorts. "Okay, then. So, how did you find out how he died? Let me guess—you Googled it?"

I don't know why it stings so much. Probably because they're right. "I'm trying," I insist. "We had a whole conversation about it, too, but Liam doesn't remember—"

"Okay, then. So who's he close to?"

I try my best to remember everything we talked about this afternoon. "He has a big friend group. And a sister, Ella, but Ella moved to St. Louis with the rest of his family. I could call her. . . ."

"God, Drew. That is literally the last thing you should do." Reece isn't even hiding their frustration anymore, and that pit in my stomach grows even deeper.

"But, if someone met my ghost, I'd want them to call you."

"No," Reece says sharply, "you wouldn't. Imagine knowing someone you loved more than life itself is just . . . is just *there*. And there's not a single thing you can do about it. Imagine answering the phone and knowing that there's nothing you can do, and you can't see them, or hear them, or talk to them—"

"But what if I need to, to make him go away?" I snap. "You can't tell me there aren't ways around it."

"Yeah," Reece says sharply, "and they require *tact*. Dree, you wouldn't know tact if it punched you in the face."

"If it punched me in the face," I say slowly, trying to keep the annoyance from rising, "it wouldn't be tact, would it?"

"Don't involve the families. The loved ones," Reece snaps. "That is actually rule number one: Loved ones rarely can deal with the reality of ghosts. And even if they could, it's not fair.

Whatever is left unresolved, it's up to *you* to fix it, Drew. It's not a problem you can just plow through, worrying about consequences later."

I blink away the tears that prick my eyes. Honestly, I don't know why I called in the first place. Of course Reece is just telling me everything I've done wrong.

I love Reece so much—I miss them every day. But that doesn't change the fact that they're my sibling, and this is something they know that I don't, and of *course* nothing I do will be good enough unless I do it exactly Reece's way.

"I don't just plow through things," I insist. "I do care about consequences."

"If that were true," Reece says, "you wouldn't be making the *corpse you're trying to help* tutor you in math. That's not help anymore. That's transaction."

There are a thousand defenses I can think of to this: Liam offered first. He's bored, and it gives him something to do. There's something to be said about a mutually beneficial arrangement. I'm not taking any more from him than he's willing to give—not even that, but I'm not taking more than he's actively offering.

And I'm not . . . I *do* care about consequences. Maybe I'm impulsive sometimes, but I'm trying. I'm not running around actively attempting to make things worse.

"Well," I say shortly. "This has been helpful."

"Drew," Reece says, softening. "I'm just trying to—"

"I get it," I snap. "You know about this stuff. I don't."

"If you don't feel up to handling it, I can find a weekend—"

"Don't bother."

Reece snorts. "Whatever, Drew. I'll be here, waiting, for when you inevitably need me to bail you out."

I hang up without saying goodbye, because of course Reece thinks I'll fail at this. Of course they think I'll just make a mess for them to clean up.

I don't get angry easily, but my sibling knows all of my buttons and exactly how hard to push them.

I drop my phone onto my nightstand and cover my eyes. Reece has probably told me before why they don't contact family members—but I never had any interest in ghost stuff. I always tried to avoid it as much as possible. When I was little, whenever I saw a ghost, I used to cry and hide in one of the upstairs rooms of our house, or get Dad or Bee to pick me up from wherever I was. As I got older, I just . . . ignored them.

But not Reece. They always went racing in. They always wanted to fix things. I guess, removed from the annoyance of the call, I can see why they think I'm going to mess it up.

But I can't. I can't let Liam keep going on like this, and I can't rely on Reece to clean up whatever mess I make. I'm going to figure this out.

Reece can keep doing things their way. I'm going to figure out mine.

CHAPTER 5

Liam appears, without prompting, as I'm putting the last of my running stuff in a drawstring bag for practice after school.

"Not worried about stunting your growth, huh?" he says, sarcasm heavy, as he nods to the thermos on my desk.

I glance up at him. Bee makes the best coffee—possibly something to do with owning a bakery with a shop that doubles as a café. She leaves a hot thermos of vanilla latte for me every morning.

"Who died and gave you a sense of humor?" I mutter.

He rolls his eyes. Despite the awkwardness of other interactions that have gone very wrong (not to bring up the exorcism again), it's nice to see that he's . . . casual with me. Relaxed. Liam waits for me to finish packing up, leaning against my desk with his hands in his pockets.

I tell myself I can do this. That my fight with Reece doesn't matter—that they're wrong.

"I have a question," he says.

"Shoot." I take a sip of my coffee. Perfect, as always. God, Dad and I would be absolutely screwed without Bee.

"I can't leave the house."

"That's not a question."

"I'm *getting there*." He shoots me a look, so I mime locking my lips shut and throwing away the key. "I've been dead for . . ." He glances at the calendar on the wall, then sighs when he realizes I never changed it from August to September, nor did I cross out dates.

I bet Liam Orville woke up every morning at six on the dot and started his day by drawing a clean dash across the date in his calendar. I bet he ironed his underwear and color-coded his sock drawer. I bet he cleaned his room without his mom asking.

". . . a while. But why have I been haunting the house, if I died in a car accident? And why can't I leave?"

"Right, you'll be unsurprised to find that haunting is not a specific science," I say.

"So you don't know."

I frown—I know *enough*. Even if I tried, for most of my life, to ignore this part of myself as much as possible. It's impossible not to know, what with Reece being such a bleeding heart—and I did learn some of it when I was little.

"I've watched Reece do this with a lot of ghosts," I say, like he didn't interrupt me with his doubt, "and we have theories."

They have theories. I don't mention how much I have stayed out of it, because I don't think that will fill Liam with confidence. I really, really hope he didn't hear any of my fight with my sibling last night.

"I'm all ears."

"We say funerals are for the living, right? Not for the dead? Well, hauntings are kind of like that, too, but they're drawn by energy—and sometimes by emotions. Ghosts usually appear in the place they felt most comfortable, which for you must've been here. But then you can't really leave that place."

He chews his lip. "So whoever kept me around . . . grieved me into a prison?"

"Kind of," I say. "As for leaving . . . I don't know. It usually is that way—ghosts don't have much range without being carried.

But yeah, Reece thinks that has to do with energy and lingering memories too. Like, you're sustained by the emotions that once lived here, even if the people who carried them are gone."

Liam looks away, silent for a long time. Something about watching him feels invasive. I take another sip of coffee and let him reason it out.

"Did you ever meet them?" he asks. "My parents?"

I shake my head. I wasn't there when Dad and Bee viewed the house, and I don't know enough about buying houses to say if they would've run into them anyway.

He sniffles a little, which is odd, because he can't cry, either. "They went to live closer to my dad's family. In St. Louis."

I nod. I already knew this because small towns are small towns.

"They talked about it, after," he says, looking down at the navy quilted bedspread. He runs his fingers over the patterns—it's homemade, a twelfth-birthday present from Bee's mom—but I'm not sure if he can feel the texture. For all the things I do know about ghosts, there's still a lot that I *don't*.

Maybe this is a good opportunity, getting to know Liam, getting to help him. Maybe it'll help me learn and understand more about ghosts in general.

"I'm really sorry," I say, but I can't really say what I'm sorry for. That he's here? That he's dead? That he doesn't remember what happened or why, and can't figure out why he can't move on? That everyone has kept going and he can't?

Another moment of quiet. "Thanks," he says, sounding a little steadier. He takes a breath, then looks at me, the corner of his mouth angling up. I realize that I don't actually dislike him, or find him annoying. There's that odd feeling again that if we'd met when he was alive, we would probably have gotten along. Maybe even have become friends.

I'm also, unquestionably, the only person who has only ever known him dead.

"Well," I say. "I take it you don't like being late, so . . . shall we?"

OF course, I know about the whole "dragging ghosts out of bounds" thing because of Reece. They had a bit of an . . . infatuation with a teenage goth who haunted the attic of one of their best friends' houses.

I have no real thoughts about the ethics of ghost infatuations, but I am very much not interested in them myself—doubtful there's a hot teenage lesbian knocking around in someone's attic here in Pine Hollow.

Besides, they're always short-lived (as is the nature of ghosts) and always painful (as is the nature of love).

Point is, I know how this whole thing works. (Maybe I *have* been paying more attention than I originally thought, which is a relieving realization if there ever was one.)

I make Liam hold my hand as we cross the threshold, and I keep track of that odd feeling of invasion and don't let it fade until we've retrieved my bike from the garage and are at the end of the driveway. Then, I let go, and when he doesn't flicker away, I know I've done it right.

"Okay," I say. "You're free."

He takes a breath, then another—I'm still not sure on those technicalities—and looks around. There's wonder on his face. Obviously, none of this is new to him. I'm not sure if Liam lived here for his whole childhood, but I'm sure he knows the front yard, the gravel drive, the twisting oak, the scatter of leaves across the grass, the pines that outline the property—I'm sure he knows all of it like the back of his hand. And now, it's the first time he's been outside in almost a year, and I wonder if it all looks new again.

"*Free* free?" he asks with an unreadable look on his face.

"Not really," I admit, snapping on my helmet. "You have to stay near me. Just like you were connected to the house, you're now kind of attached to . . . me."

Liam's smile dims. "Ah."

"I'll try not to be too boring," I promise. I nod to the bike. "Now. Handlebars or rack?"

"Excuse me?"

I nod to my bike. "You can either balance on the handlebars or sit on the rack—you have no weight, and you're not really corporeal, so it won't weigh anything down, but I'll make sure you stay with me."

He blinks, uncomprehending.

"You've been on a bike before." It's not a question—and we are now edging dangerously into "running late" territory.

"Never with another person."

I sigh, but I'm used to hauling Reece around. I get on the bike and nod to the rack behind me. "Come on. Wrap your arms around me. I won't let you go."

Surprisingly, he does what I ask.

Liam is quiet on the ride to school, which is good, because I have my own things to think about. I'm actually not sure this is a great idea, for a few reasons. First: There's no telling that Liam will find the answers he needs at school. And it's not like I can just start asking people if they knew him. And if I suddenly know stuff I shouldn't because Liam tells me about it, it'll make me look like a super creeper. I already haven't made many friends here—I was hoping running club would remedy that—and becoming the weirdo who knows too much about the kid who died before they moved here doesn't seem great for my social life.

Which brings us to my new running club—which I have today, and which Liam will now have to accompany me to, since I don't think I have time to take him home. I'm not sure what his ghostly radius is to me, but I'm pretty sure he's not a great runner (again, not sure on the technicalities here . . . maybe he can just float beside me?), meaning this might be a very bad practice session for both of us.

And third, now that we're removed from my bedroom, the reality of our plan is sinking in. Yes, I should help him move on, but I really shouldn't be *charging* him for it. Even if it's just in favors.

Isn't there, like, an ethical issue with this? There's no guidebook, of course. Reece and I have never met someone else who can do what we do or see what we see besides our mother—and it's not like we were like, "Hey, Mom, I see you're leaving . . . care to give us a detailed crash course on how this all works?"

Reece made it pretty clear, when we were little, that Mom wants nothing to do with us. It probably should hurt, but like I said, there's not really a "Mom-gap" in my heart, and Bee is the best mom I could've asked for.

Plus, Reece's ethics fill any moral gap Mom may or may not have left behind. They're still pissed with me about the trade Liam and I agreed to.

But maybe this is just a good and productive relationship. We both get something out of it: Liam gets to move on, and I get to figure out my own life.

I have to hold onto that. I'm not going to go running back to Reece, yet again.

"This actually doesn't suck," Liam says in my ear, a bit after we get going. "I didn't think I'd have any new experiences, after . . ."

"Didn't get out much when you were alive, huh?" I ask. I turn off the main road, down a side road. Back here, there's a path through the woods, a shortcut that takes me to the back of the school and avoids most of the main roads. It's like fifteen, twenty minutes tops.

"I just kind of . . . I don't know. Met expectations?"

I guess it makes sense. Straight-A student. Responsible. An older brother. "What did you do for fun?"

"I did have friends, Drew," he says, and I can hear the note of humor in his voice. His arms loosen around my waist. He has no reason to fear dying, after all. "We hung out a lot. And I liked reading, and gaming, and I did a lot of studying." A pause. "Hiking, and going around the woods. Usually with Ella. We had a dog. The most brainless golden retriever you've ever met."

"I've met some pretty brainless golden retrievers," I say. I would possibly include myself in this category.

But Liam is quiet behind me for a minute. "Do you think they miss me?"

This isn't really a conversation that I know how to deal with. I should be more sensitive, more understanding; I should tell Liam that *yes, of course they do, there's no doubt in my mind*, but the fact about life is, death is an inevitability.

Yeah, his family misses him—but they have moved on. School peers too. I know that part of it is that I'm jaded, and none of this should come out of my mouth, so I don't let it.

I wish I could give him closure, if that's what he wants—but I also remember Reece's warnings, and I know what I can and can't do. If I involve Liam's family, go seeking some sort of final goodbye, it will only make him more unstable. He might become a husk, and then, there will be no freeing him from this.

"They miss you. Of course they do," I say, because it's exactly what I should.

We get there right as the bell is ringing, and then it's not like there's much time to talk to Liam. It will just look like I'm talking to myself, and I would like to refer back to the point that I am still trying to make friends and not seem like a weirdo.

Liam follows me from class to class, walking around the classrooms and making observations that only I can hear as the minutes and hours pass. I learn that he's friends with Rin, from down the street, and also that they changed their hair since Liam died; Liam learns that they have come out as nonbinary to the rest of the school. He notices that Anna Partrelli has dyed her hair red, and he points out that two people I don't know broke up because they're holding hands with other people at lunch. He calms down for Stats, sitting quietly at the back of the class as Mr. McTavish drones on, probably so he can tutor me later—which is good, because I have no clue what he's talking about half the time.

I know I shouldn't be . . . but every time we're in the hallway between classes, I'm looking for Hannah Sullivan, or for that guy she was with. Look, I know how small towns work—Liam *had* to have known her. And if he knew her, he might know something about her that might . . . I don't know. Help me talk to her. Make me not look like a bumbling fool every time she's around.

But we don't run into her. She's in AP everything, I think, so it makes sense that our schedules don't overlap, and she has B lunch with the rest of the musically inclined kids while I'm in A lunch.

In the end, it doesn't really matter. Even though my thoughts drift to her in the middle of lessons, it feels different to walk through the halls and not feel so alone. It's . . . nice. Nice, and weird, because it's not like I have anyone *real* with me.

It feels like taking the first breath after finishing a long run, my lungs begging for oxygen. I didn't realize how starved I was for any sort of camaraderie until it's eighth period, and Liam is making some sort of snarky observation about the football team banners that makes me laugh before I catch myself.

I need to call Andie later. FaceTime with my friends. I need to acknowledge that, actually, I'm pretty fucking lonely. And my only friend here cannot be a ghost because—well, because who knows how much longer Liam will be here, and also, the rest of the world can't see him. So.

"Wait, where are we going?" Liam says after school when I grab my bag from my locker and start off towards the gym and changing rooms.

"I have practice," I say.

His brow scrunches. "What practice?"

"I'm practicing with the running club now, then in the spring, it'll be track." It's the same lie I told my dad, but it slips off the tongue. I'm not sure why I bother with it, considering Liam doesn't care if I do track or not, but maybe it's to convince myself that I might actually put in effort to find friends here. Maybe it *would* be good for me.

"Ew. Running." But he follows me down the stairs. "Do I have to . . . keep up?"

"Probably not," I say, thinking through the technicalities. "Actually—do you want to stay outside? Maybe in the parking lot or something? See if you can just be there without me keeping you? It might be a good experiment."

He agrees—probably because it means no physical activity. Again, not sure about the whole "physicality when dead" thing, but I get the vibe that Liam was pretty much allergic to exercise when he was alive. He sets up in front of the school, and I get dressed for practice.

IT turns out it's not such a big deal, and I feel normal during my run. It's weird, actually, how level I feel, all things considered. I might have to admit, begrudgingly, that Reece is right. Maybe it's better for us when we help them move on instead of ignoring them.

Which, dammit. I hate when Reece is right.

Liam comes over to find me while I'm stretching. My body feels good, limber and under control after the miles. It was the first practice, so we did a group trail run, and after my anxious running all summer, the four miles felt like nothing.

Everyone was in their established groups, so I did most of it alone, but that's okay. I will make progress eventually.

"Are you done with this?" Liam asks, distaste running thick in his voice.

I roll my eyes, pulling my foot, stretching my left calf. "It's never too late to start, you know. You could stand to bulk up—want to try my weights tonight?"

"Be serious, Drew," Liam says, but he's smiling a little. I elbow him. He's corporeal enough that it sends him sprawling on the grass.

He looks off down the lawn and sighs. "Looks like band practice is over," he says, nodding to the knots of people making their way up from the back fields.

"Were you in band? Nerd."

He scoffs. "Worse. I was a hanger-on. Most of my best friends were."

"That *is* worse," I agree.

I gather up my stuff, and Liam and I head back to the school. "We can head home after I grab my stuff from the locker room," I tell him. "And then we can figure out more of what's going on with you."

"Or study," he says, glancing at me sidelong.

I sigh. "Or study," I begrudgingly agree.

We cut through the school, and Liam waits in the hall while I pick up my bags. There's no point in changing, since I'm already sweaty and I still need to bike back home, so I'm still a bit gross when I meet him in the hallway.

"What was your favorite subject?" I ask as we head back across the gym, towards the open doors to the hallway.

He shrugs. "I was always good at English, but my real favorite was French—"

A girl's voice, sharp, rises around the corner. "You never would've said that when—"

"Things are different now. Why don't you get that?" The words are hissed, nearly, and clearly part of an argument around the corner from us as we come out of the gym. Liam hesitates, and we exchange a glance—I don't know my way around *that* well, but we need to turn that corner to go out the doors and get back to my bike.

A girl's voice says back, "You're really not being fair right now."

"What do you want me to do, treat you like you're glass?"

"No, I want you to treat me normally, like your *friend*. Like you always did, before . . ."

Liam's whole body changes. Tightens. Before I can say anything, he's stalking down the hall and toward the corner—toward the voices. He's pissed about . . . *something,* and he's a pissed ghost, so he's doing weird things with the energy in the hall. I don't even think he notices as the lights above us buzz and flicker.

"Liam," I whisper after him, trying to get his attention—anything that will get him to stop moving.

He ignores me and turns the corner.

I lurch after him just in time to see Liam as he hesitates, blinking at the scene. There are two people in the hallway, a boy with his back to me and a girl facing him, but I can't see her past him and Liam.

Liam tries to grab the guy's arm, but his fingers go through it. Of course they do; he's not real. Liam's face freezes, a mask of shock—I should've explained more to him, when I tied him to me. He can only touch me, only impact me, and only I can feel him. The corporeality that exists between us doesn't stretch to others.

Above us, the lights flicker again, and one of them buzzes alarmingly. I swear to god, if he blows the fluorescents, I am *not* going to be happy.

"What the fuck—" the boy starts, and I can see the goose bumps on his arm. He can't see Liam or physically feel his hand, but he feels the change in the air. The coldness. The energy.

"I would rather not talk about this, Caleb," the girl is saying now, as if she doesn't notice the boy—Caleb's—reaction at all. "You can't just expect things to be different, now that he's gone."

And something has changed about Liam's face, something odd and pained—and I can't bear it. Before I can think better of it, I hear my own voice, too light, saying, "Hey. Everything okay here?"

Caleb whirls around. He must not have heard me coming closer. But when he does, he reveals who he is cornering in, and just how close they were standing: It's Hannah Sullivan, her cheeks flushed and her arms crossed over her chest, looking pissed-off and too warm, and my breath catches in my throat.

"We're fine," Caleb says tightly.

"It's not fine," Liam says, his voice taking on a new edge of anger. Hannah doesn't say anything at all. She just looks down at her shoes, her cheeks going even redder.

I glance at Liam, feeling lovesick and helpless in equal measure. Crushes don't usually make me this tongue-tied and awkward, but here we are. I also feel, horribly, like I'm intruding on something I shouldn't.

Liam must somehow understand that I'm absolutely tongue-tied. "Her name is Hannah," he says quickly. "She's a friend of—Rin's. Ask her if she's going to Rin's house and say you're friends with them or something."

I swallow hard. If he were corporeal, I'd be giving him a really big glare right now. "Um, Hannah, right?" I start. It's . . . something.

Her eyes flick up. Deep brown. Agate brown.

"I, um. I'm friends with Rin. You're going to theirs tonight, right? To study?"

She stares at me, uncomprehending, for a long second.

"For physics," Liam feeds.

"For physics," I say.

"Right," Hannah says. She glances at her watch. "Shit, you're right."

Caleb looks at me blankly for a minute, but something about Hannah's face shifts for the barest second. I am briefly terrified that Liam is telling me about something Hannah and Rin used to do last year, which I wouldn't know about, and I look like a creeper.

"Um, thank you—sorry Caleb, running late!" She turns back to me. Before I can think further, she grabs my wrist and hauls me with her down the hallway. "Thank you. That was super awkward. You're Andrea, right? The new girl?"

She's touching my wrist. *She's touching my wrist.* I shoot Liam the most bamboozled look I can. *How did he know about the study session?*

"Yeah," I say. Then, reaching for any brain cell floating free: "Drew. I go by Drew."

"Drew," she says. I'm never washing my wrist.

Okay, that's a fucking lie. God—I need a shower. *God—I*

wish I showered. We are in full-throttle panic mode, and there's very little I can do about any of it now.

"Thanks so much for that," Hannah says, hauling me farther around a corner and to an exterior door I've never used before. It leads to the back lot, where a scattering of cars are parked. "That lie with Rin—that was really good. How did you know I'm in physics?"

"Guessed," I lie. "I, uh, saw you in the science hall once."

"You're a genius," she says. I look at Liam, his expression still distant and stormy—but he's kept up with us.

We're outside now, and Hannah starts off in the direction of one of the cars, a gray Honda. "Need a ride? I owe you something."

Yes. But I have my bike, and Christ, I'm not getting into a confined space with Hannah Sullivan post-run. "Nah, I'm okay. Thanks, though."

It almost sounds normal.

She offers me a smile. It's dazzling. "Maybe next time."

God.

"Thanks again—I really do appreciate it," she says, walking backwards to her car. And I just . . . wave. Like a fool. I stand there and fucking *wave*.

"Drew?" Liam asks wearily a moment later.

"Huh?"

"You gonna stop waving?"

I drop my offending hand, aghast. Tuck it in my pocket. When I turn to him, he looks just as upset—but also, there's this odd glimmer in his eye.

"Do you want to talk about whatever that was?" he asks, not unkindly. It makes me feel eleven times worse.

Do I want to tell Liam Orville that I have an inexplicable, all-consuming crush? That I know it's utterly ridiculous—I don't even *know* Hannah; there is no conceivable reason I should be this tongue-tied around her.

But Liam looks at me with this expression of—I don't know. I would call it *understanding*, but that doesn't feel quite right either.

I purse my lips. He only watches expectantly. He lets me gather my thoughts as we turn back to the school, then take the path to where my bike is. He's still waiting as I undo the chain, twist the combination lock. Then I sigh.

"Do you know Hannah Sullivan?"

He snorts. "*Drew*."

"I know," I say, prattling on self-consciously. "It's a small town—you knew everyone, I'm sure, probably from birth—"

"You don't know?"

"Don't know what?"

He looks away, but not before I catch the flicker of hurt that traces across his. "Sorry," he says, recovering. "I just thought it would be . . . well. Hannah and I were best friends."

"Oh," I say. I don't know why it catches me off guard, considering everything I know about Liam. Perhaps I've gotten so used to the reality of him as a ghost that I forgot that he was real and living and with these people, probably in my very place, just last year.

"Yeah."

There's something about this that makes me certain I can talk to Liam about Hannah—but I feel like the second I open my mouth, I'll sound like a fool. Instead, I swerve to, "So you probably know the guy she was talking to."

"Yup. Caleb DeGuise."

I swing my leg over my bike. Liam gets on behind me, and I start pedaling off on the path that leads through the woods, the shortcut back to my—our?—house.

"What was that? The argument they were having, I mean."

"I don't know," he admits. "I don't like the way he was talking about her." There's a bit of anger simmering under his tone, but I agree with him on that.

And he's right; whatever they were talking about, Caleb was being an absolute *dick*. But as Liam speaks, a chill gathers in the air, and I feel the electricity crackling along my skin, raising the hair on my arms.

"Is he usually like that?" I ask.

There's a pause—it goes on longer than Liam usually takes to think things through. Finally, he sighs, then runs his hand through his hair. "We were friends too," he admits. "But he and I . . . well. It doesn't matter. He always had a thing for Hannah, but I really don't like the way he was talking to her."

He's clearly holding onto a lot of repressed emotions here, and I very much get it. As he goes into their history, getting more and more annoyed, we wind our way deeper and deeper into the woods.

"And she didn't reciprocate?" I ask.

Liam shrugs. "Hannah's never been interested in that kind of thing," he says. Possibly, he *laments*.

"Do you think it has anything to do with—"

I don't finish the sentence—suddenly, I'm falling, and it takes me a frantic half-second to realize that something wrapped around the front wheel of my bike and jerked it roughly to the side.

I suck in a breath and turn the handlebars, but there's no recovering. I go tumbling as the bike tilts, skidding sideways. I roll three times and slam into a tree, curving around the trunk and knocking the wind out of my lungs.

"Drew!" Liam shouts.

I roll onto my back, struggling to breathe. Both of my knees are scraped, and my elbows, too, but I haven't hit my head. I can't find Liam, not even after hearing his voice—

I push up to my hands and knees, searching the place where the bike toppled over. There's something lying there, dragging itself across the path, a translucent, milky white.

My heart seizes in my chest as it raises its face, as it gnashes its dark teeth. I know what it is the second I see those teeth, the deep shadows where eyes once were, the suggestion of something human turned inside out. My stomach twists in knots, an automatic reaction to all the times I've seen them before with Reece at my side—when Reece would handle it.

A husk.

I don't have much experience with husks—they're a side effect of ghosts, and I try to avoid ghosts whenever possible. But when a ghost degrades too much, loses all of the pieces of themselves that once made them human, *this* is the result.

This is what Liam will become. It pounds in my head, too close and too real, the realization of exactly what I'm trying to prevent.

It's like looking at a piece of gossamer, both colorless and shimmering at once. The husk is the impression of a shape, of teeth that once smiled but now only grit, of claws that were once hands. It drags itself across the path to where I'm lying, moving too quickly for me to do anything but grab a fallen tree branch and wield it.

I wish I remembered literally *anything* Reece taught me about this.

"What *is* that!" Liam shouts, and my head snaps to one side. He's standing a few feet away, just at the base of another tree. He doesn't look disheveled at all, even though he was knocked off the bike when I was.

"Get down!" I shout, but it's too late.

The husk stops and raises its horrible head, like it's sniffing the air. I shakily stand and scrabble over to Liam, reaching him just as the husk starts to move. "You need to be still, and get control of your emotions," I hiss at him. Then I push him behind me and wield the stick.

The husk rises slowly to its feet. It sways gently as it approaches, like any wind is enough to knock it over, but I'm not fooled: I've seen what these bastards have done to Reece. I've seen Reece come home covered in scratches and bruises; I've sat on the counter on Dad watch while they've patched themselves up after run-ins.

And Reece knows what to do. Reece has practiced. I'll be lucky to get out of this with just scratches and bruises.

No one would look at that husk and think, *Yeah, that was definitely human once.* It looks otherworldly, demonic, a creature from my worst nightmares.

The husk shimmers when you look at it head-on, but out of the corner of my eye, I can see it more clearly: rotting flesh and weathered bones, blackened teeth against an even blacker maw of a mouth. Its skin takes on an appearance like leather, this long after, and any clothes remaining are tatters. Its hair is a matted snarl hanging down its back. Its feet, too, are tipped in claws.

Once, when Reece was cleaning themself up after a run-in with one of these, I asked them if the degradation of the ghost followed the same pattern of bodily decay, but they didn't think so. They weren't sure what metric a husk follows.

Now, facing one down, dread creeps across my skin. There's not much I can do with this stick—Reece left me behind an emergency kit, just in case anything happened, but I buried it in the back of my closet and only brought it out to use the holy water for the exorcism incident.

The husk pauses to look at me, its head cocking at an unnatural angle. Liam says again, softer, "Drew, *what is that?*"

I don't want to make the first move. I don't want to stand here frozen, either. My palms are clammy with sweat.

The husk makes a slithering lurch towards us. I skitter back, whacking out with my branch, desperately trying to remember anything Reece would've mentioned, anything they would've taught me.

The branch doesn't connect the first time, but it does the second. The husk hisses, blinking its milky white eyes at me, dark tongue snaking out of its mouth to taste the air. It reaches forward, those horrible claws grasping, and Liam is swearing behind me—

Somewhere in the woods, there's another noise, like something heavy is moving through the trees. The noise of leaves disrupted, and something slithering over the forest floor. There's a hill to our left, and the sound is coming from over the rise, where we can't see. The husk stops, turning towards it, tasting the air.

There's another sound there, under the noise of something moving through the forest, and it's enough to make my blood go cold: It's a clicking, almost-but-not-quite like computer keys, or buttons. It sounds like bones.

Or maybe even like teeth.

Liam swears profusely and grabs my arm. The husk is still looking over at the hill. Liam tugs me the other way.

"Drew," he hisses. "Let's *go*."

But I'm paralyzed, either in fear or stupidity, so I watch as the first tendrils of smoke creep over the hill—then one huge, spindly, spider-like leg slides over the rise. The husk makes a dual-toned shriek, both deep and haunting and high and shrill.

Liam doesn't have to tell me again.

We tear through the woods, nearly tripping over leaves and roots, and Liam is holding my hand so tight that I'm afraid he's going to wrench my arm off. Clearly he's discovered some sort of ghostly reserve of energy, because he's moving even faster than I am, and it takes everything in me not to recoil from the cold terror radiating off him. I glance back, and there are those inky legs moving over the ground, and a spider-like body. I can't see eyes, but I feel its gaze on me. Watching.

And watching.

And *watching*.

"Hurry!" Liam shouts, pulling on my hand, bringing me back around. Together, we *run*.

CHAPTER 6

I can sustain the pace, but Liam can't, so we keep moving through the woods in stints of fast walking and running until we collapse through my front door. Both of us sprawl across the hardwood floor of the hall, breathing hard. I'm drenched in sweat, both from the run and the terror that followed, and every muscle in me *aches*.

Liam turns his head and looks over at me like I'm going to suddenly shatter.

Even minutes later, I still don't have control of my breath yet, and my teeth won't stop chattering. Luckily, Liam speaks first:

"What was that?"

I close my eyes. Rub my face. I can't believe I need to go running back to Reece for help, but here we fucking are. "That first thing was a husk. That's what happens to spirits when they're left on earth too long."

Liam chews his lip. "That's what you're afraid of me becoming."

There's no point denying it. "Yeah."

"And I would. It's not, like, a sickness or infection."

"All ghosts who stick around become that—the process usually starts after a year or so. It's not really a matter of *if*, but of *when*."

He's quiet for another moment, so long that I think he's not going to respond at all. But then he says, "I died almost a year ago. So it's going to happen soon."

I don't really think. I reach for his hand, and I squeeze it, remembering the tether of him as we raced through the woods. The way his feet barely touched the ground. The way he dragged me out, feeling almost physical as I stumbled over roots and branches.

"Yeah," I say. "It's . . . it's a matter of time, at this point."

Another pause as Liam processes this. "And the other thing? Another husk?"

I chew on my lip. "I'm not sure," I admit. I have literally no idea what the other thing was in the woods, nor if it was paranormal or real, nor what brought it on. "What did you see? I didn't get much of it."

He shudders. "It was like a huge spider, if a spider was part octopus. And maybe part demon too."

That makes me think, at least. It's an improvement, because up until this point, my brain was just a hum of fear. I try to think this through like Reece would. "When it appeared. Were you angry?"

"What?"

"Were you angry? Or upset?"

Liam looks over at me. "I was terrified, Drew. We were being attacked by . . . whatever the fuck was happening there. And before that, when the husk appeared, I was . . . justifiably pissed about Caleb."

He has a point, and it fills me with even darker dread. I haul myself up, leaning against the wall. Liam mirrors my posture on the other wall. His legs are longer than mine, knees tented, bracketing mine.

"You look stressed," he informs me. "Spit it out."

I rub my face again. "Okay. So. When you have emotions . . . Reece is better at explaining this than I am—"

"Do you want to call them?"

"No," I say, too quickly. I want to do this myself. I want to prove that I can—that I *don't* need them. And I've already messed this up so dramatically . . . the last thing I want is for Reece to tell me that they knew all along I couldn't handle it.

"Maybe if it gets worse," I concede. "But basically, you might be able to sense things sometimes . . . or maybe not, because you've been in here the whole time. But the greater spirit world, of husks and ghosts and demons and whatever else lurks there, it can sense *you*. So when you feel a strong emotion, like anger, or anything that they consider to be tasty . . . it can attract them."

Liam draws a breath through his teeth, and maybe that's why I trust him as much as I do, even knowing that he'll be on a downwards slope of degradation from here on out: Everything he does is still so *human*. Like his soul never remembers it stopped living.

"So I'm fucked," he says. "I'm going to become that thing, and in the process, I'm going to hurt both of us because I can't control myself—"

"Hey." I lean forward, laying my hand on his knee. I don't know why I do it, but it feels right. Comforting. "We'll find a way out, okay? We won't let that happen to you."

I hold his gaze for a long moment. Finally, he nods, so I do too.

"I trust you," he says.

"Good."

Liam drops his head back against the wall, then sighs. "We should get your bike." The suggestion has my blood running cold, because it's in the woods, and there's every chance the *thing* might be there too. . . .

"Or we could leave it overnight?" I ask, not looking at him. "Just in case?"

"I would say yes," Liam says, "but your backpack is there, too, and you probably don't want to leave your books out overnight."

I sigh, but he's right. I need to face my fears and get my books—and even though I felt that creeping dread, there's no way to be sure that big thing is still there. Enough time has passed that it should be gone, and if Liam keeps his emotions level, we should be fine.

"You've never seen anything like that big spider thing before?" I ask after we haul ourselves to our feet and I lock the front door behind us. "Or anything spirit world-y?"

Liam hesitates, and I glance over at him, trying to read his expression.

"What have you seen?" I ask.

He sighs. "Well, I thought they were just shadows. Like, after all, it's not like I could really go anywhere other than the house, but there were . . . shapes. In the yard, around the house. In the treeline."

My blood runs cold. I turn, despite myself, searching the trees as we walk down the road toward the forest path. There's nothing there—it just looks like Pennsylvania in autumn, with all of its regular wooded creepiness rather than any supernatural creepiness.

"What kind of shapes?"

"I don't really know," he says. "I didn't think anything of it—just that, I don't know, maybe I saw shadows differently as a ghost. But pretty much since I died, I've noticed something in the woods."

Well *fuck*. Something has been following Liam—something has been near my *house*—and I didn't even notice. It's not like I have a sense for these things: I only know they're there when I see them myself. I can't shake the way it felt like that thing was staring at me.

I make a mental note to drag out the kit Reece left for me from the back of my closet when we get home and set up a protective perimeter around the house. It won't keep Liam out, since he already lives here, but it should prevent anything else from getting *in*.

We don't talk about anything else as we make our slow way back through the woods to the place where I dropped my bike. It's a totally normal forest, the birds chirping and rustle of squirrels darting through the underbrush, but every sound makes my heart feel like it's racing out of my chest, until I can't take it anymore.

"You said you were best friends," I say. "You and Hannah."

Liam glances my way, his lips pressed together. I try to imagine them together, side by side, maybe even laughing—it's not that hard to conjure, but something about it makes me feel like I'm sticking my entire body in ice water. "Yeah," he says.

"Since when?"

"Oh, forever." The corner of his mouth lifts. "Since pre-school, really. Inseparable. As long as I have memories, I have memories of Hannah."

I swallow hard, stepping carefully over a root. There's no sign of whatever thing attacked us before, no creeping dread following us through the trees. Maybe it's okay—maybe it's really gone.

I can't let either of us feel terror, just in case that summons it again, so I keep up the current conversation with Liam.

"What's she like?" I ask, still desperate for any sort of distraction, clinging to whatever comfort Liam has to offer.

He snorts. "Stubborn. Funny. She's probably the funniest person I know. And just wildly talented at everything she tries—except for driving. She's a terrible driver. And skiing. We went together with her parents freshman year, and it was her first time, and I swear—I've never seen someone fall so many times in one afternoon."

He's smiling when he talks about her, and two things are immediately clear to me: No matter what they were when he lived, Liam wanted his relationship with Hannah to be something more.

And with the way he's talking about her, if I let him keep steering, I have the feeling I'll be infatuated with her too.

"I think I have a huge crush on her," I blurt out just as my bike is in sight. But the bike and my backpack look normal enough, like nothing touched them after we ran. "Like, I know it's ridiculous, because I've talked to her like, twice, and there's no *real* reason for it but . . . yeah."

"I kind of figured."

I shoot him a look, horrified to be so easily caught. "How?"

"Drew, you waved at her for like, three full minutes. You had the weirdest little smile on your face—"

I'm going to cringe myself to death. "Jesus. Fuck. Right."

He's smiling when he shoulders into me. "It's fine. I've seen that kind of thing loads of times . . . you may be unsurprised to know that a lot of people had—have—crushes on Hannah."

Something about this both makes me feel better and like an absolute creeper. I cover my face with both hands. "I hate liking people," I say. "It makes me feel . . . squidgy inside."

"Gross," Liam says happily.

"I know."

"Point is, she's used to this kind of thing," he says. "And you didn't do anything super weird. So, just like, chill out a bit, and I'm sure it'll be fine. You'll probably get over it."

"Yeah," I say. "You're right." There's something about the way he says it, some odd bitterness—and I wonder, though I know it's not my place, if he's speaking from experience.

Or worse: if he's speaking about something that he had desperately wished to happen, that never did. Like he wanted to get over her. Wishful thinking.

I get my bike upright again and sling on my backpack. Liam doesn't hesitate to get behind me when I throw a leg over the seat, and when he's settled, I pedal off towards home. I don't have much else to say to him, and guilt and dread are mixing in the pit of my stomach like cement.

LIAM doesn't stick around for long after we get home, after we make sure it's safe. I wonder if he feels that his presence is a danger to me—and I can't say for certain if he's wrong.

When he's gone, I go to my closet and dig around in the

bottom, past the running shoes and the hoodies that have fallen from one of the upper shelves, past the craft projects I started and will never finish, past the three scrapbooks Andie gave me when I moved away and the shoebox of old things that used to belong to my mom. The box from Reece is a bit bigger than I remember—they painstakingly packed it while they were getting ready to leave for Boston, then put it in the stack of boxes for my room at the last minute—and I'm grateful. Even though I stubbornly told them I didn't want it. Even though I tried to give it back.

I lock my door even though Bee and Dad usually knock before coming in, and neither will be home for another hour anyway, and drag the box to the middle of my floor. I pull it open to display a selection of notebooks and three smaller boxes.

I pull it all out and lay the boxes and notebooks out in an arc around me. Of the notebooks, two are obviously Reece's—they're their favorite Moleskines in a dark oxblood, and if I opened them, I know I'd find them full of my sibling's cramped, boxy writing.

Perhaps they know me better than I know myself, and they knew that if I *did* run into trouble, I'd never call them and ask for help. I'd do this instead.

The other notebooks are older and flimsier: those nondescript, cheap composition books that we used to buy at Walmart for less than a dollar when we were little. I open the first one—and my blood goes cold.

It's not Reece's handwriting in these. I recognize the taller, spidery scrawl. Even though I haven't seen it in years, I remember it: on my birthday cards, written in my baby book, scrawled on the bottoms of pictures and DVDs, on grocery lists on our fridge.

I don't know how Reece got them or why they held onto them. I don't know if they stumbled upon them years after, or if they somehow got them directly—because these notebooks were all written by our mother.

It throws me off, knowing that Reece had them, and then that they packed them away for me. There are too many emotions within me now, looking at the notebooks. The forefront of it all is shock, but there's a layer of betrayal there, too: *Why* does Reece have these? Why did they never, ever mention them or show them to me? And why, for fuck's sake, did they leave them for me now?

The press of that paper against my skin makes me sick. It's too much, seeing her handwriting and feeling the memories that rush in with it: the brush of her hand against my forehead, pressing my face into her favorite shirt to wipe pool water out of my eyes in the summer, the smell of her perfume. It's all there, in just that glimpse of writing on the page.

And right now, I absolutely cannot deal with it. With her.

I stop what I'm doing, gather the stuff up again and shove it back in a box, then head for the bathroom. What I need is a shower hot enough to strip off my top layer of skin.

What I need is to *think*.

I turn on the water and strip out of my sweaty clothes. I wish I could burn them instead of just putting them in the laundry, getting rid of any suggestion of the husk and the shadowy spider-demon and the presence of those notebooks, but that would probably make Dad or Bee super suspicious. I lurch in under the steaming jet of water and turn my face up to the spray.

The topic of Mom is . . . complicated. Not emotionally—not for me. There's a lot to it, and thanks to years of therapy enforced by Dad, I have a healthy enough perspective on a lot of it.

The first time Mom left was right after I was born. Dad has only really talked about it with me once or twice—he said he didn't want his experiences of her to color our memories—but I know he only let her around us when she was clean. And for the first few years of our lives, it was a never-ending revolving door: Mom would show up, either right out of a program or promising she'd go into one, then when she could prove it, he would let us back around her. Things would be fine for a few months and then it was a slow decline until she left again. I don't think they were together romantically for most of the time after I was born—I think the first time she left put an end to that—but it's not like I've asked.

Point is, Mom was in and out, and then, when we were little, after yet another failed stint of rehab, she was out for good. Signed away her parental rights, packed her bags, and left. The last memory I have of her, real or not, was waking up to her lying next to me in bed, her hand against my cheek. Her eyes were closed, and there were tears rolling down her face.

I don't know why we weren't enough for her to stay. Why she never got clean, why she never came back. I don't know if the way she could communicate with ghosts had anything to do with it, if she needed something else to dull the pain, if she couldn't carry the grief of the dead all on her own. I don't know where she is or who she is now. I just know that addiction is addiction, and love is love, and sometimes the two have a gnarled, thorny relationship that I cannot begin to understand.

Reece has more theories than me on this—but I think Reece thinks about her more, and of course they remember her more. But even so, I can't believe Reece kept her notebooks. And I feel like it's a betrayal to all those therapists and Bee and Dad that I really, really want to read them.

Under the spray of water, fully and truly alone, afraid and full of grief and heavy with betrayal, I let the tears fall.

I wake up and I'm still dead. Look at my reflection
and I'm still dead. Pack my bag and I'm still dead.

(I can't sleep. I have no reflection. I cannot
move objects. I have no bag. I am still dead.)

Get on my bike and I'm still dead. Ride to
school and I'm still dead. Walk down the hall
and I'm still dead. Go to class and I'm still dead.

(This is all her, I am in the shadow of her,
I feel her trickling through my veins with her
vitality; I anger at all the things she can do and I
can't, and I can't, and I can't and I am still dead.)

Get in your car and I'm still dead. Looking in the
rearview and I'm still dead. The rain falls and I'm still
dead. It's October 31 and I'm not dead and the car races
down the road and I would wake up if I were sleeping
and it's not this car, every time I'm in a car I'm in *that*
car and in *that* moment and it's instantaneous—

I'm in school and I'm still dead. The bell rings and
I'm still dead. She leads the way down the hall, listening
as I say things that only she can hear and I'm still dead.

I see you—

I see you—

I see you and I'm still dead.

You don't see me because I'm still dead.

CHAPTER 7

Bee comes home a little while later, when I'm wearing sweats and a hoodie and studying at the kitchen table. It feels homier the second she walks into the house and drops her keys in the bowl. She comes in, kisses the top of my head, and ruffles my hair. "Whatcha doin', peanut?"

"Stats homework," I grumble. I'm trying to get some of it done before Liam decides to reappear tonight so he can tell me everything I've done wrong.

She sets a take-out coffee and a slice of coffee walnut cake down in front of me. "Don't work too hard."

"I don't think that's possible," I sigh. I take a sip of the vanilla latte she's brought me home from the bakery. "What time will Dad be home, do you think?"

Bee is in front of the fridge, shifting her weight back and forth and chewing her lip as she searches through the shelves, probably figuring out what to make for dinner. "He was in court today, so hopefully not too late." Bee shuts the door, her arms now stacked with a package of chicken, a bag of broccoli, and a head of garlic. "I'll get a start on dinner. Do you want rice or noodles?"

"Rice," I say, and there's a quick stab of loneliness when there's no Reece to automatically retort "noodles." But that is also a reminder of all the things Reece would otherwise be saying to me—and what I suspect they might've spent years *not* saying to me.

The notebooks. Is it at all possible . . . could Reece somehow still be in contact with our mother? Or were they, at any point in the last twelve years?

It's a question that makes my stomach twist. I had not thought that it could be possible before today, but now . . . I'm not so sure.

It's easier to focus on someone else's problems. Bee is well-placed, as the new town baker and coffee shop owner, to get gossip.

Ghosts stick around because of threads left untied, loose ends to wrap up. Reece never allows familial intervention because of their theory that proximity to grief speeds up the deterioration of ghosts. Reece always talks to the ghost, then spins a web around their circle of influence, picking up tiny pieces of information until they find the answer, and only then do they do anything that involves those close to the dead—finding a locket that was left by the side of the road after a car accident, then mailing it anonymously to the recipient; tracking down an orphaned dog at the humane society and finding it a good and loving home; keeping a ghost corporeal enough to watch his daughter's wedding. Reece is good at figuring out the problem, then working towards a solution.

I don't have Reece's skills or know-how. I don't have Reece's ability to work through influence—I'm as subtle as a freight train. But Bee . . . Bee would probably be good at this.

She's set up the cutting board and turned the radio on to play ABBA, humming as she chops garlic. I lever myself up onto the counter next to her, swinging my feet.

"Question."

"Answer."

"Not funny."

"You smiled," she says, and her own smile is so sunny that I can't even protest. I just roll my eyes as she goes back to her chopping.

Oftentimes, there's an object involved that needs to go to

a rightful owner—and it's the easiest thing to fix. All it would require from me is a bit of postage and a bit of sleuthing, and we'd be all good. Unfortunately, since Liam doesn't remember his death, he can't remember if he was supposed to be giving anyone anything in the hours leading up to it.

"Did you find anything left behind, in the house, when we moved in?" I ask.

Bee frowns, considering this. "I can't say for sure," she says. "Like, they left us the fridge . . . ?"

I *highly* doubt whatever Liam wanted to pass on (if that's the solution at all) lived in the freezer. "Probably not that," I say, keeping my tone as light as possible. Bee is looking at me strangely; of course she can see right through this. I curse myself and wish Reece were here for the millionth time today—and then an abridged version of the truth rushes out of me.

"The kid who lived here before," I say. "He died, when his family lived in the house."

Bee sets her knife down. She looks at me, her frown deepening. "I'm sorry," she says after a minute. "I would've told you, but Reece has always been the weird one about death. . . ."

"No, no, it's fine," I say quickly, scrabbling for something I can follow this with. "I was just, uh, wondering . . . one of his friends said he might've left some stuff behind. They wanted something to, uh, remind them of him."

Bee is too kind to point out that it's a bit of a weird excuse—which is good, because it's the best I've got. "I don't think so, hon. But I haven't checked the attic yet, if you want to try there?"

It's something—it's enough to make my heart flare with hope. "Oh, that's a good idea."

Bee reaches out, brushing the hair away from my face. "It's nice of you to try to help," she says sincerely. All of that good feeling is quickly gone—because I know, deep down, that my reasons for helping Liam aren't necessarily the most faultless.

God. I hate to admit it, but Reece might be right. Ulterior motives, in this case, are probably not the best.

My spiral only lasts a few seconds. Bee goes back to chopping for barely a minute before she glances up at me.

"Did you talk to your dad about the Stats test yet?" Bee asks.

Dammit. "Not yet," I allow. "I was going to see if I could do some extra credit first."

"Drew..."

I lean to kiss her quickly on the cheek, slide off the counter, then grab my Stats stuff. "I'm working on it, promise!" I tell her before dashing up the stairs. She just sighs after me.

A few hours later, I'm back in my room, idly doodling in the margins of a practice English essay when Liam appears next to me.

"Hola."

"Jesus," I say, hand pressed to my heart. "You scared me."

"Sorry," he says, trying to frown, but it's covered by a laugh. He just snorts and shakes his head. "I should take more pity on your nerves, after the day we've had."

"You should," I say, tucking one of my knees up to my chest. "What's up?"

"I came to help you with Stats," he says, like it should be obvious. And it probably should be—I just didn't know if he'd come back today, after what happened earlier.

I don't know why his coming back brings a lump to my throat, but it does, and suddenly, I can't speak. Because he's dead, and today sucked, and yet he's still thinking of helping me. Because I think he would give anything in the world to talk to Hannah again, and there's nothing I can do about that. Because it's actually been a really, *really* bad day, and the terror still hasn't entirely left yet.

I need to ask him if he kept anything in the attic. If he thinks that it's an object keeping him behind—maybe something for Ella, or Hannah. But if I do that, then Liam . . . well, he'll be gone. And if Liam goes—*when* Liam goes—I'll be alone.

So I don't say anything. Wordlessly, I get out my homework

and set it out. Over the next hour, he goes through every question, telling me all the things I did wrong. It's nicer, coming from him—and the care he takes makes my stomach ache.

"What do you miss most?" I ask after we're done, while I'm packing up my stuff. "Besides studying, I mean," I amend, because he is, at his heart, a complete nerd.

He's back to sitting on the end of my bed, legs stretched out in front of him. "Hanging out with Hannah and Rin, mostly. Reading. I miss that most, probably—I didn't expect to miss books as much as I do."

"What? You can't . . . read?"

He wiggles his fingers at me. "I can't hold books or turn pages, Drew. I'm not real."

It's . . . a valid point. "I mean . . . I could do that for you," I say. "If it makes you feel better. Like, I'm sure we'll figure this all out soon enough, but it makes sense to keep you happy and calm while we do, and if that relaxes you . . ."

He's looking at me oddly. "You'd really do that?"

"Of course." I go to my shelf—which, okay, only has a few books. So I lead the way to Reece's room, and Liam follows me. Reece couldn't take their whole collection with them to school, so they ended up leaving a lot of stuff here in the smaller third bedroom that'll be theirs when they're home.

"Oh my god," Liam says like I've just revealed the holy grail. "What *is* this?"

I stand by and let him trace the spines, picking out titles he says he wants, and then we carry the stack back to my room.

We sit together, cross-legged, with the book between us, facing Liam. I scroll my phone as he reads, flipping pages for him as he needs. And I have never in my life felt such happiness radiating from a dead person.

"This is the best," Liam says a bit later. "You are the best."

Maybe I'm not the only golden retriever in the room. "God, you are such a fucking nerd."

"I owe you. I owe you big time."

I roll my eyes. I didn't realize *flipping book pages* for him would lead to such devotion, but I can't say I'm mad about it either. "You're already tutoring me."

He shakes his head. "Doesn't matter. What else do you want? What can I do?"

"I want for nothing."

Liam cocks his head. "I have an idea."

I'm not sure I like the look on his face.

"I'll help you talk to Hannah."

Blood rushes to my cheeks, and I'm certain it makes me go super blotchy in the space of three seconds. "I feel like I can handle that myself."

"The three-minute wave says otherwise."

I flop onto my back, covering my face with my hands. "Oh my *god*," I groan. "She probably thinks I'm so weird."

"Probably," he agrees. "But I can help."

I peer at him from between my fingers. "You'd really do that?"

He's not looking at me when he says, "I won't be around much longer, right? Someone needs to look after her."

I'm reaching a hand out before I can think better of it. "Deal, then," I say.

He shakes, his hand like nothing against mine. "Deal."

CHAPTER 8

Against my better judgment, I let Liam tag along again when it's time for school. I tell myself it's because I really do need his help with Stats.

I tell myself it's not because I don't want to go on the ride to school, through the woods, alone.

I also tell myself it's not because he'll be within screaming distance if something catches up to me during my run.

And I definitely tell myself it's not because he can help me, if the opportunity to talk to Hannah again presents itself.

But all of my excuses fall away right before the end-of-lunch bell rings. I always leave lunch a bit early, both because I have no friends and because it's a *trek* across the building and up three flights to my Gov class. I'm at my locker, switching my books out. Liam is a few feet down the hall, attempting to kick his old locker, trying to either break into it or see if it'll rattle (this reinforces my opinion that, actually, he's a really shitty poltergeist).

I'm just pulling out my books for Gov and Enviro when a soft voice behind me says, "Drew, right?"

I whip around (so much for being cool), and Liam is there by my side in a half-second. Hannah Sullivan stands before us.

She's wearing those Converse again and jean shorts and a Pitt T-shirt that's too big for her.

"Say something," Liam hisses.

I try to smile, and I probably look like I swallowed a lemon. Her own smile falters. "Hi," I say, hurrying to cover this up *somehow*. "Um. Sorry, you caught me off guard."

"Sorry about that." She nods down the hall. "I didn't mean to—anyway. I just wanted to say thanks again. For yesterday."

For a half-second, my brain is perilously blank—Hannah is *really good* at doing that to me. I can't remember what she's talking about. What happened. It's been blocked out, overshadowed by tentacle-like legs and shining black teeth and my own too-fast heart and the deal with Liam—which she *definitely does not and cannot know about*.

"Drew," Liam groans, like he can read my mind. Maybe he can. Maybe this whole ghost-corporeality-shit is making us too close. "She's talking about Caleb."

I swallow hard, scrabbling for words. "It was nothing." I try to style it out, leaning back against the lockers, but I'm pretty sure I just look like a jackass. "Are you okay? Was everything . . . ?"

What? Do I *want* to know about this fight with her . . . with her what? Her boyfriend? I wish I could ask Liam. I wish he *knew* what happened in the last year, but he only knows what happened in the walls of his own house. He's as useless in this as I am.

"Oh, uh, yeah." She laughs a little, not meeting my eyes. "Sorry, I know that probably looked . . . well. It probably looked pretty intense."

"He shouldn't talk to her like that," Liam says.

"He shouldn't talk to you like that," I say. Liam takes a quick, panicked look at me.

But Hannah takes the bait. Her top teeth sink into her bottom lip, dimpling its fullness, and—

Stop it, Drew.

"I know I don't really need to explain it. But my friend, Caleb— you met him at a bad time, I promise he's usually better than that—he's just worried about me. I swear it wasn't anything weird or . . . I don't know. Please don't go to the guidance counselor?"

I blink at her. "Why would I go to the guidance counselor?"

"And better yet," Liam says over my shoulder, "why doesn't she want you to?"

Hannah shrugs. "I don't know! Sorry, I'm making this so much weirder." She closes her eyes, takes a deep breath. Regroups. She's flustered, and I'm flustered, and I very *highly doubt* we're flustered about the same thing or for the same reason.

"Are you always this good with girls?" Liam deadpans. While Hannah's not looking, I elbow him in the ribs. He isn't able to dodge the jab, but he says, "Tell her you liked her poem. It's hanging in the library."

We had English in the library yesterday, so that must be when Liam saw it. "I liked your poem," I blurt.

"Delivery could use work," Liam says. Hannah is looking at me, though, so I can't deal out any more un-physical harm.

"Thanks," she says.

"What inspired you to write it?"

She glances away. "It's about, uh, my best friend."

"Oh, no way!" I say, thinking of Andie, who would literally die of laughter if I wrote a poem about her. Hannah must just have much nicer friends. "Did they like it?"

"*Drew*," Liam says, aghast.

Hannah just looks at me for a moment, her smile cracking. "I have to go back to class," she says quickly. Before I can say anything else, she's rushing away, down the hall, and not in the direction she came.

"Oh shit," I say. "I messed that up, didn't I?"

Liam is leaning against the lockers with his head in his hands. "Holy fuck, you are so bad at this."

"I don't even know what I said!"

"It's for *me*, Drew," Liam groans. "*I'm* her best friend. And no, she wouldn't have been able to show it to me herself. She can't know if I like it or not. Because I'm *dead*."

"Oh my god," I say, the whole conversation clicking back into place. "Oh my *god*."

Before I can recover, the after-lunch bell rings, and the hall is flooded with other students. I shove my books in my bag and zip it up, heading down the hall with Liam hot on my heels. "I didn't know," I say. "I mean, I did know, but I didn't think. . . . Oh my god! This is so hard! Why am I like this? I'm *never* like this."

"I don't know enough to say," Liam says flatly. Probably because I just made his best friend/my crush cry. Maybe because I am, to his knowledge, statistically a moron.

"I would like to die," I lament.

"Doubtful," Liam says. "Look. We can fix this."

"Fix it *how*?" I whine. A group of sophomores turns to look at me, and I remember too late that, to everyone else, I am talking to myself. A touch lower, I add, "I've definitely ruined it. She will never speak to me again."

"Again, doubtful," Liam says, but he's not as convincing this time. "Besides, we need to talk to her—Hannah might be the only person who can help us figure out why I'm still here. The only other person would be Ella, and you have no logical reason to call her, nor any real way to get ahold of her. So, as far as I know, Hannah's our only chance to send me on my way before I become . . ."

He doesn't finish his sentence. He doesn't have to. We both know what will happen to him if we can't figure out why he's still hanging around.

"You might be here for a while, then," I say darkly. And the husks might eat both of us before Hannah's willing to talk to me again.

"Look," Liam says, following me up the stairs. "Just . . . let me steer, okay? If you just let me tell you what to say, it'll work."

I glance at him sidelong. "You'd really do that?"

"It's probably easier than letting you do it," he says. "It's nothing against you, Drew. But realistically, we need to get closer to Hannah to figure out what's going on with me, and that means we can't . . . well. We can't send her crying down a hallway every time we see her."

I hate that he says it so plainly. I hate that he's right. I hate that part of me relaxes, relieved at giving him control.

"Okay," I say. "Lead the way, then."

ANDIE tries to call me after running club, but I'm in the middle of Reece's journal—and besides, I know there's nothing new, she's still doing great, and all of my friends are doing great, and they're planning their annual back-to-school camping trip, and I definitely don't feel like shit for missing it.

I would ask Dad if I could join, but it would mean either driving two hours back (and I *hate* driving) or asking him or Bee to take me. I can't deal with inconveniencing them like that. Maybe I'll get up my courage before the trip and find a way there . . . or maybe I won't.

And I can't pretend that I don't feel a stab of guilt there. But also resentment, because all of my old friends are together, and I'm just not.

But it would've happened in a year anyways. I keep telling myself this: I'm just speeding up the process.

Afterwards, I shower, and Bee's home by the time I'm out. It's Wednesday, so Dad has some sort of career development session with a few of the interns he's mentoring, meaning it's just the two of us for dinner. When I go downstairs, she's stirring a big pot of soup and singing along to ABBA again.

"Hey, peanut!" she says, her face lighting up when she sees me. "How was school?"

Awful. "Fine," I say, hoisting myself up on the counter. Liam is nowhere to be found—I'm not really sure where he goes when he's not here, but maybe he just perceives time differently or something—so I'm able to have an evening to myself.

"Have you made any new friends?" Bee asks, a note of hope in her voice. When I said I was fine to move, Dad accepted it joyfully without any protest—but Bee knew better. She knew what it meant to leave my friends and the only school I'd ever known; she knew I was doing it because it would make everyone else happy.

It sucks, but I've always been the fixer out of the four of us. The one who just wants to smooth everything over, keep everyone else happy. And realistically, if I said no, what would've happened? They would've moved in a year anyway. I probably still would've had shitty grades. Bee would've missed this opportunity, and we'd go another year of barely seeing Dad, and he'd spend at least three nights of the week sleeping on the couch in his office because he's working too late to come home.

The move just made sense. It sucks, but it's true.

And I don't want to lie to Bee—but I also don't want to disappoint her. "Oh, you know, Rin is cool. They live down the street?"

"Oh, good! I'm glad. Do you eat lunch with them?"

"Er—" I haven't talked to Rin besides a few comments in the hall every now and then. "Nah, I've been eating with my friend Liam."

Shit. I know it's a mistake the second the words are out of my mouth. Because Bee remembers everything, including all of my friends' names, and she will *notice* when this "Liam" never comes over, never hangs out, never materializes.

"How did you two meet? Is he a part of that running club?"

"Just at school," I lie, wincing, because I'm digging a deeper and deeper hole. "He's, um, in my Stats class."

Shit shit *shit*. I need to stop. I need to stop *now*.

"How's the bakery?" I ask quickly, trying to cover it all up. "Do you need me to do any shifts over the weekend?"

Bee smiles at me, looking up from the bacon she's chopping to garnish the potato soup. It's not quite cold enough for soup season, but the second August turns into September, Bee's big Strega Nona pot comes out, and no one can stop her.

"Are you around tomorrow afternoon, actually?" she asks.

"If you don't have practice, can you cover a couple of hours after school? I need to have a meeting with one of my suppliers."

"Yeah, I can do that," I say.

"And maybe Sunday morning, if you're up for it," she says. "And tell Liam to come by! Pastries on me. It'll be nice to meet your new friends."

Absolutely fucking not, and I have *so many* regrets. "I'll mention it to him," I lie.

I'M not mentioning it to Liam, even though he's there when I go upstairs after dinner. Bee is thoroughly occupied testing out a new recipe downstairs, and Dad won't be home until late, so it's the perfect time to figure out what's in the attic.

Liam doesn't protest as he follows me to the attic, which is accessible through a door in Reece's room that leads to a creepy staircase.

"This looks like a fun evening," I deadpan, as Liam gazes into the gathered dust.

He only sighs. "Do you have a flashlight?"

I flick on the one on my phone. We both stare up the stairs. "You should go first," I tell him. "You're already dead."

Liam rolls his eyes, but he reaches for the banister—probably more out of habit than anything else. "What do you think we're going to find up here?" he asks.

"I don't know," I admit. "Maybe your mom left behind a bin of baby clothes or something."

Liam glances at me over his shoulder. "But she still lived here for months after I died. She had every chance to get them herself."

He has a point, and I feel my face heating. I know I'm not any good at this—Reece has already pointed it out loads of times. I don't need to hear it from Liam too.

"Did you keep any stuff up here?" I ask, and I know some of the acid has crept into my tone.

"Not really," Liam says. "Ella and I used to play hide and seek up here when we were little, but I haven't been up here in years."

"Then maybe there's something older of value here—but you're the only one who will know that," I say. We get to the top of the stairs, where a string hangs down from a bare bulb. I pull it, and the light buzzes slowly into a dim glow. It's not enough to light the corners, but I can see the boxes at the far end, covered in cobwebs. There's not much else up here, but it's a start.

I nod to the boxes. "Let's go through them, then."

Liam sighs, but he heads off towards the far corner. "Is this one of Reece's theories?" he asks as he reaches the wall, then leans against it—he can't pick up any of the boxes or go through them. He'll just have to watch me, and stop me if anything catches his eye.

The first box is a bunch of old sweaters, but they're not anywhere near his size. "It's not," I say as I pull the first few out; he shakes his head and waves a hand, so I move to the next. "With ghosts, lingering often falls into three categories: something ungiven, something undone, or something unsaid." The next box holds photo albums. Liam glances over my shoulder as I start flipping through them, but they're clearly from some time way before Liam or I was born.

"Right. So you think once I give something to someone, do something, or say something, I'll be able to go."

"Not particularly," I say, flipping through the second album. A little closer in date—but not by much. I wonder if one of his baby albums is here, if his mom just couldn't find it before he died. If she lies awake thinking of the first picture of her newborn, now lost, or a lock of his hair, wrapped in plastic, pressed into a page. No such thing materializes. "You can't actually do any of those things. It's my responsibility to solve it for you."

"Ah," Liam says, his voice a little rough. I glance up at him and see the stiffness of his expression.

"Let's talk about something else," I say, eager to change the subject. If he gets emotional and attracts a husk, I have no desire to fight them in this creepy attic. "That Caleb guy. What's his deal? You said he's into Hannah?"

Liam shrugs. "What's the deal with anyone?" he says imperiously.

I shift to a new box; there's nothing in this one that's from the last century. "That's not an answer."

Liam sighs. "You're not going to like it," he says.

"Oh, goody," I say. This box is full of moldy shoes, and possibly spiders. We're eliminating boxes at an alarming rate—and I have to admit, it might be an exercise in futility.

"It's . . ." He frowns, chewing on his lip. "Okay. We were all friends. Rin, Caleb, Hannah, me. A few others I don't think you've met—you probably will."

"I shouldn't be surprised you had a lot of friends," I say, "but yet."

Liam rolls his eyes. "Anyways. In, like, eighth grade, Caleb decided he wanted to ask out Hannah. But he knew I, uh, liked her. So he got me and Rin together, and we made a pact."

My hand stills. Of course, I suspected this, but there didn't seem to be much point in saying it. "Right."

"And we knew it would ruin the friendship, and the friend group. So Caleb and I decided that . . . neither of us would ask her out, and Rin would hold us accountable, and we'd all be happy."

He's right. I don't like this. "You didn't think to make this . . . oh, I don't know. Hannah's decision?"

Liam holds my gaze for a minute. I see the irony. I feel the awkwardness growing between us. "Right," I say, going back to my box.

"Caleb broke the promise for Homecoming last year," Liam says quietly. "But Hannah said no. So."

My hand stills on the box before I rip through the tape. "So he violated the terms of your deal? And that's the last night you remember?"

"Him asking her isn't the last night I remember," he says sharply. "I remember . . ." He shakes his head. Folds his arms over his chest. "I drove her to a party after Homecoming. And since he violated the truce, I could do it too."

"You asked her out," I say, some of the pieces fitting together. But—if he already made that confession, that's not something left unsaid, is it? He *said* what he needed to. So why is he still here?

"In a word," Liam says, staring at his shoes. "I told her how I felt, and it went badly. I guess none of it mattered, and Caleb and I were even."

"It's kind of shitty," I say slowly. "Being her friend for years, I mean, only because you wanted to date her."

Liam covers his face with his hands. "That's not the only reason I was friends with her," he groans. "And I . . . I would've gotten over it. I probably *was* getting over it. That was the promise I made to myself: that it wouldn't ever impact our friendship if she turned me down."

I swallow hard—but also, I recognize the peril of my own situation. Because, by using Liam to get close to Hannah . . . aren't I doing something much, *much* worse?

"Hang on," Liam says, so sharply I jump. I look up at him, but he's looking at the box in my hands. "That is definitely Caleb's hoodie."

I look down at the fabric folded in the box. It's gray, with a rather distinct '90s-style Steelers pattern.

"Huh," I say. "You sure?"

"He used to wear it all the time," Liam insists.

I pull the hoodie out of the box, wrinkling my nose at the odd smell—and then we both realize at the same time where it's coming from: the bottom of the hoodie is stiff and dark, crusted with blood that has long since dried.

A SOLILOQUY

By Liam Orville

When I was a kid, I couldn't imagine dying. I know, I know—I'm seventeen, not much older than a kid now. Seventeen and never eighteen, in that weird tragedy of unknowing that is spinning out of control.

Let's start over—when I was a kid, my cousin died. He was sick for a while, the type of thing that's mostly a matter of waiting for a call, waiting for the other shoe to drop. I don't know if I'm explaining this in any sort of sympathetic way, but since I'm dead too now, I guess it doesn't much matter.

When I was a kid, my cousin died, and he was twenty-seven. I was nine, probably, and Ella was seven or eight, and we got the call late at night on a Tuesday when I was supposed to be in bed but was reading under the covers of my—Drew's—room with a flashlight propped against my chest. I remember Mom crying, first quiet, and then too loud, as if she suspected that it didn't matter if we heard her anyways.

I snuck down the stairs, avoiding the creaky ones, and sat in the shadows so I could better hear Mom and Dad as they whispered about his death. As they planned the drive for the funeral, Mom just kept saying: "He's so *young*. I can't believe it—he's so *young*."

He had ten years more than I did, didn't he?

I think back to the night of my own death—I wasn't there when Mom and Dad heard the news at first. I woke up, opened my eyes, and it was a new day and I was still in my clothes from last night and Mom was crying downstairs and I didn't know that I was already dead. I went downstairs and Mom was on her knees in the kitchen, sobbing. Dad was out—I later learned that he was at the hospital, making the official identification, making sure it was actually my body there.

"Mom," I said. "*Mom*."

But she didn't know. She didn't hear me.

There was something, then, like a hand on my shoulder—and I turned, and for the first time in almost a decade, I saw him. My cousin, Tommy, twenty-seven still. Shaggy hair hanging into his eyes, meek smile curving one side of his face, looking just like he did when I saw him the Christmas before he died.

That's when I realized I couldn't remember the night before.

I don't know if Tommy's ghost was really there or if I only imagined him. I don't know if you're still around. I don't know if Drew is listening to me now, or if I'm talking myself into oblivion—

I don't know where the memories go, when I'm gone. When I was seventeen and not dead, I would sometimes lie awake in bed at night and think about death in an abstract way of something that was so far off, it could never happen to me. My grandparents are mostly dead, too, but that's a far-off kind of thing. I found myself thinking of Tommy, of his crooked smile and the oil on his hands from fixing his motorbike and the band T-shirts he used to wear before it got bad, before he no longer saw the light through the haze.

Where did all of him go? Where did all of his himness disappear to? Where did the things vanish to, the thoughts and hopes and dreams, the fears, all of that person in one stable period in time, in one stable shape?

I wonder if he's knocking about at Aunt Martha's, or if maybe death actually was the end for him. The reprieve. Maybe he finished everything before he died and didn't hang around like me. Maybe he made peace with the fact that it all would be over at some point—maybe he craved it.

Do not go gentle into that good night. It's Hannah's favorite poem.

I don't want to go gentle. I don't want to go at all. I'm here, screaming, and I think I'll be here, screaming, until the end of time. I don't seek peace—I seek *more*. I want *more*.

I want to be alive more than I've ever wanted anything before, and I fear—

It's too late, isn't it? It's all over.

CHAPTER 9

"Can you smell?" I ask Liam on Thursday afternoon. He's sitting on the counter of Bakerbee while I lean against it, mindlessly doodling on a napkin.

Liam wrinkles his nose. "Of course I can."

"Well, how am I supposed to know? I'm not a ghost."

He sighs, kicking his feet. They go right through the cabinets. I asked him, the other day, how he can sit on some things and go through others—he didn't have a good answer for me. I've been prying on other things, attempting to lock down the parameters of his understanding.

We are doing everything possible to avoid talking about the hoodie.

I know we should—after all, there's a very good chance it was covered in Liam's blood. It's still in his attic, long after he died. But I can't forget the look on his face when I pulled it out, when we saw the blood. It was utter betrayal.

If Caleb had something to do with his death . . .

"Did you have a job?" I ask next, a minute or so later.

"Nah," he says. "Made a bit of extra money tutoring, but that's about it."

"Huh." I can't relate. Reece and I have been working for Bee as long as she's been in business—don't worry, she pays us. It's minimum wage, but we also get free pastries and coffee, so I'm not complaining. Plus, she doesn't care if I do my homework or doodle when I'm back here.

It's been pretty quiet, as far as afternoons go. We're all still figuring out what it's like here, and when people want what: So far, Bee's busiest time is (unsurprisingly) the pre-work and pre-school coffee rush. She was expecting to get more of an after-school crowd, but that hasn't built up quite yet.

And with the lull, of course my brain slips back to Caleb.

Reece told me, when we were younger, that most ghosts weren't murdered. Usually, the murdered spirits become husks pretty quickly—it's the rage, they said. The fear. All that emotion, pent up? Yeah, that's not lasting long.

And I've met Caleb. Sure, he didn't look super nice, but I can't believe he would've just *killed* Liam. Someone he cared about. And every time there's a lull, every time I know Liam is thinking about it, he has a sick look on his face.

The best thing, at this point, would be to call Reece. To tell them, officially, that I've bitten off more than I can chew. I'm thinking about texting them, nearly reaching into my apron for my phone—

Except the bell dings over the door, and when I look up, my heart drops to my stomach.

"All right, game faces on," Liam says when he sees Hannah Sullivan and Rin Mendoza come through the door. There's a change in his face, a flicker—and I wonder, if this was last year, in another universe, if it would be Rin, Hannah, and Liam walking through.

And maybe Caleb. Caleb, who could be a murderer.

"Hey you," Rin says, a wide smile splitting their face. They're one of those people who have time for everyone, at least on the surface—I haven't yet discovered if they're genuinely nice, or if they just give the impression of niceness. This might have a lot to do with my own cynicism. "I've been meaning to drop in—your stepmom brought over cinnamon rolls last week, and they're all I can think about."

"She makes the best cinnamon rolls," I confirm. Going great. Nothing weird yet. Good job, Drew.

"You two know each other?" Hannah asks.

"Be cool," Liam warns me. I can already see the concern building on his face as he waits for me to mess this up.

I paste on a smile, leaning on the counter. I show off my forearms, because girls love forearms; *I* love forearms. "We're neighbors," I say.

Hannah does a double-take, and I again realize my mistake. Next to me, Liam groans. "You live on Percival?" she asks. "What house number?"

"You have to tell her now," Liam says. "It's weird if you don't."

"Forty-eight," I say, but it comes out as more of a squeak.

Rin glances at her unhappily. Hannah's expression shutters for a moment, but then the corners of her mouth are turning up in a smile that doesn't reach her eyes. "Well," she says. "It couldn't stand empty forever, could it?"

"Don't say anything," Liam cautions, which is good, because my lips are forming questions about her and Liam and who he once was. I realize, after he corrects me, why that is a bad idea. "Offer her a cinnamon roll. One for Rin too."

"So those cinnamon rolls," I say before the silence can go on too long. And because Liam can't chide me for being nice, "And can I get you a coffee?"

"Ooh," Rin says. "Caramel latte for me, please! And yes—I promised Mom I'd bring a roll home for her too."

I package up two cinnamon rolls for Rin and start on their latte before I turn to Hannah. "Anything for you, Hannah?" I ask.

"Crushing it," Liam praises me. He should be glad there are other people here, because otherwise I'd kick him in the shin.

Hannah comes closer, looking at the desserts in the display case. Today, she's wearing a gingham milkmaid sundress with her

Converse, and the same gold necklace from the other day. Her hair is pulled into a messy fishtail braid. I wonder if, when she looks at me, she *sees* me. I wonder if she takes me in like I take her, or if I'm just this awkward point of discord in her life.

"What do you like?" she asks, looking up at me. There's something about the way she looks at me that immediately makes me flush.

"Be cool, Drew," Liam says.

I swallow back anything else I could say. "The lemon tart is so good. It's one of Bee's—my stepmom's—specialties."

Hannah nods gravely, like this is the most difficult decision she's making today. "A slice of that, and a cinnamon roll for home."

"Coffee?" I ask.

"Chai latte," she says with a hint of a smile, "if you have it?"

"Coming right up," I say.

"Wow, a normal conversation for once," Liam says. He's smiling, which is a change—he's smiling, but he's also looking at Hannah.

I should be asking her something that will eventually get us to talk about Liam, to figure out what he needs, to get him moving. But Liam is right—we've finally had a *normal* conversation, and that feels like a precious thing.

Because when Liam moves on, I'll still be here, and I'll have to figure out how to deal with Hannah on my own. I'd prefer it if she doesn't hate me when that time rolls around.

Rin and Hannah pay for their stuff and grab a table while I work on their drinks. They're talking about something in hushed voices, but I'm trying hard not to eavesdrop until I hear *Caleb* and *Homecoming* and something turns in my stomach.

"Drew," Rin says when I come over with a tray. "Settle something for us."

"What's up?" I ask, setting their drinks down, then the pastry boxes.

"If one of your friends kept asking you out even when you

said no, would you see that as a reason to nuke the relationship or would you be like, oh yes, of course you can be my boyfriend?"

"Um." I look at the table for a second, and I feel that blush creeping up—but honestly, I haven't been quiet about being a lesbian since, like, ninth grade. "I'm not really the boyfriend-having type?"

"Girlfriend, then," Rin corrects. "Partner."

"Then no, I don't think that would fly," I say. I've got a towel looped over my apron, and I use it to wipe crumbs off the table next to them, partially to look busy, partially to have something to do with my hands. "Probably a full nuke situation. After I told them off."

"Full nuke sounds harsh," Hannah mutters. "I don't really feel like losing more friends."

"*Who???*" Liam shouts across the room, as if anyone but me can hear him. "Drew, ask who it is!"

I shoot him a glare, because the other two can't really see my face, and that is actually fairly bad advice from Liam.

"Is this about the guy from the other day?" I guess, aiming the question at Hannah.

She winces. "Caleb didn't mean anything by it, first of all," she says, mostly to Rin. "Yeah—it was a mistake. He knows that."

My stomach drops to my toes.

I aim another look at Liam. He leans back against the display case unhappily, folding his arms over his chest, but he stays quiet. I wonder if he's thinking about it, too—if he's imagining Caleb at the scene of his death, doing . . . something that would involve that much blood.

Rin is already firing back. "He knew you were vulnerable, and he pretended to be supportive just so he could get in your pants. Does nothing that happened last year matter? You think that's acceptable behavior?"

I feel like I'm intruding on this conversation, so I try to move away as subtly as I can.

"You saw their conversation," Rin says to me, dragging me

back in. Hannah and I exchange a glance, both of us looking scolded, and I think that, for the first time, we're actually on the same page. "The other day, when Caleb was an ass. Right, Drew?"

It looks like Hannah told Rin about how I interrupted. No idea how that conversation went—maybe they did have Physics to study after all, or Hannah just went to Rin's house anyways. I twist the towel in my hands. "I really didn't mean anything by it," I apologize to Hannah. I'm on my own right now—I feel Liam, simmering with fury somewhere behind me. It's making the electricity go all weird, and he needs to calm down, because if he summons any more husks or that weird spider thing, I will actively feed him to them headfirst.

"He just had a tone," I say. "If there was something going on, I was happy to stay out of it, but I just wanted to check if you were okay."

"Han, if even the new girl sees it, it's a bit fucked," Rin says, their voice going softer. They reach out, laying a hand on Hannah's arm.

"He was there when I needed him," Hannah says, not looking at either of us. I am definitely not meant to be in this conversation. "He just thinks . . ." Hannah sucks in a breath. "He thinks I'm holding on too tightly. To. . . . That I should let go."

There's a pause. A beat. Hannah doesn't look at me.

"You're not," Rin reassures her. "You're going at your own pace. But even if he was there for you when you needed him for emotional support, it doesn't mean you owe him anything at all," Rin says. "Not a kiss. Not a date. Not a second of your time."

I take that as my cue to go back behind the counter. Rin and Hannah continue their conversation, quieter, as if neither have noticed I left. I don't eavesdrop. I focus on packaging up the last pick-up orders for tonight and avoiding Liam's mounting fury.

Unlike me, he *does* eavesdrop.

"I can't believe this," he says, stomping back over to me as Hannah retreats to the bathroom, covertly wiping tears from the corners of her eyes, and Rin turns to their phone. "Are you listening to this, Tarpin?"

I shake my head, just a fraction, as I uncap one of my Sharpies and write the name on the box for one of the orders.

Liam hoists himself back on the counter, his fingers digging into the edge and going right through. "It sounds like, when I died, he really put on the pressure. Started buying her flowers. Bringing her snacks. Coffee. Taking her out, to 'take her mind off things.'" He shakes his head. "It's just fucking predatory, really—"

"Hey, Drew?"

We both freeze. I spin around from the prep counter. Hannah is there, holding the box in front of her.

"Say something," Liam hisses.

"I didn't mean to overstep," I blurt. "And I'm sorry."

She smiles, and this one is sunnier than the last. "No, I do appreciate it. I, uh. If you're going to the game tomorrow, a few of us are going to a bonfire after. Do you want to come?"

I blink at her for a second.

"Say yes!" Liam shouts.

"Sure," I say, the word falling out of my mouth without any conviction. I swallow, clear my throat. "Yeah, I'd love to. Thank you."

Hannah smiles. "Thanks for this," she says. "You're right. The lemon tart is really good."

"Bee's a magician," I say, which sounds ridiculous, but is also kind of true.

Her smile widens. She has dimples, and the corners of her eyes crinkle, and I'm going to die.

"Sounds it. I can't wait to try more of her creations." Hannah gestures with the box and nods as she turns to go. "Meet us in the back lot after the game, yeah?"

"Sounds good," I say.

At least this time around, Liam waits until they're out the door and down the road a bit before he celebrates. And if they turned around and saw me dancing by myself, high-fiving the air? Well, I can't answer for that.

Until Liam and I turn to one another, and the rest of the conversation returns to us. "Do you think Caleb hated me?" he asks, deflating against one of the fridges.

I sigh, crossing my arms over my chest. "I don't know," I admit. "I don't know *him*."

Liam looks away, a muscle in his jaw ticking. "Well," he says. "Do you think he liked Hannah enough to kill me to get close to her?"

We both look out the glass window, down the street, as if we could still see the memory of Hannah Sullivan walking down it.

"I don't know that either," I say.

LIAM comes back around when I'm showered and dressed in my PJ's with wet hair dripping down my back, just in time to review Stats for the evening. I have to give him credit: He's holding up his end of the bargain, even if I'm doing a shit job at mine.

He tucks himself in the chair I dragged in from Reece's room even though he doesn't really need to sit down. He and I work through the problems one at a time, and Liam doesn't even make fun of me when it takes me a few tries to get the correct answer.

I don't mind it either. It's oddly companionable. I have my calls with Andie and texts with the rest of our friend group, but not true friendship these days. It's nice, to be comfortable with someone—even if he's a ghost.

"So, tomorrow," I start as we work through the last problem on my homework set.

"Mm?"

"What should I expect? And do I have to go to the game?"

He snorts. "You don't have to go to the game. But isn't it your thing? You seem to like . . . sports."

I roll my eyes. "I like *select* sports. Running. Track. I will watch hockey, and sometimes soccer. Football doesn't really do it for me."

"Same," Liam says. He leans over to check my work when

I finish the problem, then nods. I smile, despite myself—he is actually good at this. "I hate football. I only went to the games when Rin or one of our other friends dragged me along, or when Hannah was doing something important. She's in the band."

"I know," I say, blushing despite myself.

Liam goes to sit on the edge of my bed. I follow, going up and crawling under the covers, leaning against the headboard.

"But no, you don't have to go to the game. Sometimes they do a bonfire. Sometimes we all end up at Steak 'n Shake or Eat'n Park. You know, an all-night diner situation."

"We didn't have many of those where I'm from."

"Welcome to the big city. The wonders never cease."

I throw a pillow at his head. It goes right through him. "We live in the suburbs, you ass."

He just smiles, draping an arm over his knee, and that's when I realize that, if he were still alive, there's no questioning it: We'd be friends. Maybe even good friends. Maybe we'd have this same conversation, or one similar, and the pillow wouldn't go right through him. Maybe he'd still help me with my Stats homework. Maybe we'd help each other talk to girls.

I glance at my hands, picking at a cuticle on my left middle finger. "I have a question. About Hannah."

"Yeah?"

"Is she, uh." I don't know how to ask it, and I don't know how it'll be received. "Is she into girls at all?"

Liam is quiet for a long moment, long enough that I look up at him. If he were alive, he'd be blushing, too, I'm sure of it. He's not quite meeting my eyes either.

"We didn't really talk about that stuff all that much," he says. "And, obviously, it's been a bit since we've *talked*. Things might've changed."

"Ah," I say, wincing.

"But she was definitely bi-curious, if nothing else," Liam says. He'd be beet-red now, I'm sure of it, and I'm pretty sure I'm not far off. I feel my pulse in my ears.

"Oh," I squeak. "Well, that's good news."

He nods, still not quite looking at me. "I just . . . I can't believe Caleb would be such a dick," he says finally. "That he would be that possessive with her." He does not say, *I can't believe that Caleb might've had something to do with my death.*

"It's not cool," I agree.

"Can I ask a favor of you?" Liam asks, and the tone of his voice is odd.

"Yeah, of course." We're already neck-deep in favors. What's one more?

"It's also about Hannah," he says, rubbing his left hand with his right. "I can't do much. I know. But something about Caleb is really making me feel . . . not great. Can you just, I don't know, keep an eye on her? Intervene if need be?"

"Well, it looks like our interests are, again, united." I hold out a hand for him to shake. He hesitates before he takes it. "You have yourself a deal."

"Thanks," Liam says, not meeting my eyes.

"Liam," I say. We can't keep doing this. We can't *not* talk about it. "Do you think . . . do you think he was involved, at all, on the night that you died?"

Liam closes his eyes. His expression is unreadable, but I've spent weeks studying him—and I think I can see the fear there.

"I . . . I can't rule it out," he says.

I nod. I guess it's what I suspected. And I can't say it surprises me too much, in a grim, awful way; it makes sense that he'd still be here, lingering, if his death wasn't just random after all.

CHAPTER 10

In the end, surprise of all surprises, I do go to the game before—but not of my own free will. Rin comes to my house after school and drags me first to Bee's to get more cinnamon rolls, then back home to change, then back out to the game itself. I don't mind; they can drive, and they're fun to hang out with, and, like I said, I could use the companionship with a living person.

Liam is out doing ghost things until tonight. He explained to me the other day that it takes him a lot of energy to keep up with me, and in between, he essentially "sleeps." I don't know what that means or where he does it or if I'm going to find him hanging from the bathroom ceiling like a bat one day.

(He was horrified by this suggestion and broke one of my lightbulbs.)

((It was worth it.))

At the game, Rin and I shout our lungs out and eat shitty nachos washed down with hot chocolate, even though it's still well over seventy degrees and will be for another couple of weeks still.

When we make our way to the back parking lot to meet the others after the game ends, Rin has their arm slung around my shoulders, and we're still laughing over one of the kids we saw in the student section, dressed in one of those blow-up dinosaur costumes, who tripped on their tail and nearly fell out of the bleachers when we scored.

For the first time, I feel accepted. Embraced. It dulls the ache of being here, alone for my senior year; it makes everything a little bit more manageable. Like I can breathe again.

Between one blink and another, Liam is on my other side, hands shoved in his pockets, a smile playing on his face. He glances at me and Rin sidelong, and it's almost like he's really here.

The back entrance of the school is chaos, with band kids going in and out, half dressed in uniform and locked in rowdy discussions. Rin and I lean against their car while we wait, and they identify different people and feed me tidbits of gossip. Liam supplements sometimes, adding context that Rin doesn't provide, and I nod along as I take it all in.

When Hannah comes out, she brings three other people along with her. Her hair is in two French braids, the baby hairs sticking out haloed in the bright lights of the parking lot. She crashes into Rin, happier than I've ever seen her, and Rin nearly falls over.

"You must be Drew," one of the people with her says. He's got curly hair and dimples and a kind smile.

"That's Danny Martinez," Liam says at the same time the boy says, "I'm Danny." Liam continues, "And Sophia Allman, and Adam Hill. There are a couple others, but that's most of the friend group."

"Nice to meet you," I say as Sophia and Adam also introduce themselves.

"I'll take Danny and Sophia if you take Adam and Drew?" Hannah says once we've all finished pleasantries. "You'll probably beat me there anyways, so you should have Adam."

"Sounds like a plan," Rin says. "Is Caleb going?"

"Of course he is," Sophia says.

Rin gives Hannah a look, which Hannah studiously ignores. I shoot Liam a glance. "Caleb is part of the friend group, unfortunately," Liam says, looking at his shoes. "I imagine the others would find it odd if he wasn't invited."

Before we split off, Rin puts a hand on Hannah's arm. The

others are messing around, but I'm close enough to hear Rin ask, "Holding up okay?"

"Fine," Hannah says tightly, ducking out of Rin's grasp.

"What do you think that's about?" I whisper to Liam as we turn toward the cars. Hannah takes Sophia and Danny, but Adam stays with us, getting into the passenger seat as I let myself into the back of Rin's car.

Liam crowds in after me. "Not to be a narcissist," he says, and I give him a look, "but there were things we always used to do, at the beginning of the year. Like this—Adam does a lot of bonfires, and we always used to go together. Sometimes, we used to go to the Steak 'n Shake in the next town over, the one the football players don't go to, and we would stay out too late and eat too many fries and inevitably someone would reveal something embarrassing they did over the summer and someone else would confess to a new crush." He shrugs. "We just have *things* we do: post-game fries, and bowling in the winter, and volleyball in the summers—"

"Wouldn't peg you for a sportsman," I mutter under my breath, quiet enough so the others don't hear.

Liam rolls his eyes and presses on, "And Hannah's band contests and Rin's field hockey games and Caleb's track meets—"

Fuck, looks like I'll be spending more time with Caleb than I want to.

"—and Adam's swim meets. And whatever else comes up that we all want to do. We sit together at lunch. We hang out after school. And Hannah and I are attached at the hip." He catches himself, in the present tense. His throat works when he looks out the window. "Were," he corrects.

I reach out. Lay my hand over his. When I squeeze, he squeezes back.

"I imagine," he says, after a moment of listening to the laughter from the front seat as Rin puts on a particularly heinous remix of a Run-DMC song and cranks it up so it pounds through the speakers, "she's struggling with . . . me not being around."

"I imagine she is," I agree.

We do beat the others there. Adam goes inside to set up drinks and snacks, and Rin nods towards the edge of the trees. "I'm the fire-builder extraordinaire," they tell me, winking over their shoulder.

I snort. When we used to go camping, Andie was always in charge of the fire, but I'm not completely clueless. I help Rin gather sticks and then sit by as they start building the fire in the rock-lined pit.

"Are you going to be okay for a bit?" Liam asks, rubbing his head. "I'm feeling a bit . . . yeah."

Rin is thoroughly occupied, heading back to the edge of the woods for a few more scraps. "Are you okay?" I ask.

"Yeah. I think the distance is getting to me," he admits. "I'll try to meet up with you again in a couple of hours, if you can fend for yourself until then?"

"Go," I tell him, surprised by the tenderness in my own voice. "I'll be okay. No reason for you to overexert."

He gives me a weak smile and vanishes into nothing, but I'm still looking at the space where he was when Rin returns.

"You okay?" they ask.

I blink back into the present. "Yeah," I promise.

Rin and I keep working on the bonfire, and it's not long before Hannah's car arrives—followed by a whole bunch of people I, unsurprisingly, don't know. I stick close to Rin as they introduce me to most of them. I forget most of their names.

I wish, weirdly, that Liam were still here—it makes the world a bit more approachable when he's next to me, whispering info about these people in my ear, giving me context and all the gossip I could ever want.

Rin is great with names and sometimes okay with context, but they never give me the true gossip. I have a pet suspicion that they might be too nice for that.

There's music pumping and snacks and drinks and sticky-sweet punch weighed down with vodka that someone's brother bought. It's not too different from the gatherings I've been to with Andie, and maybe that makes it all the lonelier.

We're sitting on the back porch, looking down at the fire and talking to Sophia and Danny, when another group rolls in. I recognize Caleb immediately, and another girl from my English class—from Liam's usual monologue during class, I know her name is Paige—and there's a new round of intros. Caleb's expression hardens when he sees me, and he doesn't quite smile so much as tighten his mouth when he says hi to me.

It's almost like he knows I don't trust him.

And—I can't say I *don't* have ulterior motives for being here. If I can figure out where Caleb was that night, maybe I can find out if he was anywhere near Liam when he died—or if he had anything to do with it.

"Where did you move from?" Danny asks once we're all crammed in on the porch swing and outdoor sofa.

"I moved from Fairhope Creek," I say. "Southeast of here. Almost West Virginia. Past Seven Springs, and not really *near* anything."

"Can't say we're near much," Danny says.

Sophia throws a pretzel at him. "We're literally twenty minutes from the city."

"Not with traffic," Danny whines.

Rin rolls their eyes. "Such a first-world problem."

"Well, if you had to get to youth orchestra practice every week—"

"Danny made the Pittsburgh Youth Symphony," a familiar voice says directly into my ear. I jump, turning—and Hannah is there, leaning down. She moves to perch on the arm of the chair next to me, so close I can feel the warmth of her skin. She must've come out a minute ago, covered by the noise of the party.

"And he will not let any of us forget it," Sophia says cheerfully.

"That's actually really cool!" I say.

"We know," Hannah and Sophia and Rin say, almost in

sync. They exchange this little look, like this scene has happened before—

And I miss Andie so much. Or maybe even Liam. Or anyone else who doesn't make me feel like I'm just on the outside of this.

The door behind us swings open. I turn—it's Adam, carrying a tray of plastic cups. "I thought you guys were out here," he says. For a second, the noises of the house slip out, the music and the clamor of voices. I don't know how many people are here now, but it's just our group on the porch, and the few people hanging out by Rin's bonfire are out of earshot.

Adam clears his throat. "I thought," he says, a tone softer, "we might have a toast."

Silence descends. Next to me, Hannah looks down at her hands, throat working; Rin lets out a heavy breath.

"It's the first game of the season," Adam says, as if that's an explanation. "I just thought . . . well. It's just weird, you know? Doing the bonfire without him, sitting around without him being grumpy in his chair, doing all of this as if it's normal and not . . ."

His breath is ragged for the barest moment. Sophia gets up and wraps an arm around him, careful not to disturb the cups. She leans her head against his shoulder.

Adam takes a few breaths, then he starts to hand out the cups. "I don't want to forget he was here," Adam finishes.

"We won't," Rin says. "We can't."

Hannah still isn't looking up. I can't tell if she's crying—even next to me, it's hard to say if she's breathed at all.

We all take a cup. They have a bit of that sickly punch in it. Hannah opts instead for her can of Coke, and I wish I had a different drink, too, but I'll drink to this. To him.

"I love you guys," Rin says. I have the sense that maybe I should leave, move on before it's clear that I don't belong here, but it would be too obvious now. "And no one else would've been able to get through what we did and come out on the other side. But fuck, I miss that kid."

"Me too," Danny says.

"Yeah," Hannah agrees, her voice a little choked.

I keep my eyes on Caleb. Watch him for any sign of guilt. He doesn't look at anyone as he takes his cup—his eyes are focused on his shoes, on anything but the scene happening before him. I can't say it's a sign of guilt, but when everyone else is leaning in and searching for connection, I can't help but notice that he's doing everything in his power to set himself apart.

Adam raises his cup. "To Liam," he says. "Wherever he is now."

Closer than you think.

We all drink. The punch burns like poison all the way down. As soon as it's finished, Caleb takes his empty cup, excuses himself from the circle, and goes back inside alone.

I leave the circle when it's appropriate and not weird and make my way down to the fire. There, it's easy enough to make small talk with a girl I barely know from my Gov class until she goes to find her other friends, and then I'm alone, sitting in a camping chair, staring at the flames.

"Hey."

I look up—it's Hannah again, and my stomach goes leaden with anxiety. "Hey," I say back, which is pretty good as far as starting points go.

She grabs one of the other camping chairs and pulls it closer. "Sorry if that was weird for you, up there."

I snort. "You don't have to apologize to me. He would want you to . . ."

I catch myself halfway through the sentence, because what? *He would want you to miss him* is what I was about to say, or *He's afraid you forgot him*, and all of those sentiments are no-nos, considering Liam is dead and I never actually knew him.

I backtrack. "It's nice, what you all did. You clearly cared about him."

"Yeah," Hannah says quietly, poking the fire with a stick. She takes a long, shuddering breath. "Sorry, that's not what I came down here for." She shakes her head. "You must think I'm so . . ."

"What?"

Hannah blows a breath through her teeth. "Dramatic. Just, like, with the Caleb stuff, and the dead best friend, and—Christ. We haven't had just a *normal* conversation, have we?"

And what does it matter what I think? I don't ask.

As if he can sense my heart rate rising, there's a shimmer in the air across the fire for a moment, and then Liam steps into existence, as if he were just waiting on the other side of the universe and only a half-second away.

"Sorry," he says quickly, coming to sit cross-legged by my chair. "I had to figure out how to get back, and—" He catches sight of Hannah next to me, just the two of us, and says, "Oh, perfect timing."

I smile too wide, with too many teeth. "It's okay," I say to Hannah. "I don't think you're dramatic."

"She kind of is," Liam mutters, trying to pull out grass, and finding he can't. "Did she say you can't have a normal conversation?"

"It's just," Hannah says, "I crave the banal."

It's *such* a fucking Liam-like thing to say.

"Ask her what kind of music she likes or something," he says.

"Okay," I say, "then what kind of music do you like?"

Hannah snorts. "Banal, delivered. Oh, you know. I like all the things everyone else listens to on the radio. Though I'll never, *ever* admit it to her, I also love my mom's old CDs—Paul Simon and Alanis Morissette and Green Day. So yes, I am basic."

"Basic and sad," I say, nudging her shoulder.

She laughs. "Can't argue with the facts."

I can't say for certain why it catches my attention. Maybe it's because I have Liam on one side of me and Hannah on the other, and I'm trying not to look at Liam so I'm looking straight ahead—maybe because there was movement that I didn't realize I was looking for until it happened.

I realize, though, that there *is* movement in the woods across from the bonfire, just ahead—this creeping fog across the ground, white-shadowed.

Except it's not a fog at all. Of course it isn't. It's a husk, slinking across the forest, and it's coming for Liam.

Not in front of Hannah—I can't let this happen in front of Hannah. I move like I'm stretching my legs and hit Liam with my foot. He takes the hint and looks out at the woods—then swears profusely, echoing what I can't say.

"We have to get out of here," he says decisively.

He's right, but Rin was my ride, and I saw them drinking before I came out here. . . .

"Is Rin planning on staying over?" I ask Hannah, keeping my eyes focused on that husk. It's not strong like the other one in the woods, not fast. It must be much older, drained of energy, seeking Liam—but there are other shadows in the woods, and I can't bear to risk it.

"They were," Hannah says. She glances at me, then reads something in my face. "Oh, do you wanna go? I can drive you, if you want. . . ."

She thinks I don't want to hang out with her, I realize, which is *so* far from the truth. I'm trying to think of something else, but the husk has already reached the line of the woods and is now crossing the grass, dragging itself along, and I think there's another swirling shadow in the forest.

The more I look at it, the worse it gets. This far away, I can't see that dripping maw of teeth, or the milkiness of its eyes—but I know. I know the musky way it smells and the way it rots and the decay that clings to it. I know what it can do to me—and even worse, what it can do to Liam.

I know we need to get out of here, and *fast*.

"Do you mind?" I ask.

Something flickers across her face—I can't tell if it's hurt, or what, and frankly, I don't have the time. I get up from my chair. "I mean, if not, I don't mind calling an Uber—"

"No," Hannah says quickly, getting up too. "I, uh, didn't want to stay late."

It's awkward, especially when I turn and high-tail it out of there towards the drive, Liam hot on my heels. He's muttering a litany of profanity under his breath, his fists clenched at his sides. He keeps glancing over his shoulder.

"I'll just say goodbye," Hannah says, nodding to the house.

"Cool!" I say. As soon as she's out of earshot, I turn to Liam. "Well, we fucked that up."

"Drew," Liam says, looking pale, if a ghost *can* look pale.

I turn in the direction he's indicating—and there's something dark and shadowy at the edge of the woods, something reaching out to take the husk. Liam and I both watch the husk—it's almost reached the bonfire now—as a tentacle of darkness wraps around its lower legs. Slowly, slowly, that shadowy tentacle drags it back into the woods. We both watch with equal expressions of horror.

The shadows move to cover the husk, and there's this horrible screeching sound—I'm pretty sure the others can't hear it, but *I* fucking can—as whatever the hell that was devours the ghost.

"Oh, *fuck*," I whisper.

"What the hell is *that*?" Liam asks.

I shake my head. I don't know. I can't begin to know. But if it's following us . . . if it wants Liam like it wanted that husk . . .

Well. I imagine, energetic as he is, *vital* as he is, he'd be a lot tastier.

It only takes Hannah a minute to get her coat and say goodbye, but even still, I'm bouncing on the balls of my feet when she comes out. I lurch into the passenger seat too fast—

"I just really don't like parties," I lie to Hannah when she gives me a look.

She snorts, shaking her head, and I can't tell if she's annoyed. She turns the car on, and it immediately starts blaring Taylor Swift from the speakers.

"Sorry," Hannah says, reaching for the volume dial.

I grab her fingers. "Leave it," I say. I'm desperate to say

anything that will cheer her up at all, even as I see those inky tentacles still moving at the edge of the woods, and my need to get out of here and my desire to stay on Hannah's good side are all tangled up—

But she smiles at me, and when she starts singing the lyrics as she backs down the drive, I'm surprised to find myself joining along.

Tagged Posts
l.i.am.orville03

ella-orvilleeeeeeeeeeee: I miss you I miss you I miss you I miss you I miss you I miss you

comment by 2hansondeck: <3 miss you, miss him, give my love to mom and dad

comment by ella-orvilleeeeeeeeeeee: love you, hannah <3

rinmendozazodemnir: Found this picture the other day, and the first thing I wanted to do was send it to him. Posting here instead. Fuck. Miss you forever and ever, L.

heyyyyitssophia8792: happy birthday wherever you are, Liam <3

2hansondeck: six whole months without you, liam. we visited you yesterday and called el from your grave. There's a willow growing a few graves down from yours, and it reminded me of that summer we chased fireflies around your grandma's yard and hid in the big tree behind her house. Nothing is the same without you.

CHAPTER 11

It's past midnight when Hannah gets to my house, but I told Dad and Bee I'd be out late, so all the lights are off minus the porch and entryway.

There's no sign of husks or that terrible, shadowy husk-eater. Even Liam notices this. "I think we got away from the Watcher," he tells me—and I make a mental note to ask him why he's calling it *that*. It makes my skin prickle.

"You didn't ask for directions," I say to Hannah as she pulls into the drive.

Liam groans behind me. "Drew, this isn't rocket science."

Hannah puts the car in park. "I was friends with the person who lived here before you."

"Drew—" Liam cautions, but I overrule him for once. I don't think she needs me to tiptoe around it.

"Liam," I say, his name odd on my tongue. I never really say it out loud—after all, it would be weird if I did. "Liam Orville. Right?"

A shudder goes through her at the sound of his name. Behind me, Liam closes his eyes. Tilts his head back.

I shouldn't speak of the dead to those who love him—but for Hannah, his presence is everywhere. There's no way to avoid it. To avoid *him*.

She bites her lip. Nods. "You know what happened to him, right?"

I knot my hands together on my lap. Maybe this is the opening we need—and in the back seat, I feel Liam holding his breath. His hands are on our seats as he leans forward, his semi-translucent face hovering between Hannah and me over the center console.

"Kind of," I say.

Hannah draws a knee up to her chest. "Car accident. It absolutely sucked."

"You were close?" I ask. It feels like a natural thing to say.

"He was my other half," she admits with a vulnerability that I feel guilty about—I haven't really earned it, not on my own. "I'm sorry—I know I've been totally weird with you. It's just, you say things sometimes, and I know you never met him, but you have this knack for reminding me of him."

I wince. Perhaps it's because I am a vessel, and Liam's behind the wheel. "I'm sorry," I say, which doesn't quite fit, but I don't have anything else.

She shakes her head. "It's nice, sometimes. And you also—" She cuts off, shakes her head.

"Ask," Liam says.

"I what?"

She looks at me, and the light from the porch deepens the shadows of her face. She is so beautiful it hurts. "You don't look at me like I'm going to break," she says softly.

Not even Liam has anything to say to that. I have to take over. "You don't seem like the type," I say.

The corner of her mouth turns up. "Do you mind if we go to the treehouse?"

I glance at Liam.

"It's in the backyard," he says. "Just past the treeline. My dad built it."

"Is it structurally sound?" I ask Hannah, maybe Liam, maybe both. Maybe I ask because I can't get over the chill on my skin from seeing the Watcher again, and I don't really feel like going into the woods right now.

But Hannah's smiling, laughing like I said something funny. "It was fine last time I checked," she said. "Come on."

There's the chance that there's something *in* the treehouse that she needs. It feels like a more promising lead for Liam's personal effects than the attic was.

It's odd, to have someone who knows your own yard, your own *house,* better than you. But Hannah turns off the car and leads the way down the side of the house, down the little hill, and into the trees. It's dead silent besides the crickets and the babble of the creek and the occasional sound of trains far off in the distance. She doesn't even summon her phone light, and I nearly die tripping over a root—Liam tries to catch me, and of course he's useless, but then there's Hannah's hand on my arm, holding me up. A shiver runs down my spine.

"It's here," she whispers, coming to the bottom of a tree. Then, she does turn on her light—

"Absolutely fucking not," I say, looking at the monstrosity precariously perched above us.

"It's not like I'll add weight," Liam says. I flip him a rude gesture behind my back, where Hannah can't see.

But she's already halfway up the ladder (note, when I say ladder, I mean the *fucking planks nailed to the side of the tree*, and they're not even nailed securely). It's against my better judgment, yet I cannot help but follow a girl I like, even when she's putting me in a situation that might get me killed.

You don't have to point out the irony to me.

I grit my teeth and climb. Hannah pulls herself up above me, and I hear a scraping sound from within the ramshackle collection of boards she calls a "treehouse." It's more involved than a hunting stand—there are actual walls, and a roof, but I don't trust it.

I glance over my shoulder to check if Liam is keeping up, but he's right below me. He rolls his eyes at my look, definitely reading my mind on this one.

"Upper body strength is much easier to use when you're dead," he says. I don't kick him in the head, no matter how much I want to.

When I pull myself up, Hannah is already settled in the corner, comfy as can be. She doesn't seem to mind the spiders in the corners—I have had a new unhealthy respect for spiders, since the whole Watcher situation—or fear for her life. I doubt we'd escape without injury if we went hurtling out of the tree now.

I sit on the other side, a bit away from the wall to avoid contact with any stray arachnids. Liam folds himself up in one corner, arm slung over his knee, looking as comfortable as I've ever seen him. I imagine they spent a lot of time up here.

"This is . . ." I swallow hard. "Quaint."

Hannah smiles. She opens a box to one side and pulls out a battery-powered camping light. She turns it on and hangs it from a little loop on the ceiling.

"We fit better when we were ten," she admits.

"When were you here last?"

Hannah looks away. She's quiet for a moment. "Ella and I came up here after the funeral," she admits.

"I wondered where you went," Liam says—it's not for my benefit.

"His whole family was here, everyone I'd heard about my whole life and never met, and some I had—and we just couldn't do it anymore." She laughs, but there are tears in it. "Ella—that's Liam's younger sister—she stole a bottle of vodka and dragged me up here. God, I can't believe I made the climb, I was still in so much pain."

"Pain?" I echo.

Hannah rubs her eyes. "Shit," she says. "I'm sorry. Yeah. I still had, um, a bunch of stitches. There was a lot of glass when they pulled me out of the car."

Liam and I are both silent for a moment—I think it hits us at the same time. There were *two* people in the car, after all.

"You were in the crash too," I say, aghast, before Liam can tell me otherwise.

"Yeah," Hannah says.

"Fuck," Liam says.

"Fuck," I echo.

I guess it shouldn't be a surprise—I'd forgotten, really, that there was someone else in the car. But if Hannah was there . . . well, there was only one other person in the car, and it was Hannah, and yet Caleb's bloody sweatshirt is upstairs in my attic.

It's not a promising image, honestly. I don't know how it got there, nor why it was like *that*. Could it be possible it's unrelated? Probably not. Could it be possible Liam was wearing it during the crash? I glance over at him, but he's in the same outfit as always, and if he had been wearing it when he died, he would still be in it now.

As if she can feel the force of my wheels spinning, Hannah looks away. Changes the subject. "But yeah, we got—well, we got super drunk, and Tom—that's Mr. Orville—had to come up and carry us down. They couldn't even yell at us. Just loaded me up in the car and sent me home with my parents. You wouldn't believe the hangover—I already had a concussion, so I would not recommend."

"Take her away from that day," Liam says, but there's an odd note to his voice.

"And the time before?" I ask. "When you were up here?"

Hannah tips her head back, thinking, and the smile grows on her face. "Probably like this," she says. "After the first game of the season. I remember we wanted to come up here, to see if we still fit."

For a second, I pretend Liam isn't here. "You don't have to talk about him," I tell her. "If it hurts too much. If you don't want to, or can't."

But she shakes her head, and the expression on his face is so rife with yearning that I have to look away. "It's . . . nice," she says. "I can't really talk about him with anyone else. They either miss him, too, or they're choking on sympathy, and I can't handle the way they look at me." She glances up through her lashes, and I do my best to keep my expression blank. "If you don't mind."

"I don't mind," I say. I hope this doesn't all go straight to Liam's head. After all, on paper, I'm only here to figure out why he's still around.

But she doesn't talk about him—she goes back to the crash. Hannah laces her hands together, unfolds them, laces them again. "I don't remember it happening," she tells me. "It's so shitty, actually—we were supposed to hang out that night. He had to tutor in the morning. But it was one of our friends' big Halloween parties and—well." She shrugs. "I wanted to go, he didn't. And I drank way too much, and according to Rin, I got into a fight with another one of our friends, and I wouldn't calm down until he came to get me. So I called and I called, and he came—and I don't remember any of it. All I remember is spinning around in my costume, covered in glitter. Next thing I knew, I was waking up in the hospital."

"Oh, Hannah," Liam says, or maybe I do—it's hard to tell where he ends and I begin right now. He reaches forward. Tries to put a hand over hers. Can't.

There are tears streaking down her face now. "They told me at the hospital that he was driving. That we crashed into a tree—he swerved. It was cold, and raining, and maybe the roads were slick. He wasn't speeding."

"I never speed," Liam says. "But that doesn't make it her fault."

"It's not your fault," I say. I process the way Liam is sitting, and then I reach forward, like he is, and lay my hand over Hannah's.

"No matter what happened," Liam says.

"No matter what happened," I repeat, "it wasn't your fault." He didn't finish it, but I can infer the rest. What I can't infer is the pain itself, and how much it has shaped who Hannah is now—or who she was before.

Hannah sighs. "Hard not to feel like it was." She turns her hand up, squeezing mine tight. "God, I'm so sorry—this really is the opposite of banal. You probably never want to hang out with me again."

"Of course I do," I say, before I can think better of it, or Liam can feed me a line that isn't so vulnerable.

She laughs, then sighs. "I'm not glad for what happened—I don't think I'll ever get over what happened. What I lost, and what he meant to me." She aims a look at me, and her eyes are glassy with tears.

I need to ask about Caleb. I need to figure out if he was there, with them, during the crash, or at the scene afterwards. I need to figure out why Liam's still here. Except Hannah is looking at me, and she says, "But I'm really, really glad you're here, Drew."

I press my lips together. Liam sits back on his heels; he doesn't look at me. I can't change the subject back. I can't go down that line of inquiry when we're just past the worst of it.

"You can tell the truth," I say to Hannah. "It's because of Bee's lemon tart, isn't it?"

This time, her laugh is real. "Of *course* it's because of Bee's lemon tart," she agrees.

AFTER I go inside, I shower away the clinging scent of bonfire. Now that Hannah's gone, my brain keeps returning to the thing in the woods, the thing Liam called "the Watcher." Every time I close my eyes, all I can think about is the way the smoke enveloped that husk, the way it consumed it, the way the husk disappeared.

There's no way around the dread. But there's another realization: There's no way I can let that happen to Liam—and that means I need to stop fucking around. I need to be serious about saving him.

Even if it means reading the journals.

After my shower, I wrap my hair up in a towel and get dressed in one of Reece's oversized crewnecks and a pair of my own sweatpants. I stare at my closet for a long time, shifting my weight. Maybe I wish that Liam would appear and . . . I don't know. Reason his way out of it.

But he already looked exhausted when Hannah left.

And he won't be around forever. At some point, I have to start facing my problems myself.

The box is where I shoved it when I put it back last time. I take it out, unpacking it in the same way, setting out the journals and the different kits. There's no way to quickly figure out if Reece or our mother has seen the Watcher before—although Reece's journals have glossaries and keys, I don't know what they would have called that apparition. And Mom didn't use the same organization as Reece.

I need to read it. I need to read *all* of it.

If I care at all about Liam, it's a sacrifice that has to be made. So I gather up the first of Reece's journals, tuck myself into bed, and start on the first page.

CHAPTER 12

After staying up with the journals, I sleep in an extra hour on Saturday, but it doesn't change our routine too much.

Dad is ready for our weekly Saturday morning run when I wake up. He pretends to read the paper while I have a bowl of cereal and stretch. When he sees me going for my shoes, he jumps up, already ready to go.

We've been doing weekly runs since I joined the track team as a freshman. Reece and Dad may bond over case law and *Jeopardy!*, but he and I get each other best when we're running side by side, quiet besides the sound of our footfalls and breathing. We log five miles before slowing down for a cooldown, which is when we actually talk.

"Bee said you made some friends," Dad says, still a little out of breath.

I definitely regret bringing any mention of Liam to Bee. "Yeah," I say. "It's not so bad, you know. This school."

"Who were you out with last night?"

I shrug. "Just some kids from school—you met Rin, who lives down the street. They brought me out with their friend group."

"Have fun?"

I think of Hannah in the dark, tears running down her face.

The toast to Liam, the crackle of the bonfire—the shadows of the husk and the Watcher. "Yeah," I say. "They're nice enough."

"And how are classes?"

There's a chance Bee already told him about my Stats test, since I'm dragging my heels so much. I have no way to know, but I figure the best way to get through this is to aim for nonchalance.

I shrug. To be honest, they've been much better since Liam started helping, but there's not a good way to explain any sudden improvement to Dad. He knows me too well. "I'm managing," I say instead, which is as close as I can come to the truth.

When we're not talking, I'm thinking about Reece's journal. There's nothing salacious in there—it's clear that my sibling wrote it with the intent of passing it down to me, and that makes me feel warm and soft inside. It makes me miss them more than I have since they went to school.

In the first weeks after they left, when we were still at the old house, I often found myself unable to sleep. Reece's room was mostly packed, but the furniture was still there. I don't know what made me do it, but on those nights when I couldn't settle, I tiptoed down to Reece's room and slept in their bed.

Reece and I know death, and of course, I know they're just a call or flight or long drive away. They're not gone. I can't imagine the person I would be if they were.

But there's no pretending there's not distance between us now—and maybe it's partially caused by my own stubbornness. If I asked for more help dealing with Liam and the thing in the woods, they would come running.

But Reece isn't here anymore, not physically, and they *want* me to solve my own problems—they just don't think I *can*. They wouldn't have left me those journals, both the ones they wrote and the ones Mom did, if they wanted me to come to them with every little thing that went wrong.

It's not Dad's and my best run—I keep feeling my brain trailing away, prodding at that loneliness that's settled over me and the things I read about in Reece's journal. The journals started from the beginning, from definitions that I already knew: what makes a husk, and why ghosts stay around, and common ways to send them moving.

But there was also information I didn't know, like how quickly a ghost can degrade into a husk, and ways they can degrade faster, besides emotional exposure—and ways to preserve them, to slow down the degradation.

Liam has already been dead for a year. We're already low on time. And by bringing him around people, I feel like I'm only speeding things up.

I *need* to figure out how it all connects: The husks. Hannah. Caleb. The Watcher.

"You okay, peanut?" Dad asks. "You're awfully quiet today."

I grimace. "A lot on my mind," I say.

"Everything okay at school? Grades okay?"

And—I haven't told him about the Stats test. There's no way to get extra credit. But if Liam helps me enough that my grades go up anyway . . .

I can't tell him. Not yet. Not until I give myself the chance to fix it. "They're fine," I say through my teeth. "Just an adjustment period."

We swing by Bee's to see how she's facing the Saturday rush. She's laughing when she hands over a bag of cinnamon rolls and almond croissants, along with a cappuccino for Dad and vanilla oat latte for me. She's too busy to talk, so we head back home, and I ask Dad questions about his cases—most of which he can't answer.

We're almost home when I realize that, maybe, Dad has access to information I don't. "So I was talking to Bee the other day about the family who lived here before. That car accident. Any idea what happened?"

He shrugs. "There's not much to know, but a few of the neighbors talked about it to Bee. Good kid. Just one of those things—hydroplaned into a tree or something."

It's not the most helpful explanation, though it does cement that no one thinks there was foul play involved. Dad is always speculating about that kind of stuff.

But even if no one suspected it, it doesn't mean it didn't happen.

"Was he alone?" I ask, even though I know he wasn't—but I don't know if anyone else was in the car with them, and I don't plan to bring it up again with Hannah.

Dad looks at me sidelong. "Why are you suddenly so curious about it?"

"Morbidity."

He sighs. "You kids and your true crime." Shakes his head. "Not everything is some conspiracy, Drew. Sometimes, sad stuff just . . . happens."

"I know," I say. I sip my coffee, debating. There's something about Liam's death that doesn't sit right with me, even though I know Dad is probably correct. I think about telling him about the bloody sweatshirt in the attic, but I'm worried that'll freak him out, or he'll throw it away, and I might need to use it later. "I just, I think one of the girls I was out with last night was there too. Curious if anyone else got hurt."

"Ah." Dad frowns. "No, just the Orville kid, and one of his friends. A real pity. You have to feel for his parents."

It's a weird position to be in, seeing the reality of grief and feeling none of it. For everyone else, Liam is gone forever—there's nothing left of him in this town, especially now that his family is gone. Even for Hannah, there's just the space he left behind.

But not for me. In my life, Liam is here, and as vibrant as he ever was alive. I'm still thinking about the incongruity of it as I shower and change into a pair of running shorts and one of Reece's old musical T-shirts. Liam is waiting on my bed, eyes closed, stretched out in the sunlight. I grab a seat at the desk and poke at the cinnamon roll I brought up with me.

"Are they really as good as everyone says?" he asks without opening his eyes.

"Better."

"Dammit." Liam's lips thin to a line. "This is one of those times when I wish I just had taste buds."

"A tragedy, to be sure." I poke at the roll again. "Yesterday wasn't too much for you?"

Liam sighs. "What part? The time we watched a ghost get eaten, or when all my friends toasted my death, or the part when I found out my best friend almost died with me?"

I wince. He has a point. "Yeah, now that you say it, it was a lot."

Liam nods, looking down at his hands. "I just don't see what the point of all this is. If I'm staying behind for some reason, I should know what it *is*."

Usually, ghosts do have more of an idea of why they're lingering. But we're not any closer to figuring out why Liam is here.

I eat some of my cinnamon roll and try to figure out how to say what I want to. "I was thinking we should make a list. Of everything we know, and why you might still be here."

He opens his eyes, finally, and he can't hide the sadness there any longer. "So eager to get rid of me?"

Honestly? No. Against my better judgment, I actually *like* Liam, and I don't want to think of what it'll be like when he's gone, when I'm facing all the challenges of a new place and new people by myself again.

At least now, I have some sort of ally. A protection from faux pas, when I'm otherwise so good at getting everything wrong.

"I just want you to be at peace," I say, probably sounding too sincere.

"Right," Liam says, and I don't think I'm making up the flash of disappointment across his face. "Okay. What do we know?"

I grab one of my notebooks. "You had a good friend group, right? They all cared about you."

"Yeah."

"And you're not keeping secrets from anyone. Nothing that you wanted to say when you were alive."

A pause, then, "No. Not that I can think of."

I chew on a hangnail on my left thumb. "Okay. That's usually the most common—something you wanted to say when you were alive, that you never managed. Or maybe something you never got around to . . . you don't have a library book or something still out?"

He gives me a long, level look. "If I did," he says, "I imagine it would now be with Ella, in St. Louis."

"An unfortunate point, but true all the same." I think over doing this with Reece in the past; we used to solve these based on a checklist that they'd made when they were younger. Unspoken words? Crossed off. Unresolved business? Maybe—I don't know if I can fully rule that one out yet.

But Dad's words come back to me—yes, sometimes tragedies are just tragedies. But sometimes they're not.

"Caleb's sweatshirt," I say finally.

He looks down at his hands.

"Do you think there's any way your death could be . . . wrongful?"

"Well, I don't think it was *rightful*," Liam scoffs. "But as far as I know, it was a car crash. Hard to murder someone while they're the one driving."

Hard . . . but not impossible. "But you don't remember it," I say, tapping the end of my pen against my desk.

"It's the brain trauma," he says flatly.

I wince, but I'm moving past that. "And neither does Hannah."

That makes him quiet, even for just a minute. Liam frowns, thinking it over. "So you think . . . what? Someone cut my brakes?"

"I don't *know*," I say. "It just doesn't feel as straightforward as everyone seems to think it is. Don't you agree?"

"I don't know what to think," Liam says, flopping over on his side. "I think it's wildly suspicious that his hoodie is here, but it's not like we can just *ask* him about it. It was buried under boxes, so someone wanted to hide it, and if he actually is dangerous . . . it doesn't seem like a great idea to just approach him and ask."

He's right, unfortunately. I look at my scant list and sigh. "I guess the best thing to do is just keep working on Hannah," I say. "If she remembers something, that's our best bet."

He gives me a look. "I'm sure that has nothing to do with your desire to get to know her better."

I roll my eyes, but I'm instantly scarlet. "Oh, give me a break."

"She was telling you about my death, and you were *flirting* with her."

"I wasn't!" Kind of.

"'He's in a better place,'" Liam mocks.

I throw my pen at him. "*Rin* said that, not me," I say, doing my best to defend myself. "I know better—you're in the same shit place, still here with the rest of us."

He snorts, but then his expression clears, turns serious. "How can you be so sure there's something else after this?"

I shrug. "I can't." And I'm not. Maybe, after we figure out what's keeping Liam here, he'll disappear and go—nowhere. Maybe it's better to let this all go, to let him stick around. But as much as I want to keep him, I'm not sure how long he'll be able to sustain himself, and ghosts who do stick around get weird after a few years. Either they get super angry and powerful and poltergeist-y, or they just get sad.

And if he's already drawing things like the Watcher, it's probably not a good idea to let him stick around for much longer.

CHAPTER 13

I don't see Hannah again until Tuesday. Liam is scarce, too—recovering from the weekend, he says, when I catch him lurking around on Monday night.

But I still don't fully trust myself to talk to Hannah without training wheels, so when I literally run into her in the hall while I'm grabbing my bag, the first thing that comes to mind is *shit*.

She doesn't seem ruffled in the slightest—in fact, she's happy to see me, which does weird things to my heart and throat and makes my palms sweaty.

"Drew!" she calls, spotting me down the hall.

I slow down. "Hey," I say, trying to artfully lean on a locker or something—I trip over my feet and end up slamming my shoulder into the metal.

"Oof," Hannah says. "Paige said she saw you at the bakery on Sunday—when are your shifts? I'll come by sometime."

"Ah, Bee usually manages to run things herself," I say. Hannah's face falls, and I realize how that sounds. "Not that I don't want you to come!" I hurry to say. "I just don't have, like, a consistent schedule. I go when I'm called."

And then, for some *fucking reason*, I salute her. Like a little soldier.

God I miss Liam.

"Ah, that's cool," Hannah says. She adjusts her grip on the books she's holding. "Are you busy?"

"Now? No, not really. Just have to shower—running and all. Sweat. You know the drill." My god my god oh *hell*—

"After that," Hannah says, moving swiftly past my awkwardness, "do you want to go for a hike or something? There are some trails by your house that are really nice. We can see if Rin's free, too, if you want."

I plaster on a smile, trying to not mess up this interaction any further. The second I get home, I'm dragging Liam back from whatever purgatory he's haunting and hauling his ass out for a walk, just to make sure I don't make a fool of myself, *again*.

"That sounds great," I say, already plotting.

Friday night wasn't the right time, for an abundance of reasons. But now, if I have Hannah alone, maybe I can figure out what really went down with her, Caleb, and Liam. Maybe I can find out what's keeping him here—and if Caleb has something to do with it.

RIN isn't free, so it's just me and Hannah, and unbeknownst to her, Liam. He caught me while we were heading out the door and pointed me towards the stash of cookies Bee keeps at home. When Hannah comes to get me, I'm waiting at the door with a giant chocolate chip and toffee cookie in one hand (Liam's suggestion), and her eyes go wide and joyful when I hand it to her.

"This is so good," Hannah groans when she takes a bite.

"Using me for pastries again, eh?" I ask. *It's permitted,* I don't say, because Liam is already giving me a look with one eyebrow raised.

"Hey, leave me and my ulterior motives alone," Hannah says.

I slide into the passenger seat and start snooping through the detritus of her car; it was too dark to take much of it in the other night. "It's never been clean for a day in her life," Liam tells me, his voice weighted with affection.

"No judgment permitted on my CDs," Hannah says as she steers out of my road. "Half of them are my mom's."

"Who uses CDs anymore?" I ask, aghast.

"That counts as judgment," Hannah whines.

"She likes to understand 'the whole cohesive work as a movement,'" Liam intones from the back seat.

I put in a white disc with *Paul Simon* written in spiky handwriting. Immediately, "You Can Call Me Al" starts blaring.

"A woman of taste," I say.

Hannah smiles. "She's the best."

"Don't listen to a word she says," Liam says. "Yes, Mrs. Sullivan is great, but she and Hannah fight like feral cats."

"Hmm," I say, noncommittal. "So you two are close?"

She shrugs. "I mean, we fight. But everyone fights with their mom, right?"

I wouldn't know. I decide it's better not to say that, though. "Bee is pretty cool," I offer, letting Hannah read between the lines.

She's more tactful than I am. "She's your stepmom, right?"

"Yeah," I say. "But she's been around for ages, and our birth mom didn't stick around."

"You have siblings?"

"One older. They're a freshman at BU. Studying something that will eventually lead to law."

"That's cool," Hannah says. "Just me. But I've basically always had friends around, so my mom says it's like she has loads of kids. . . ."

She smiles tightly, and I glance back at Liam.

"You're being really quiet," Liam says. "Ask her—"

"Where are we going?" I ask, because it feels harmless, and with all the oddness in my stomach, I'm not sure I want to factor him in right now.

"There's a nature park just up the road," Hannah says. She gets in the turning lane and signals. We're on the one-lane highway that runs out of town, thick forest on both sides of the road. The leaves are turning, shifting, throwing up a riot of colors. She sighs, taking it in like I am. "I can't believe it's October already."

"You can ask about her favorite season or something," Liam says.

And I almost do. But there's a choice to be made here—I need to know what happened on the night Liam died. I need to figure out what Hannah remembers, and I need to know if Caleb was involved.

So I ignore his suggestion, and go plowing right through into what I instinctively know is the worst thing possible: "What are you doing for Halloween?"

Next to me, Hannah stiffens. Liam sucks a breath through his teeth. I know I'm gambling here—if Hannah thinks I'm just a forgetful jerk who can't remember that her best friend is dead and it was traumatic, she probably will never want to see me again.

But if I don't figure out what's wrong with Liam, if I keep letting him degrade into a husk, just to keep from losing Hannah's friendship . . . I don't see how that's a better option.

"I . . . I don't know," she admits, feigning lightness. Probably nothing, because the one-year anniversary of her best friend's death is the next day.

"Drew, ask about *anything* else," Liam says, a little desperately. I feel the hair prickling on my arms and shoot him a glance. He needs to get himself under control, or else we might attract something worse in the woods.

I know it's risky, doing this with him here. But I don't know how many chances I'll have to get Hannah alone before she decides it's too much, or that my curiosity goes too far. And right now, I have to put Liam first.

Even though it makes my stomach hurt.

"What do you usually do?"

Hannah shrugs. For a minute, I don't think she's going to answer. Hannah parks, turns off the car. We sit there in the silence for a moment. Then, finally, she says, "Like I said the other night. I went to a party. At Caleb's house."

She doesn't add more than that, but the shortness of her tone makes my heart beat faster all the same. I exchange a glance with Liam in the rearview as Hannah unbuckles her seatbelt. I sense she's shutting down—but it confirms that Hannah and Caleb were together on the night Liam died. There is every chance he could be involved.

"Don't push it," he says quietly.

I nod, just for him, and open the passenger door. Hannah is already out, head tipped back, looking up at the blue sky.

"I love Pennsylvania in the autumn," she says, clearly changing the subject.

"It's the best time of year," I say, allowing her to.

That gets a smile out of her, and I think we're back on level footing. I follow Hannah across the parking lot. We're in a little clearing with a lot and a map of the trails. There's a swing set a little ways away, and a lake past the copse of trees farther down.

"This is really nice," I say. I shoot a glance at Liam.

"This place has nothing to do with me," he says, so we're in safe territory, probably.

"Do you come here often?" I ask.

She glances at me, giggling, and I realize it's a pick-up line a beat too late. My face flushes.

"Often enough," Hannah says, still laughing. She leads the way past the swings, toward the lake. The water is green at the edges with algae. Hannah leans down when we're close, searching for a stone to skip. "I like it here," she says. "I really started coming . . . last winter, maybe? After I had healed physically, and I was supposed to be okay again." Hannah shrugs. "I would come here and walk, and think. It was the only place where I could be by myself."

She skips the stone. It makes, like, two jumps and sinks. I go searching for my own flat stone, because I'm nothing if not competitive.

"I used to have a place like that at my old house," I tell her. "My best friend—her name is Andie—she and I used to call it Big Tree."

"Let me guess," Liam says, at the same time Hannah guesses, ". . . because it had a big tree?"

"A beauty *and* a scholar," I say. I find the perfect stone and take my time. It jumps five times, nearly the whole length of the pond.

"Good shot," Hannah says. "But back to Big Tree."

"It was a bit like this—Pennsylvania is Pennsylvania, after all." I tuck my hands in my pockets, watching as she goes for another stone. "But whenever my parents were pissed about my grades, or if I did really bad at a track meet, I used to go there. Any emotional stress, really, was solved by a trip to Big Tree. And sometimes Andie would come find me there, and we could just . . . be."

"Do you miss it?" Hannah asks, taking another throw. It goes worse than her last. "Your old school. Your old friends."

"Of course I do," I say. "But it was just delaying the inevitable, really. Because they were going to move on, leave and go to college, and I wasn't. That's never really been my plan. Better to rip off the Band-Aid and split up earlier, ease the ache a little bit."

"God," Liam says.

"That's . . . kind of depressing," Hannah says. She starts off on the trail, and I walk by her side without hesitating. "Why don't you want to go to college?"

I shrug. "Not my thing," I say. "I prefer working with my hands rather than my brain."

Hannah looks at me like this is the first time she's considered another alternative. I'm used to that reaction: I got it a lot from friends at my old school who had never thought of *not* going to college. It's like some pre-determined path, like we all have to do the same thing, follow the same choices, make the same mistakes. "What will you do instead?" she asks.

"I don't know," I admit. "Maybe I'll go to cooking school, or pastry school—I'm sure Bee would love that."

"I wouldn't mind it either," she mutters under her breath, and for the first time, I realize that there's a possibility that our friendship doesn't end the moment Liam disappears.

"You're not worried about the future?" Liam asks, like he's here and in the conversation, and I realize he's looking at me with the same confusion Hannah is.

They really are the same person sometimes.

"Maybe I'll wait tables," I say. "Maybe I'll take up woodworking. Maybe I'll become a car salesman."

"*God*," Liam says again, with feeling.

I kick a stone from the path, feeling a little judged (and that's valid: They're both judging me, but unlike one half of my company, I am alive and able to make my own life choices, thank you very much).

Drew, my dad would say at this point in the argument (because this is always an argument, with him), *get serious*.

But Hannah only looks at me for a moment longer, and then she shrugs. "At least you won't have to worry about student loans," she says.

"Precisely." Or grades. Or exams. Or roommates. Yes, maybe it means I won't be able to get the same kinds of jobs, but maybe I'll be able to *breathe* for the first time in forever.

There's a burbling ahead, and we come to a creek. Hannah turns, switching to the path that follows the creek. "There's a swimming hole down this way," she tells me, and I follow her lead.

It doesn't take long before the creek grows bigger, then opens up into a little burbling pond fed by a small waterfall. Hannah claims one of the larger rocks by the edge, still warmed by the sun. The weather will turn, at some point, but it's still warm enough that I unlace my shoes and pull off my socks, then dip my feet in the water. We sit side by side, kicking our feet, not saying much of anything—but it's not awkward. It's companionable.

"You can talk to her," Liam says, but I'm not sure I have anything to say. Maybe their relationship was more quick-fire, always challenging one another, always in need of the last word.

Maybe I don't want that. Maybe I want something quiet, comfortable.

"What are you planning to do for Homecoming?" Hannah asks.

"Hmm?"

"Are you going?"

To be honest, I hadn't really thought of it. Andie and I went to our freshman winter formal before we decided it wasn't our scene; our only exception was junior prom, and only because we thought it would be funny to wear thrifted suits and show up looking like '30s mafiosos.

"I wasn't planning to."

"You should come. With us, I mean." Hannah is looking at her hands, tracing the line across her left palm with her right thumb. "We usually go to Sophia's first and then we go to the dance, and after we always go to Danny's or Caleb's—" She catches herself, probably senses she's rambling.

I glance around, looking for Liam—and that's when I realize he's gone. Maybe it's been too long since he rested. Maybe he just decided this was all boring. Either way, he's not here to tell me what to do now.

"Yeah," I say, because what excuse do I have to *not* go? And worse—why wouldn't I? Even if she's asking me as a friend and nothing more, even if there's no way she sees me that way or ever will, she's asking me.

And if she's asking, then yes, I'll go.

I think I understand why Liam never could get over her, why everyone else seems to turn toward her in every room that she's in. She smiles, and that dimple shows, and I think my heart starts up in double-time.

"Great," Hannah says. "I think it's going to be so much fun."

OCTOBER 25

DRAMATIS PERSONAE

LIAM ORVILLE, 17, not yet dead,
HANNAH SULLIVAN, 16 going on 17, very much alive

Scene I

A car parked in an unfamiliar driveway. Blue. Beige interior. Smells faintly of cigarette smoke and lemon-lime cleaner. LIAM ORVILLE is behind the wheel, hands clenched, knuckles white. HANNAH SULLIVAN sits in the passenger seat.

Liam: I'm sorry. I just—I need to say it, Han.

Hannah: Please don't. I told you what happened with Caleb, and I just can't—

Liam: I can't change how I feel.

Hannah winces. She presses her lips together and a muscle in her jaw clicks.

Hannah: If you say it, you'll ruin everything.

Liam: Well, that's not quite true—

Hannah: It *is*.

Liam throws his hands up.

Liam: I'm sorry. I tried so hard to be the person you wanted, okay? I tried and tried and tried, and I *failed*. But we need to talk about it—maybe we just need this one thing, this one big fight, and we can say all the horrible things we need to say to one another, and it'll be over.

Hannah looks out the window. One tear slides down her cheek.

Hannah: I have nothing horrible to say to you.

Liam: I *love* you, Han. Okay? I know you don't want me to, and I'm sorry—if I could just stop, I would stop, you know?

Hannah: I get it. I'll never be enough for you.

Liam: That's not what I'm saying at all. You're already enough—you're too much. I am not going to sit here and act like I can just . . .

Hannah: What? Make me love you?

A pause. Long.

Liam (*slowly*): I would never ask you to lie to me. No, I'm not, like, trying to make you love me, or go on a date with me, or anything like that. Fuck, Hannah, I'm not Caleb. But I can't hide it from you, okay? I need to figure out who I am without pining for you. I need space.

Hannah: I won't be weird if you're not—

Liam: I *know* you won't be weird about it. That's not it. It's not—sorry, this is pathetic. It's not you, okay? It's not the whole "it's not you, it's me" but—Jesus.

I would follow you to UNC, if you got asked. I would give
up CMU. I would follow you anywhere. I would give up
gaming. I would be a vegetarian. I would dye my hair. I
would change my name. Literally, Hannah, if you asked me
to do any fucking thing, I would drop everything to do it.
And that's the *problem*, okay? I can't be this person who
bases every single part of my identity on you. And that's
not because you don't love me back, or because you don't
see anything with me—it's because it's unhealthy, and I
can't keep following you around, waiting for the day that
you decide you actually care about me.

Hannah: That is such bullshit. I care about you *so much*—

Liam: Never in the way I want. Never in the way I care
for you.

A silence.

Hannah: So that's it then. You'll give up our friendship
because you just can't deal with the fact I don't love you
back.

Liam: That's not what I said at all. I need time, Han. A
week. Two. God forbid, a month. I need to get over it.
Get over myself.

*Hannah pulls off her seatbelt and gets out of the car.
She turns to slam the door.*

Hannah: I just thought you were better than him.

*She slams the door before Liam can respond. He watches her
go. When the house door shuts behind her, he sighs, puts
the car into drive, and backs out of the driveway.*

CHAPTER 14

It's not until I get home that the dread starts to unfold.

Firstly: Liam still isn't around, even though I whisper-call his name in the corners of the house in an attempt to rouse him. But the more I look for him, the more it gets me thinking: I don't know if Liam can sustain his appearance for the entirety of the pre-party next week, then Homecoming itself. There's no way I'll be able to rely on him for the entire thing, and I also don't know if it's fair to expect that of him—especially knowing how close Homecoming was to the end, for him, and what kind of emotions that could dredge up. Especially since I'll be there with his friends. With *Hannah*.

Secondly: It's been . . . a while since I've been at a school thing and not overtly out. I've been skating under the radar here, and no one really knows I'm queer, but I'm not actually sure . . . I don't know. I don't know if they'd care, but I promised myself I wouldn't play it straight again. I'm not close enough to anyone else to read the room, if you know what I mean, and I don't feel like I know Rin well enough to ask them what their experiences have been like, because that shit is traumatic when it goes badly.

And I could ask Liam, but if people had been shitty, I can't say for certain he would've noticed.

It's a lot to worry about, but it's only one of a million things I need to worry about.

THE worries—and avoidances of them—keep me going all the way to Saturday. I'm able to dance around the topics with Liam, and the simple agony of keeping himself going seems to take up enough energy that he doesn't really notice any extra stress on my part.

Dad and I do our Saturday run, and he heads to the office to finish up some work. After my shower, I am faced with the day stretching out ahead of me with no way to fill it. Andie doesn't answer the phone when I call—she texts me to say she's out and she'll call me later, which has to do. I consider calling Reece, but that feels too much like admitting defeat or asking for help.

And if I call Reece, I'll need to ask them about the journals. I'll need to ask them about Mom.

There's this thing between Reece and me, something they always make fun of me for. Reece always cried over dropped ice cream cones and stressed over lost phones. They struggle to let relationships drift apart; they would rather chew off their own arm than end a friendship.

Point is: Reece doesn't let things go. I have never had that problem—quite the opposite, actually. It's easier to cut things loose before anything gets too complicated.

And I wonder, now, if that inability to let things go is why Reece has held onto Mom's journals for so long . . . and if, at the same time, they're also holding on to *her*.

I know I said it's fine—it is. But it's fine in the same way a long-healed wound is fine. The scar is there, and sometimes you might see it and say, "Hey, look at that scar—what a shitty thing that happened." You might poke it. But you don't take the knife and carve it open again. You don't purposely get scurvy and dissolve all that collagen that keeps you from bleeding.

Point is, I don't think of Mom because I spent years figuring out a way to make peace with her not wanting me.

If I call Reece, if I open that wound, if I take up the blade and start carving . . . I don't know what I'll find, or if I'll like it. For all I know, Reece is in communication with our mom. Maybe she lives in Boston. Maybe they see her regularly.

And I fucking *hate* speculating about it. But if there is something . . . I hate that they kept it from me. There is so much about those journals that makes me uneasy.

Maybe that's why, faced with the reality of a day spent knocking around the house, I grab one of Mom's journals and chuck it in a tote bag with my wallet. I leave my hair to dry loose over my shoulders in a wet tangle of red curls and pull on a hoodie and jeans.

There's another coffee shop in town besides Bee's bakery, and I decide to size up the competition. I tell myself that's all it is, and it has nothing to do with the fact that reading something of Mom's feels like an active betrayal of Bee, who may or may not be the reason a lot of those wounds have healed so neatly.

It's a short bike ride to Hallowed Grounds, the coffee shop across town from Bee's. There's a plaque on the wall right inside that says it used to be a nunnery.

Sigh. Competition or not, I do like a pun.

I grab a vanilla latte—point to Bakerbee; Bee's is better—and settle in at one of the corner tables. There's a bit of a rush since it's Saturday: students from the local college, a mom with a baby in a stroller, a few kids I know from school.

I put on my headphones, even though the music is pretty okay—but I need to focus. Block everything else out. I open my own notebook to a new page and tap on it a couple of times with my pen.

Mom's composition book is black and white, printed in that not-quite-cow print that some of them are. The first date in it is February 12, 2004—I wasn't even born; Dad wasn't even out of law school.

I can't put it off any longer. I need to know what's in these journals, and why Reece thought it was worth me having them. They wouldn't have just left them for no reason at all.

I scroll to a dad rock playlist and set it to repeat. It's easiest to think with music on, and even better when the music is already familiar and playing in a loop.

A deep breath. Thirty seconds of uninterrupted Lynyrd Skynyrd. Then I open the journal up and start to read.

February 12, 2004
Picking up where we left off. 278 Orchlee called in today. Got the referral from Mom. Went to handle it after visiting Dad in Presby. Not much to report—a minor haunting. I talked to the ghost and found the lost locket to pass on to his daughter. Easy peasy.
Dinner in Oakland, back to Presby, then drove Mom home.

We all know math is not my strong suit, but I find myself frowning down at the dates. I don't know too much about Mom's side of the family—her mom, my grandma, is still around, living in Oakmont. I don't see her that much, but like us, she keeps the sacred covenant: She doesn't talk about Mom either.

Not to me, at least. I don't know if she talks to Reece about it.

February 14, 2004
Did a walk around Squirrel Hill to follow up on a lead, but nothing much of importance there. Froze my ass off, though. Dad thought it was hilarious when I walked in, glasses all fogged, cheeks red, eyelashes frosted over. Nearly coughed himself into an episode. It was funny until it wasn't.
Met Harry for dinner at Joe's. I fucking love their gemelli. It used to be Dad's favorite too.
Fuck. Can't talk about him like that. It is Dad's favorite.

I skim over the next few entries, which are more of the same: She deals with ghosts, which she refers to by their street address; she sometimes writes about where she eats. She spends a lot of time at one of the bars in Oakland between stints at Presby. The entries take place when Dad is at Pitt for law school, I realize, and she talks about grabbing drinks with him at Fuel and Hemingway's after his classes.

The other running theme: She writes, almost every day, about visiting her father at Presby. I know what she's referring to; Presby is the hospital on Pitt's campus, one of the bigger ones in the city.

I chew on the end of my pen, trying to remember when Grandpa died. It was before I was born, I'm certain . . . but I'm not really sure when.

The entries start to skip a bit more. She writes that she and my dad are engaged, and how they just want a small thing for the wedding. It's a wedding they never went through with—they stayed engaged for a while, and then she had Reece and me, and things went off the rails somewhere in the middle of it all.

But she's not there yet, not in her life. She hasn't written about the wedding in a while when I hit the beginning of 2006, where an entry sticks out:

> Dad at Presby, again. I'm sitting here next to him, writing one-handed, holding his hand with my other. Mom is out checking on the dogs, so I'm on lunch duty. Harry said he'd drop by after work. I heard Har talking to Mom last night in the kitchen. They were saying that I need to get ready. I don't know how to talk to either of them right now.
>
> Dad's on a ventilator. Every time he breathes, it sounds like

That's where the entry cuts off.

The journal picks up a week later, and my heart drops.

I can't stand to write. Dad's funeral is tonight.

I can't say he's manifesting or if this is wishful thinking but, every time I turn, it's as if I can see him out of the corner of my eye.

It's never happened like this for me. Usually, when they appear, they just appear.

Something twists in my stomach—guilt, or anxiety, or fear. I know my grandpa died before I was born. I know my mom could see ghosts. I know she struggled with a lot of things. Depression and addiction, and the links and intricacies between the two.

I don't know when or how it started. How do you just ask about that? And who would I ask? It's not like I'm going to go dredging it up for Dad, bringing up the worst parts of his life. . . .

And if to remember Mom is to remember what happened to her—well. I don't know if I want to read any more. There's something sick twisting in my stomach, and it only gets worse with the next entry.

He's manifested. I saw him upstairs, in his study, when I went to go get one of his sweaters. He was there at his desk. Smiled at me.

I can't bear it. I can't make him go.

I talked to him, like I always do, and I didn't ask how to make it easier.

I can't lose him again. I can't do it. I won't.

We talked about nothing, and I got his sweater, and then I went downstairs. I went to the room that used to be mine and shut and locked the door and then I lay facedown on my bed and wept.

I can't let Harry see me like this. God. He will think I'm insane. He doesn't know about . . . it. About the things that I see.

When I got up, dark was falling. I looked outside and there was

Ok. I see ghosts. That is rational. That is something I understand. But the thing I saw in the yard? The thing that waited?

That wasn't a ghost. Not like anything I've seen.

The next entry is the last, and it is one single line:

There's something in the woods.

I almost spill my coffee. "Oh fuck *that*," I say out loud, probably *too* loud with my headphones on. She might've written more, but it's gone now: There is a line of ripped paper, pages torn out, and no way to know if it was Mom or Reece who got rid of them. But I can't get rid of the prickle, the chill that runs down my spine, because. . . .

What was it, Mom? *What* was in the woods?

But the worst feeling of all is that I'm pretty sure I already know.

LIAM doesn't show up until that night, after dinner, while I'm in bed scrolling through my phone.

"Hey," he says quietly, folding himself at the foot.

"Hey," I say back. I don't really know what to say to him. I've been a knot of anxiety since this afternoon. Bee and Dad know something's up—Bee asked me if I was okay, after dinner, and I had to make up some excuse about missing the friend group camping trip. Now she feels like shit because she couldn't drive me, and I feel like shit because my mom saw a monster in the woods, and what if it's connected to—

"The thing we saw the other night," I say to Liam before I can lose my nerve. "The shadowy demon. The Watcher."

He immediately goes tense. "Yeah?"

"You said you've seen it before, or something like it. A shadow in the woods."

Liam looks at me for a long, long time. He sighs. Gets off the bed and goes to the window. He leans against the frame, palms pressed to the sill, and leans his forehead against the glass.

"Not close," Liam admits. "Not like the other night."

I close my eyes. Press my palms against them. There's an edge of a headache starting somewhere in the back of my skull.

This is so, *so* far above my pay grade.

"How often?"

"Not very," Liam says. His voice wavers slightly. "Not—well. It was more frequent at first, and then I went a while without seeing it, until you came."

I nodded. I didn't know what I'd expected. Somehow, this feels a million times worse than anything I could've predicted.

I've been through Reece's journals backwards and forwards, and they don't mention *anything* like this, not even in reference to Mom's journals. The only record I can find of anything similar at all is in Mom's. And knowing what I know of what happened to Mom, I really, *really* don't like this.

I don't even know if involving Reece would help at this point. Reece knows ghosts, yeah—but I can't say for certain a ghost is what we're dealing with anymore.

CHAPTER 15

I can't dwell on it. That's what I think on Sunday morning when I wake up after a restless night of tossing and turning.

The Watcher is probably some way to remind me that Liam needs to move on—so if I can shuffle him into the afterlife, I can make it go away too.

I tell myself that *has* to be the secret.

Because the other alternative . . . maybe it's hinting to us that there's something darker at play. That Caleb really *did* have something to do with Liam's death. And I can't dismiss the possibility, especially with how weird he's been since Liam died, according to Rin and Hannah.

I think, to get to the bottom of it, I'm going to have to find some way to talk to Caleb.

Liam shows up again on Sunday morning. I'm already getting dressed to do a shift at Bee's, and I nearly jump out of my skin when I look up at my own reflection in the mirror and see him standing behind me.

"Jesus!" I shout, dropping my left shoe.

He smiles at me, sitting back on the bed on his hands. He looks . . . tired. I don't know what to think of it, because I rarely see ghosts looking anything other than ghost-like. I haven't spent enough consistent time with one to notice these kinds of changes.

I make a mental note to read more in Reece's notebook on degradation and signs that a ghost is becoming a husk. I don't want to think of Liam getting worse, but it is inevitable it'll happen sometime.

I just hope we can find a way for him to move on naturally before that.

"Sorry I ran off on you," he says, rubbing his eye. "I think it's harder for me to stick around, the farther we get from here."

I recover easily enough. "It makes sense," I say. "Based on what I know, the . . . core of your energy is focused here. So, since you've been here for so long without leaving, it's probably due to that. I imagine you can sustain here better than you can with me."

"Ah," Liam says. "So I'm a dying battery. Need to be connected to the charger at all times."

He's a *dead* battery, but there's no point adding insult to injury.

"Pretty much," I say. "Look, I need to go to work, and I'll probably be run off my feet and not actually good company—do you want to stay back? Hold down the fort? I'll be home by three."

He looks relieved, and then annoyed at himself for being relieved. "Sick of me already?"

Surprisingly, no, but I'm not going to let Liam know I've grown fond of him. "We'll have a debrief after, I promise," I say, going for my bag.

"As long as you promise," he agrees.

THE biggest surprise about Sunday rush at Bee's? I *know* people now.

The first Sunday I was working, it was all awkward smiles and pauses. But now, I know people from my classes, and I have an entire chat with Danny and Sophia when they come through the line. Bee takes on the bulk of making coffee orders while I work the register—she's far more introverted than me, and I think that's the main reason she has me in to work every now and then—and I keep turning around to find her smiling into steamed milk.

There's a lull near the end, though. I tucked my notebooks into my bag in case there was downtime, and after I restock the pastry case, I pull out my bag. There's no one in line, and only a couple of people lingering, so I take out both Reece's journal and my mom's. Before I can think better of it, I flip back to that last entry in Mom's handwriting:

There's something in the woods.

It sends a chill up my spine—but it doesn't contain any more information, or context.

I switch over to Reece's notebook. I'm sure there's something there about ghosts getting weaker, but I hope there might also be something about how to keep them around longer, to give them a natural end.

I'm still flipping through, finding nothing, and I'm nearing the end of my shift when Rin comes in with their mom. I shut the notebooks and shove them between two stacks of folded takeout boxes before Rin can ask me what I'm reading.

"Here for more cinnamon rolls?" I ask, already getting a box ready.

"You know it," Rin says. Their mom goes to grab a table after a quick chat with Bee. "What time are you off?"

I glance at the clock, but Bee intercedes. "Drew, you're good whenever," she says. "I can handle it from here."

"Now, I guess."

"Amazing. Look, Hannah said she invited you to go to Homecoming with us."

I bristle, preparing for rejection. There's something about the way they keep shifting their weight, the way they're not quite meeting my eye.

"I don't have to go—"

"Oh! It's nothing like that." Rin accepts the box and pays for the rolls and coffee. "Do you have anything to wear? We can go shopping, pick something up." They must see the look on my face because they quickly amend, "Don't worry, I also hate shopping. But it's something to do."

That it is. When I finish up and do a few last tasks, Rin is waiting for me. "Mom left the car," they say, swinging the keys around. "Do you need to stop home?"

"Nah, I'm good." I tip into Rin's car, and they start in the direction of one of the last big (god forbid) malls on our side of the suburbs. "What did you want to talk about?"

Rin chews on their lip for a minute. I can already feel my palms sweating, and I kind of wish Liam were here—which is bad, because I need to stop using him every time I run into some sort of emotional turmoil.

"It's Hannah," they say finally. "Look, I don't want to make things weird or anything, but I think . . . well, not think. She's into you."

Everything in my head goes quiet.

"Like, as more than a friend," Rin qualifies.

"Oh," I squeak. "Really? Like, actually?"

Rin barks a laugh, and I bury my head in my hands. "Really."

"And she wouldn't be mad at you for saying it?"

"Absolutely not," they say. I exhale, relieved, and Rin continues, "Sorry. I just—she's had a rough one. I just can't stand to see her get hurt again. Do you, er, like her back?"

Do I like Hannah back?

Is the sky blue?

Is my house haunted?

"Oh, definitely," I say. "I just didn't know . . ." I wave a hand at nothing, gesturing to the whole institution of sapphic attraction.

And honestly? Thank god for Rin.

"Great," Rin says. "Then, like, no pressure, but it might be nice to do something for homecoming. I don't know. Buy her flowers? Not sure what y'all do with feelings."

To be honest, I'm not sure what to do with them either. But as

I sit back, accepting Rin's gentle ribbing, I can't keep myself from smiling.

It's enough to forget, for a while, that everything else is a clusterfuck.

We both complain the whole time, but overall, it's a successful trip: I end up with a navy blue jumpsuit, and Rin picks out a hot pink suit that I wish I could pull off. It's already dark by the time I get home. I don't see Liam at first, but when I'm hanging up my dress, I catch sight of a shadow outside—and I realize that he's sitting in the backyard, looking out at the treehouse.

Bee and Dad are downstairs, watching TV. "Whatcha doing, peanut?" Bee asks when I cross through the room, towards the kitchen and the back door.

"Uh, supposed to be some cool stars," I lie. "Gonna check them out."

"Ooh, fun," she says, but neither of them look inclined to join me, which was definitely, 100 percent part of my master plan all along.

I'm sure he hears me crunching through the leaves, but he doesn't say anything as I come up behind him. He's just looking out into the darkness, and just beyond the edge of the forest, I know the treehouse is there, waiting.

"Do you want to go up there?" I ask.

"Do you think they care I'm gone?"

It takes all my effort not to roll my eyes—it's a harsh reaction, but it's automatic. "I'm sure they do."

"I don't know how you can be certain."

I sigh, then reach a hand down and haul him up. "Come on," I say, heading off in the direction of his deathtrap treehouse. "Let's make a plan."

He doesn't protest. Liam just follows me across the yard and through the trees, so quiet that I have to look over my shoulder twice to make sure he's still there, because there's no way I'm going up in that treehouse for no reason, by myself. But if he *is* still tied to an object, there's the chance it's there—and we can discuss what might've happened with Caleb while we look.

Liam lets me go up first. I tuck myself in the corner, next to the box of stuff he and Hannah shared.

"There's nothing valuable in here," Liam grumbles, folding himself up against the opposite wall. "If you think I have some love letter for Hannah hidden up here, you're wrong."

I sigh, running a hand through my hair. He's not being the easiest to work with right now. "Right. Then let's figure out what we can about Caleb. Have you thought of anything else that might be useful?"

"No," he says. "We both liked her. Caleb and I had a disagreement, but no huge falling out. It's not like she chose me instead or anything like that. It was all tame, and then it was all over."

I chew on my lip. It seems too simple by far.

"Where were you all day?" he asks, his tone even more despairing.

I glance up at him, taking in the miserable expression on his face. I desperately want to go through the stuff he and Hannah kept up here, searching for any trace of what can solve this, but I have the feeling that will only make him feel worse.

"I. . . ." The truth burns on my tongue, along with the realization that it will remind him of all the things he's missing out on. I swallow hard. "I was, uh, shopping for Homecoming stuff. I'm going with Rin and Hannah." I clear my throat. It's better to just say it now, to rip off the Band-Aid, to get it over with. "I guess Hannah told Rin that, uh, she likes me. . . ."

I trail off when I see Liam's face. There's an expression on it I've never seen before, and it takes me a second to realize that it's anger.

"What's wrong?" I ask weakly, because I already know.

"What's *wrong*? Oh, I don't know. I've been waiting for you for hours, and you were just off gallivanting with *my* friends—"

"Whoa, whoa now," I say, gripping the edge of the wooden bench I'm sitting on. "They're my friends too."

"Because I helped you trick them!"

I turn my face away. There's nothing much I can say to defend myself here—and I can't even say I'm surprised he feels this way. When I left him this morning, he was tired, but otherwise didn't seem to be in a bad mood. Nothing like this.

Softer, but no less hurt, he says, "You definitely didn't use me so you could slip right into my life, like I never existed."

"That is *not* what happened—"

"You even went after my *best friend*—"

"You knew I liked her!" I explode. "From day one!"

"I didn't mean to—"

Liam's voice cuts off. His face is pallid with anger and twisted with shock as a clawed hand reaches up through the hatch in the floor and grips his thigh—and then he's gone. Pulled. Dragged.

There's not even a thud. He's not corporeal; his body doesn't make a sound as it falls.

"*Liam!*" I shout, lurching across the treehouse. I throw myself down the ladder, launching myself off when I'm close enough to the ground that I won't break anything. My knees smart from the impact.

I spin in a wild circle, but I don't see any trace of him at first. And then there's a garbled shout from somewhere close by, and before I can think, I'm running.

If a husk feeds off him . . .

If he becomes a husk *now*, under my watch . . .

If there's actually nothing I can do for Liam, and this argument is the last thing he ever does . . .

None of it. I won't be able to forgive myself for any of it.

And then I see him: He's on his back, his feet kicking, trying his best to fight off the husk that lurches over him. It's a terrible, ghastly thing, milky white and dressed in rotted clothing, its hair a dripping black tangle against its back. Liam catches sight of me, his face twisted in terror.

"Drew!" he shouts.

I am so, *so* glad I read Reece's journal last week. Because I don't go straight for Liam: Instead, I grab two fistfuls of dirt, rich with rotten leaves and detritus, and launch them at the husk. Liam covers his eyes on instinct.

"What the hell are you doing?" he shouts.

"They love pain," I seethe, grabbing for more. My hand squishes against a rotting bit of wood from a fallen tree. "But they hate true decay."

This time, when I throw the rotting leaves and wood at the husk, it lurches back, hissing. It turns its awful eyes on me, filmed over with that hazy jelly of decay. When it reaches for me, I call on all of Reece's training.

I go for the solar plexus first, where Reece thinks their energy sits. After that, I give a swift kick to the shin, knocking the husk off balance.

"Get inside," I snarl to Liam. He hasn't moved, and I don't know how much time I can buy him—but I know he'll be safe in our house, in the perimeter of where he was once contained.

"Drew—" he starts.

But the husk is getting up, regrouping, coming back for me—and I can't focus on both this and Liam. "*Go.*"

For once, he doesn't fight me.

I focus entirely on the husk as its eyes go weird and dark, dripping down like inky molasses. It moves towards me, slow and sinuous, making some sort of odd hissing-clicking noise. It's clear its attention is focused on me.

I put my fists up. If I were smart, I would keep any sort of religious objects on my person—not because husks believe in anything, but because there is an odd kind of power in an object of collective faith. I would also probably benefit from a knife, but I don't have that either.

What I *do* have, after I take a moment to regroup, is a very large stick. And I do my best with it.

I jab at the husk as it comes close. It bares its teeth at me and slips into a hunch. Claws catch me across my ribs, and it fucking *hurts*, but I land a swing with the stick that makes the husk screech. It manages a bite to my thigh, but I recover quickly enough to slam the stick into their skull.

The husk explodes.

It's gross—just because they're not corporeal doesn't mean my brain doesn't *think* they are, and it feels like the awful slime of its body mixes with my own blood. I am covered in dirt and sweat, and I'm bleeding where it got me, but it's gone.

I drop the stick. Tilt my head back and look up at the leaves. The space between them. And then I lumber back to the house, to figure out what the fuck we're going to do next.

I manage to slink by Bee and Dad by going the other way, through the dining room and up the stairs. Alone in my bathroom, I strip off my shirt, turn on the water, and stare at my reflection. The cuts against my ribs are ugly and jagged, and the twisted shape of teeth mar my left thigh.

Then there's a hand against my ribs, like he can catch the blood that weeps from the wound.

I glance up, meeting Liam's gaze. He's still too pale. "You didn't . . ." He swallows hard, his throat working. "You didn't have to do that for me. You could've just let it have me."

I close my eyes. When I open them, he's still there, and I feel no better. I find the thing of antiseptic that Reece kept under the sink at our last house, the one I dutifully unpacked here, and pour some onto a cotton pad. It fizzes against my skin, and I bite down on my lip so I don't make a noise.

Finally, I say, "I wouldn't do that to you."

"You'd have a right to," Liam says quietly.

I sigh, moving to the wound on my thigh. "I'm sorry," I say. "I . . . I promise I didn't go into this thinking I was taking your spot, or anything like that—I've *never* thought of it like that, and I appreciate every single thing you've done for me—"

"I know," Liam says, his voice twisting.

I throw away the bloody cotton pads and sag to the floor, curling in on myself, sitting back against the door. The cold of it bites into my spine. I need to shower, but I'm not going to do that in front of Liam. "I think you should stay inside for a bit," I say, unable to meet his eye.

There's a long, long pause. "Are you even *trying* to figure out why I'm still here?" Liam asks, his voice dark as the grave.

I wince. Close my eyes. Rest my forehead on my knees and wrap my arms around my head. "I promise, I'm doing my best," I say.

But Liam doesn't answer. And when I unfold, open my eyes, and look for him, he's already gone.

Liam's Afterlife Notebook
(if it existed)

Notes for Mom

- I'm sorry I lied about breaking your terracotta mint pot on the patio. I'm doubly sorry I blamed it on Ella.

- I'm sorry I didn't read that book you really, really wanted me to read the summer before I died. I know I would've loved it. I know we would've thought the same things. I watched you put it in the donation box before you left, because it was in my room when I didn't come back, and even though you loved it, you couldn't stand to look at it anymore.

- I think you're the best mom that has ever existed. I wish I could've folded myself up small in one of those boxes, hidden amongst the old cookbooks and folded up sheets from the linen closet, or maybe in the hope trunk you inherited from your grandma. I wish you didn't have to leave me behind.

- I'm sorry I didn't come home.

Notes for Dad

- I know I wasn't the kind of son you wanted. We didn't play ball and I didn't have a love for the Steelers and I always took a book with me to hockey games. I'm sorry I always changed the radio station when you were trying to listen to commentary.

- I'm sorry I wasn't interested in engineering, like you. I know how badly you wanted me to love it— I know you know I did the Westinghouse Honors thing for you, to see if there was even a miniscule thing that could keep my attention. I'm sorry it didn't. I promise I tried.

- I wish I'd told you I loved you more. I wish you'd said it back.

Notes for Ella

- I used your toothbrush three times and didn't tell you.

- I also stole your shirt that Mom got you from the Globe, but to be fair, it's back with you now. I saw how much of my stuff you took from the donation bin without Mom seeing, and how many times you wore my clothes after I died, so I think we're square. I hope you still have that awful Margaritaville shirt you took from my drawer.

- I'm sorry I made things weird with Hannah. I hope you don't blame her. I know I don't.

- I'm sorry that I've become, like, this *thing* for you. This trauma. I am perhaps being narcissistic about this but I don't think I am, because I watched Drew stalk you on socials the other night, and your posts are so sad. Ella, I didn't mean to cause this. You're so much better than me, El. So much brighter. You are so much more than the space I left behind and I desperately wish you would move on from me, if you could. If it's possible.

Notes for Hannah

- I'm sorry that you wear the scars, literally.
- I'm sorry about October 25th.
- I'm sorry about November 1st.
- I'm sorry that I still loved you, in the end.
- I'm sorry that, in the end, you did not love me.
- I'm sorry that I even cared.
- I'm sorry I still do.
- Love you, I mean.

CHAPTER 16

The only thing more annoying than being haunted is *not* being haunted.

Liam doesn't come back. I try all the tricks I know: leaving out an offering, a Ouija board, burning incense. I call Reece to try to figure out some sort of ritual, but they're too busy with classes to help me with "pointless ghost shit."

I feel guilty enough to avoid everyone for a few days. It doesn't much matter, in the end: Paige ropes most of the group into helping with Homecoming setup, and Hannah has extra band practice to get ready for the game. Rin asks me to hang out twice, but I manage to dodge them by begging Bee for extra shifts.

By the time the Homecoming game rolls around, I haven't seen Liam in a week and Rin keeps looking at me oddly when we sit together in study hall. They're waiting for me at my locker when the bell rings after eighth period—there's no way to grab my stuff and get my bike without talking to them.

You definitely didn't use me so you could slip into my life, like I never existed.

"Hey," Rin says when I come close. "You okay?"

"Ah, yeah," I lie. "Sorry—I've just been super busy lately."

They glance down the hall at the clots of other student

surrounding us, then step closer. "This doesn't have anything to do with what I said last weekend, right? About Hannah?"

"What? No, of course not. I just—I got into a fight. With a friend back home."

"Ah, shit. I'm sorry, Drew."

I dig for my books and switch them out, then swing my bag over my shoulder. "It's fine," I tell them. "Just feeling a little meh, you know?"

"Are you coming to the game?" they ask, keeping stride with me.

"I don't know if I'm feeling up to it, honestly," I say, which, for once, isn't a lie.

"No worries. Just—Hannah's coming over to mine tomorrow to get ready, if you want to join us. No pressure. But we can all go to Paige's together, then."

I think about telling them no, that I'll just meet them there. I think about backing out entirely. But actually, Rin has always been nice to me, even before Liam and I had any sort of agreement. I can be mad at him, and mad at myself, too, but there's no point taking it out on Rin.

"Yeah," I say. "That sounds really nice. Can I bring anything?"

"Just yourself," Rin says, smiling with relief. They must've genuinely thought I was mad at them, and my stomach twists with guilt.

I make a mental note to help Bee with a batch of cinnamon rolls, because I'm not going to show up empty-handed. "Can't wait," I lie through my teeth.

It's already dark outside, and I'm playing a game with Andie over Discord when there's a knock at the door. It's not Dad, because of course Dad wouldn't knock, and it's not Bee, because she's doing the dreaded weekly deep-clean of the espresso machine.

It's also not Liam because he's 1) dead, and 2) still ignoring me.

I'm expecting an incorrect pizza delivery when I open the door, but it's Hannah, catching me completely off guard. Her eyes are red and puffy.

"Hi," she says before I can recover.

I blink twice. Try to look cool. "Hey," I say, leaning against the doorframe. "You okay? What's up?"

She rubs her eyes. "Yeah, I—god, sorry, this is so dumb." She laughs into her hands, but there's no humor in it. "I tried to stop at Rin's, but they're out, and then I just figured . . . well. I thought you would be—"

"Yeah," I say, agreeing, because whatever she thinks I'm up for, I probably am. "Come in—did you come straight from band?"

She follows me inside as I lead the way to the living room, though I'm pretty sure she knows the way even better than I do.

"Yeah," she says. "Sorry—this may be super weird. It's just, my mom's not home, and I'm just feeling a bit rough, you know?"

I hesitate as she sinks into the couch, because I think I know what this is about, and the idea of talking about it with her and *without* Liam after our fight the other night feels odd. But if I was a normal girl and not a haunted one, of course we'd be having this conversation without Liam, and the fact I feel odd about it makes me feel even worse about the extra layer of manipulative fuckery that's usually happening.

So, "I get it," I say instead. "Do you want water? Tea? Anything?"

"I'm okay," Hannah says. She curls into a little ball on the corner of the sofa. Outside, it's drizzling—we've entered that period in autumn where it's raining as often as it isn't. Her hair is wet from it, from practice. "Sorry, I probably shouldn't have come."

"It's fine," I say, some of that exasperation with the situation leaking out. "We're friends."

The corner of her mouth turns up.

"So what's bothering you?" I ask, even as I'm searching the shadows for Liam. I'm torn between wanting him here and wanting him to stay as far away as possible—I'm torn between knowing what's best for Hannah and what's best for me.

Hannah folds her hands in her lap, unfolds them, folds them again. "This is going to be too much, probably," she says, not quite meeting my eyes. "Like, I haven't even told Rin—but I don't know if it's because you live here, and that makes me feel like you're closer to him, or just because you say things sometimes, and it's like what he would say."

Somehow, my smile doesn't falter.

"I just still can't believe he's gone," Hannah says. "Like, it's easier to believe he just up and left town—I don't know if I can let go of him."

I swallow hard, moving to sit on the other end of the sofa. "Did you guys . . . did anything happen? Before he died, I mean?"

"Just Homecoming. Last year, we had this huge fight afterwards, and that was the last real time I talked to him, you know? We had a huge blowout after the dance, when he drove me home, and then two weeks later he was dead. And I don't remember it— amnesia, or brain trauma, or whatever went wrong at the point of impact just *erased* those moments for me—so I don't know what happened. I don't know why he picked me up, or what I said, or if we were still fighting. And that's all I can think about: that when he drove off the road, what if we were fighting? What if it was me?"

"Hannah," I say, my voice sounding as raw as I feel. "I highly doubt that."

"It's just," Hannah says, "that week—it was bad. We never fought, not like that. And I can't get over the feeling that, for whatever reason, for him to answer the phone, for him to come for me—something really bad must've been happening, you know?"

My stomach feels odd and knotted. "He cared about you."

She's quiet for a moment. "Maybe," she says, her voice cracking down the middle. "But doesn't that still make it my fault?"

"No," I say quickly—maybe too quickly. "Absolutely not."

"I guess that's the thing. And, like, the party—it was at

Caleb's house. We'd all been drinking, and there was no one else to call but Liam, and Caleb is the one who did it. That's why Caleb and I were so close afterwards, at first. Why I let it get too far. Some fucked-up version of survivor's guilt," Hannah says, dropping her head back to her hands. "This is so messy."

It is, but so are people. I only shrug. "It's okay. It will get better." I want to ask more about Caleb, but there's no way to do it without being suspicious—but if Caleb called Liam, then he knew Liam was coming for Hannah.

Could he have done something to the car?

She shakes her head. "Everyone keeps saying that—that I'll move on. Like you said. That it will get better. But it won't. It *can't*."

It's the closest thing to an outburst she's had. I feel myself flushing, and I don't know if it's because there is nothing I can say . . . or if it's because there are a dozen things I want to.

"I'm sorry," she says, after a moment of quiet. "I didn't mean to . . . yeah."

"It's fine. Is there anything I can say to make it better? Anything I can do?"

Hannah thinks, then shakes her head. "Just . . . thank you for listening. I really do appreciate it. Honestly."

"Any time."

Another moment, then, "And . . . maybe we could talk about something that isn't Liam? Maybe we could do something?"

"Do you want to bake something?" I ask. I'm not nearly as good as Bee, but it always makes me feel better: the tactile nature of measuring and kneading, of mixing and whisking and tempering. "Bee is going to be a while still, and who knows when Dad will be home. So we can turn the music on loud and make something, if you want."

"Oh," Hannah says, like she hadn't considered it. "Yeah, actually. That sounds great."

She leads the way to the kitchen this time, and scrolls through the music on her phone once I connect her to the speaker. Soon enough, a blare of '80s music starts while I'm reaching for the flour.

It's nice, actually, focusing only on the measurements in Bee's careful handwriting on the laminated sheet. We settle for her lemon tart, which is kind of technical but doesn't require anything to rise or wait for too long. Hannah sings along under her breath as we bake, and she *is* a good singer.

And through it all, all I can think—I want *this*. I want all of those smiles to be mine, I want to know every quiet laugh. I want to dance around the kitchen with her without having to talk about the most traumatic thing that's ever happened to her first. I want to help her move on, which is so shitty—because the very person I'm helping her move on from is the person I need to keep close.

There's no sign of Liam. That almost makes every second of the guilt worse.

At the end of it, it's almost midnight, and the tart is cooling on a tray, and Hannah is sitting on the counter drinking a mug of hot chocolate I made using another one of Bee's recipes. I lean against the counter next to her, and my forearm just barely touches her thigh, my hand only just grazes hers. My heart speeds into overdrive when she reaches down and laces our fingers together. As if it's nothing at all. As if it doesn't change everything. As if it doesn't fill me with hope that, just maybe, everything will be okay.

CHAPTER 17

"*L*iam." I try to summon him again, one last time, before I head over to Rin's to get ready for the dance. I haven't seen him since our fight. I know it's not fair to assume he'd be at my beck and call, especially knowing exactly why he's upset—but I don't think it's fair to *me* to leave me in a lurch.

Nothing.

I sigh, but I'm out of time. Actually, I'm already late, and Rin has texted me at least four times. I gather up my things, sling my duffel for later over my shoulder, and head downstairs.

"Heading out?" Bee asks from the kitchen. She has Meat Loaf blaring, and she's rolling out dough for a new recipe. Dad is out at his office, working on a trial he's arguing this week.

"Yeah, going to Rin's to get ready."

Bee wipes the flour off her hands and comes over to kiss me on the cheek. "Text me when you're ready, and I'll come for pictures, yeah?"

"Yeah," I say, blushing a little, but I appreciate the fact she's involved. The fact she cares.

It's not like I'm mad at Dad for missing things—it's moot, at this point, and he's been absent more than he's been present for, in terms of events. Piano recitals, track meets, Reece's mock trial competitions (mostly—he would try to be at those, when he could). It hurt Reece more than it did me. I think I've just accepted that this is who he is, and this is how we are, and that makes everything easier.

But it would definitely sting more if Bee weren't here to pick up the slack.

She hands over the box of cinnamon rolls we baked yesterday, and I head for the door. I'm putting on my shoes when I feel the faintest brush of cold. When I look up, Liam is leaning against the wall, arms crossed.

Bee is still in earshot, so I can't say anything. I just look up at him and offer a tight smile. Liam nods back, his expression not quite clear.

When we're outside, I say, "Look, about yesterday—" just as he starts, "I was unfair to you."

That's enough to stop me in my tracks. "Not really," I say. "Like, genuinely, watching everyone keep going . . . it must *suck*."

"Oh, it does," he says, without any sort of malice. "But, Drew, *you're* not the one who killed me. And you're right. Especially with Hannah. I told you I'd help."

There's a weird lump in my throat, maybe relief, and though I swallow it down, my face still feels too warm. "Still," I say.

"It's okay," he says, a note softer. "The other day . . . when Hannah was talking about me being gone . . . I would hate for her to feel like that all the time. You take some of that away. I'm only mad at you because I can't do it myself."

He's a better person than me. I think I always suspected it, as long as I've known him, but it's true. Liam Orville is kind, and mature, and he always says the right thing—and the fact that he's here as a ghost and not a boy is a damn tragedy.

"Thanks," I say.

"Anytime." He sighs, rolling his shoulders. "So, let's seal the deal, eh?"

I don't know who's more thankful for the cinnamon rolls: Rin or their mom. Both look more delighted to see the box than me, but that doesn't matter, because when Rin whisks it off to the kitchen, Hannah is there in the doorway to the living room, and she's smiling.

She's smiling at *me*.

Rin comes back and slings an arm around my shoulders. "Right," they say. "Let's get the party started."

"Getting the party started" apparently just means going to Rin's room with a cold two-liter of Diet Coke and more chips than we can ever hope to consume, listening to musical soundtracks, and watching Hannah paint her nails as they gossip about people they know.

I don't mind, honestly. It's nice to be in a room that's not mine, in a house that's not mine; it's nice to feel included; it's nice to get up-to-date information from a source with a heartbeat. I perch on Rin's big circle chair, and Liam squeezes in next to me, making observations about people and giving me context to back up the gossip.

"Sorry, Drew," Rin says at one point. Hannah has finished her nails, and she's now swinging her hands around, willing the paint to dry. "You probably don't know any of these people."

I shrug. "I've picked up more than you think," I say. Next to me, Liam snorts.

"We should get dressed," Hannah says. She goes for her dress. "Do you mind if I take the bathroom? I want to curl my hair."

"Nah," Rin says, opening their closet and pulling out their pink suit. "Drew and I will hold down the fort. Holler if you need anything."

She smiles and darts off. Rin turns to me and says, "Well? Feeling okay?"

"Feeling fine," I say.

They pull off their T-shirt, and Liam turns to face the wall. He's a good kid. Respectful.

"Are you going to make a move?" Rin asks as they pull their

silk tank top over their head and tuck it in. I fiddle with the zip on my jumpsuit.

"Eventually, yeah," I say. Liam shoots me a look, sees more skin than intended, and turns around with a gulp. "I just . . . I'm nervous, okay? Waiting for my moment."

"Do you want me to set one up?" Rin asks, too serious.

"God." Everyone is very interested in my love life, or lack thereof. "I'll figure it out," I say.

They give me a sympathetic look, and we settle into talking about other topics. A few minutes later, when Hannah calls, "Hey, can I get a hand?" Rin basically rips my arm off getting me through the door.

"Drew's coming!" they call out. "Be cool," they say to me.

I am certain, together in life, Rin and Liam were a force to be reckoned with.

Liam hesitates outside the bathroom door as I open it and peek in. Hannah's hair is curled, and her dress is on, but the zip is only half up, and the buttons at the cuffs of her sleeves are undone. She meets my eye in the mirror.

"If I do my buttons," she says mournfully, "I will ruin my nail polish."

"Ah." I make a sign to Liam that there is no offensive flesh on the other side of the door. "Hang on."

He follows me in, and I shut the door behind us. I stand behind her, palms going sweaty as I do up the back of her dress, clasp the hook and eye at the top, and do the button over the cut-out. She meets my eyes in the mirror.

"Drew," she says.

I drop my hands. "What's up?"

"Really?" Liam asks, leaning against the glass of the shower. "That's the best you could come up with?"

She turns. Her hands on the counter, curling over the edge. She leans back. Looks up at me. I'm not that much taller than her—an inch, maybe—but it feels like an uncrossable distance.

"I, um, heard a rumor."

"Right, breathe, and don't say anything impulsive," Liam says. "Repeat after me."

I nod, then realize I haven't said anything—but Liam hasn't said anything either. "What rumor?" he says, and I repeat him.

Hannah searches my face. Her dark eyes are liquid, gold eyeshadow shimmering. She is beautiful. She is the most beautiful girl I have ever seen.

"Do you like me?" she asks, her voice caught.

"Yes," Liam says, but the word catches in my throat. There's a line here, one that I'm not sure I can cross.

"If I say it," I say instead, "I can't take it back."

Hannah sucks a breath through her teeth, turns her head. "Would you want to take it back, if you said it?" she asks, her voice carrying a note of hurt, and I remember again why I usually let Liam steer the ship.

I take a half-step closer.

"Let me," Liam murmurs. He takes a deep breath. "I just— I'm not used to being with people. To getting what I want, and having it reciprocated."

I repeat his words, watching as the meaning hits Hannah's face. She looks up at me again, and this time, there's no hurt. "I know what you mean," she says. "But you can tell me. I think— no. I know, I probably feel what you feel. But you have to tell me what that *is*."

Liam is next to me now. I feel the cold of him, the chill raising goose bumps on my arms. "I don't know if I have the words," he says, and I echo. I reach out, taking one of her hands from the counter.

She looks down at her hand in mine. "I know, I get that. But I'd like to hear them, if you do. I—" She bites her lip. Looks away. "If you can find the words, then I want them. I want all of them."

Next to me, Liam is statue-still. "If I speak, everything will change between us." He's not looking at me, he's looking at her, and I know I should stop this—

But I just repeat after him. His puppet. His body. His words in my voice, these stolen words heavy in my throat.

"Then change it," Hannah says.

Something shifts. Changes between us. It's like Liam and I are one, like he is me and I am him, like there's not a gap between the words he's saying leaving his mouth and coming out of mine. And maybe there isn't. Maybe this is possession; maybe this is truly what it is to be haunted.

"I desire you," Liam says, or I do, "in ways I don't know how to name. I adore you. I want you. I need you. I think of you, constantly, from the moment my eyes open in the morning until they close at night. Even in my dreams, you're there, haunting me." I take her hand in mine and start the buttons on her sleeve, unable to look at her. "Every time I hear your name, I listen closer, hoping to know something more of you, something that you yourself haven't shown me. I just—even last week, at dinner. You wore your hair differently, in two braids, and I thought to myself that I would study you, every move and every breath, every parting of your hair. You're imprinted so deeply in my brain, when I look away from you, it's all darkness. Nothing more than an afterimage. Looking at you is like looking at the sun."

I set her hand down. Take up her other. Do the buttons at her wrist.

"Every time I look at you, it's like my blood is on fire." Her hand in mine is clenched into a fist, and I fear that we've pushed it too far. That we've said too much.

And I know—the thing we've done, that I've let Liam do, *that* has pushed it too far.

Because I *like* her, yes—I have that old, nameless infatuation, that fire in my blood. But what we just said, what *Liam* just said, alludes to years of study. To a lifetime of desire. Not to my silly, teenage infatuation of a couple of months, but to Liam's careful construction of a love that followed him all the way to the grave and beyond.

My confession is certainly a truth—but I'm certain that only part of it is *mine*.

I let go of her wrist. Step back. But then Hannah's hand is

on my waist, and the other goes to my neck, curling around the back. I only have a second to look up, to see her face, and then she is pulling me down.

Whatever is left of Liam in me leaves in one violent rush. It's like resurfacing, coming back to myself, in full control and finding myself in Hannah's arms.

She brings my mouth down to hers, tentatively at first, and I am frozen—Hannah breaks away, looking at me wild-eyed, as if she has made some sort of mistake, and that's when my sluggish brain fires into action.

I pull her against me, hard and close, and I'm pressing her back against the counter. Her hands are tangled in my hair, and my hands are on her waist, fingers digging into the velvet of her dress, and her mouth is on mine.

Her mouth is on mine, and I taste the strawberry of her lip gloss.

Her mouth is on mine, and I have been imagining this—and yet nothing compares to the sweetness of it now, in reality.

Hannah gasps, breaking away, leaning back. I stagger back, too, putting space between us. My heart hammers in my chest.

She looks at me, one hand going to touch the edge of her lip, as if she can't quite believe what just happened. What she did. What *we* did.

"I'm sorry," I blurt. "That was a *lot*. Are you okay? Was that okay?"

I know I'm rambling, and glance around—and it's only then that I realize that Liam is gone.

Her cheeks are high with color, and she takes a deep breath. "I liked it. I, um, I like *you*, Drew. I feel like you stripped the words from me. Like you siphoned them directly from my brain."

I am, unfortunately, familiar with the feeling.

"I didn't mean to come on so strong," I say, reaching to brush her hair back. I can't stop touching her. The fact that I even get to touch her is—well. It's astounding.

Liam would have better words for this, but that thought makes my stomach do something odd.

"It's fine," Hannah says. "I like knowing where we stand."

She leans up, brushes her lips against mine. I cannot believe this is real—this is happening. And she's right; I also like knowing where we stand.

It just feels a bit hollow, because I can't be certain she's falling for the things I've said, the way I've acted, the way *Liam* has told me to be—or if she actually sees past that. If she sees me at all.

CHAPTER 18

The dance itself rushes by in stolen touches and covert smiles. By the time it's over, my veins are fizzing with electricity.

It's not like anything spectacular happens; we don't kiss in the corner of the gym or hold hands out by the tables laden with cookies and punch in the cafeteria. In fact, I spend most of the time spinning between my new friends, winning a dance-off against Adam by the skin of my teeth and then joining Hannah and Rin as Sophia teaches us new dance moves.

We swirl in a circle, letting in random other kids from school and letting them pass through just as quickly. Liam sticks around for only a few minutes before he disappears.

Nothing much is different until the very last slow dance. I see it happening—I see Caleb turning to Hannah, his lips forming the words, and then before I can even really think, I'm reaching for her hand. She turns to me, a question on her lips—and then she smiles.

"Wanna dance?" I ask. My heart pounds in my throat.

"Yeah," she says.

There's a whole stack of clichés I can apply to this moment: how Hannah's highlighter glimmers in the lights from the DJ's booth, how her hair falls over her shoulders as she reaches up to loop her arms around my neck, how her waist feels under my hands when I loop mine around, my fingers only just touching against her back.

"Have you danced with a girl before?" she asks, a note of wryness to her tone.

"Yes," I snort. "Have you?"

"No," she says, lowering her gaze. A flush rises in her cheeks. "I'm not experienced with much of this, actually."

I swallow down the dryness in my mouth. "That's okay," I say. I step away to spin her once, twice. Her grin is even wider when she spins back into my arms. "Hey, I have a thought."

"Yeah?"

"What if we skip Caleb's tonight?"

She hesitates. "Why?"

I shrug. Because I can't bear to think about Liam's death and the circumstances of it, or the weight in my chest whenever I think of what happened between the two of us—between the *three* of us. "There's just this pretty girl, and I was thinking I could ask her on a date."

Hannah still looks suspicious. "We could go on a date at any time," she says, and she's right. But—

"Maybe this pretty girl doesn't have the best memories of this night," I say, watching her face carefully. "And maybe the party will only make things worse, will be like prodding a bruise. But I happen to know an Eat'n Park that's sure to be open, and a quiet night might do you good."

She searches my face. "You'd really do that?"

"Do what?"

"Blow off the party. Go out with me instead."

I scoff. "I can't think of anything I'd rather do. I'm not much of a partier."

Hannah bites her lip. Then, even though there are people all around, even though we're not really much of anything at all, she leans onto her tiptoes and presses her lips to mine. It's only a chaste kiss, the barest of touches, but it makes my veins feel hot under my skin.

"Yeah," Hannah says, launching into another spin. "Yeah, I'd like that."

We ditch the party and go to Eat'n Park instead. It's the one in the next town over, and they don't have Homecoming, so it's just us, a few overnight drivers, and a couple of kids our age playing a board game across the dining room. Hannah doesn't even look at the menu before she goes for grilled stickies and an Oreo shake. I, a woman of class and good breeding, take a Pepsi and fried ravioli.

"That's literally two desserts at once," I say, regarding Hannah as she takes a sip of her shake.

"And I will have no slander from you, Tarpin," she says. "Did they have an Eat'n Park near your last place?"

"Yeah, not too far," I say. "It might be a bit of a trek, but Eat'n Park is a Pennsylvania institution."

Hannah pushes the ice cream around her plate. "You really don't want to go to college?" she asks. I'm a bit caught off guard by the sudden change in subject, but I can roll with it. I take a bite of my ravioli, thinking about the best way to answer.

"I guess I don't really see the point," I say finally. "It's just, well, it's a lot of money. And I don't really see myself doing something that requires a degree—I like working with my hands, and being outside, and doing stuff outside a classroom. I don't really like class at all, actually."

"There's nothing wrong with that," she says quickly.

"I know," I say. I shake my head. "I know it'll take me a while to figure things out, but I think it would be nice to just be free for a bit, you know? Travel or something, just throw a dart at a map and go there. See what it's like, get a job and a place. Maybe I'll move around for a few years. Maybe I'll get a dog."

"It just sounds . . . unsettled."

I shrug. "Maybe," I allow. "But I can always go back, if I decide that's not what I want to do, if I change my mind. But I won't be eighteen again."

"You won't miss your family? Your friends?"

"Sure," I say, "but I can always come home. I've been working for Bee for a few years so I have savings, and I can get a car and put down first month's rent on an apartment. But I haven't seen much of anything outside of this place, you know? There are so many things out there that I've just never had the chance to experience."

Hannah looks at me, and it's like she's stripping the layers away, peeling back every one of my answers. "You're a lot braver than I am."

"That's doubtful," I tell her. I finish the last of my ravioli and move the basket to the end of the table. "What do you want to do?"

"I've always wanted to go to UNC," she says. "My dad used to work there, right after he and Mom divorced. I'd go down there for a couple weeks every summer, and there was just something about it."

"Is he still there?"

Hannah shakes her head. "Toronto now, but it doesn't have the same feeling. Or perhaps *he* doesn't have the same feeling." She folds her hands in front of her. "So, your parents. Are they . . . divorced?"

"They were never married," I say. "My mom left when we were really, really little. We being me and my sibling, Reece."

"Ah." She traces circles on the table. "It's a bit of a weird one. Most of my friends here—their parents are still together, and have always been, and always will be. Like the Orvilles, and the Mendozas—they just have these perfect family units. Like, divorce is super normal, but it was like they always looked at me and pitied me because my dad wasn't around anymore."

"I'm sorry," I say, and I mean it. "I don't know—well, I can only speak for me. But things are a lot easier now. Dad is happier. And Bee is great. And I imagine my mom is happier, too, wherever she is."

"Does she not talk to you?" Hannah asks, her gaze flicking up to mine.

I shrug. There's that creeping memory of her handwriting in her journal, like she'd never left, like the wound had never healed. But I haven't spoken to her since that last night when she left my room over ten years ago. If she's spoken to Reece—well. I guess that's none of my business. If it's none of my business, it can't hurt.

I wish I were mad at her. I wish I knew how to be. I get desperately not fitting into a life that you've stumbled into. I get searching for a way out. And I know what she can do, I think—she can see spirits like Reece and I can. I can't imagine what we were like as kids, the two of us. Maybe Mom hated the talent, and that had something to do with it.

Maybe she wanted us so, so much, but the addiction was a black hole she kept getting sucked into. Maybe there is a moment where you realize that, actually, you're not going to get better.

Maybe I'm making excuses, and I should be mad at her. But late at night, when my thoughts turn to her, I can't find it in me to be angry.

"She doesn't really want much to do with us," I say, and it's the truth.

"Drew..."

"It's okay," I say, because it is. It's an old wound.

Hannah reaches across the table and lays her hand over mine. I flip mine up under hers, so I can knot our fingers together. She doesn't pull away.

I pay for the food—a date is a date, after all—and Hannah drives me home. Liam isn't here with us. I don't know what to make of this—I don't know if there's anything to read into it at all. Maybe he's just tired, burnt-out in that dying way he is when we're away from home for too long.

Maybe he hates me for kissing Hannah.

Maybe he knows, in another life, it would be him here, in her passenger seat. Maybe even him here, with her fingers entwined with his.

I try to push those thoughts away as I sit back further in Hannah's passenger seat. This, too, is familiar to me now: the clean cotton smell of the air freshener clipped to the vent mingling with the leather polish she uses to keep her band shoes shiny. She doesn't talk at first, but she drives with one hand on the wheel and the other loosely knotted in mine.

"There's still so much I don't know about you," she murmurs as she pulls out of the lot, her thumb skimming over mine. "Can you drive? I've only ever seen you with your bike."

I snort. "Yeah, I have a license, but I hate it. I'd much rather bike everywhere I can. When Reece was around, they'd drive all the time."

"Passenger princess," she says, squeezing my fingers. I look out the window at the trees racing by, wishing I could bottle this moment, this night, forever. Her voice is softer when she asks, "When did you, um, know you were . . . not straight?"

"I'm not straight?"

"*Drew.*"

I laugh. "Always," I say. "I don't think there was a single moment when I looked at a boy and thought, *yeah, I could do that.*"

Hannah's laugh fills the car. "I can't relate, unfortunately," she says.

I run my thumb over the back of her hand. "Have you ever been in a relationship before?" I ask, tentative—I don't want her to think I'm assuming that *we're* in a relationship, but I just want to know. I want to know everything about her.

"I had a boyfriend, freshman year," she says, risking a glance over at me, as if I'll judge her. "For the briefest of moments."

"Hannah. You're bi, right? I know boys exist—chill."

She takes a shaky breath. "It's just, sometimes when you're with a boy, it's like it erases that other part of you, you know? Like, there's a 50/50 shot you'll end up with anyone, but it just so happens that I've only dated boys. Maybe I haven't been brave enough to cross that line with any other girls I liked. Maybe I didn't know how."

"I get what you mean," I say. "I'm not bi, but—well, people assume, right? That, like, if you're with a boy, it means you're just . . . always going to do that. Or that liking girls was a phase. Or that you're just not into girls that much after all."

"Yeah," Hannah says, relief clear in her voice. "But, uh, yeah. There was one boyfriend, and then whatever was going on with Caleb—but that was more of me leading him on than anything else." Her face is flushed when she admits this, so I don't respond—I don't think anything I have to say will make it better. She's quiet for a moment. "I've . . . liked other people. Flirted with other people. Maybe even loved one or two of them. But I don't think I actually know what love is, what it feels like. I think my emotions are too wobbly, too uncertain to really *know*, you know?"

"I think so," I say.

"What about you? Any girlfriends?"

"Just flings," I say. She swallows hard, and I realize the connotations of that—I don't know how to tell her that she's not just a fling to me, or if that would make things worse. But this is how I always am around her: searching for words I can't find. That's why Liam's helpful. He takes the guesswork out, removes the fear from the equation. Even if what he says isn't exactly what I feel, it sounds *better*.

I might actually be a horrible person. But that's a concern for tomorrow.

"It's just hard to get a read on people sometimes, you know?" I continue, fighting to make sense. "There's just so much dancing around, so much will-they-won't-they. But I find it so hard to just . . . come out and say it."

"You didn't have that problem earlier," Hannah murmurs, but I catch her smirk.

There's no point saying that the words weren't mine, that the feelings were, but the actual development was on Liam. The guilt is growing deeper, echoing in my stomach.

We get to my house, and Hannah pulls into the drive. The

lights are all off besides the hall and front porch, which Bee always leaves on when I'm out late. Hannah looks at the house, something unreadable in her expression.

"Do you, um, want to hang out for a bit?" I ask. Then, realizing how that sounds, "If you're not tired, I mean. We don't have to go in. We can just talk."

"I . . ." She glances at the house, then at me. I wonder how weird it must be, to walk into this place again where she's been a million times. To layer the memories of Liam's parents and sister over my family. The uncanniness of it.

I wonder if she felt it the other night, the oddness pressing on her heart. If she looked up, expecting Liam, and found me instead. I wonder if she would see the scuff on the wall of my room and immediately remember how he looked, leaning back in his chair, limned in sunlight.

"We can go to the treehouse," I say, even though that thing is a death trap, and I'm still wary of it after the other night—but I can't imagine putting Hannah through more of that uncanny overwriting of who Liam once was, and I'm not ready to say goodbye to her tonight. This seems to be the right thing to suggest, because Hannah turns off the car and starts across the grass.

"It'll be hard to climb in my dress," she says when we reach the bottom. She leans over, undoing the ankle straps on her heels.

"I'll go first," I offer, even though the "steps" are the actual devil. "No weirdness, I promise."

I scrabble up the ladder and go looking for the camping light. It's right where Hannah left it—but there are other things in the box too. I pull out two blankets, a stuffed notebook in a Ziploc bag, and a canister of bug spray.

Hannah pulls herself up and sees what's in my hands. Her expression flashes for just a second, and I know that, no matter how much she's ready and able to share with me, there are some parts of Liam she wants to keep for herself.

I set the bag aside between us, acting like it doesn't interest me. I'm not going to go trampling over Hannah's boundaries, especially when it comes to the things she shared with Liam—not just because it's Hannah, but because it feels invasive to unpack these, the articles left behind of his life, without him here to give me permission. Against my will, I'm reminded of the ugliness in his voice the other night when he accused me of stealing his life.

Instead, I unfold the blanket, draping half of my shoulder. "Good thing the spiders didn't get into this," I say.

Hannah snorts. "We did so many bug bombs to spider-proof this place," she says. "But still. I'm amazed it worked." She comes to sit next to me on the built-in bench, huddled against the warmth of my body. I wrap the blanket and my arm around her shoulders.

She's so close I can feel her breath against my cheek. There are two thoughts within me: first, that this is a perfect moment I don't know if I'll ever get again—there's every chance that I'll mess up.

And second? That I didn't earn any of this, any of Hannah's trust or affection. That there are so many reasons why this is wrong, why I should abandon ship, why I shouldn't press further—but there's no way I can tell her about Liam or what we've already done.

And the way she's looking at me . . . Hannah has the faintest smirk on her lips, and she keeps glancing at me from the corner of her eye, like she's expecting me to take control of the situation. And god, I would. I *want* to. My palms are slick with sweat, folded in my lap, but I can't imagine crossing the space between us.

I am too nervous for any of this.

"So, um," I say, grasping at straws. "Have you kissed a girl before?"

She blinks at me. "Drew . . . hate to break it to you, but I've kissed *you*."

"Before," I stammer.

"Once or twice, at parties," she says. "Why? Are you thinking of kissing me again?" Her gaze flicks to my lips. She reaches forward, one of her hands finding my waist under the blanket. I feel more present now than I did earlier, in the bathroom, probably because there's no trace of Liam in this. Probably because this is all me, all us—it's a relief against that niggling doubt that she doesn't actually like me for me at all, but it doesn't put the fear fully at rest. There's too much of Liam in every other moment we have shared.

"If you would like to?" It comes out as a question, my voice hitching in the middle. If Hannah had any preconceived notions about me being cool, I'm pretty sure I've dismantled every single one of those tonight.

Hannah doesn't answer. She just leans forward, nose brushing mine for the barest moment before she leans in.

When I was fourteen, I won my first event at a track meet: It was the 800 meters, and my coach wasn't sure about putting me in because I was a freshman on JV filling a gap for varsity.

During the race, I remember the quiet stillness as everything around me seemed to narrow, the background fading away until all that remained was one key point: the track ahead. I could breathe again, the measured pace of it muscle memory, so well-rehearsed that I could practice in my sleep. I felt the exhilaration of the race, the wind in my hair, the blood pumping in my body.

It was like no one else was even there. And then, when I crossed the finish line, there were Reece and Bee, screaming my name, swallowing me up into a hug so tight my bones creaked. I remember the elation. The pure joy of it.

Kissing Hannah brings all of that back. There's no wind, but her hands tangle in my hair, her fingers twining through my curls. There's no thought of losing, with her mouth against mine. There's just the reality of her, and the press of her mouth, and the grip of her hands.

I don't know how long we're like that, but I kiss her until I get used to the idea that I *can*. Desire runs hot in my veins, but it's mingled with the sluggish understanding that we're not doing more than this now, that we don't *need* to. That everything has already changed, shifted incrementally and then flipped on its axis all at once. That I'm finding out the shape of her, the shape of what we are, without Liam's involvement. That I'm figuring out how to stand on my own with her. The best I can do is cling on as everything between us settles back into solidity, into a shape I can comprehend and understand.

She pulls away finally, laughing, weighted with exhaustion. Nips my lip, then kisses my cheek. It's late—I know it's probably a ridiculous hour, and she should head home and I should go to bed so that I can lie in the dark and pray that everything won't be different between us when I see her next.

But she doesn't make to leave. Instead, she reaches for the packet I set to the side.

"What is that?" I ask.

"Oh, just some stuff we thought was important, at the time," she murmurs.

"Like a time capsule?"

Hannah snorts. "Maybe, if we'd put more thought into it, or had more patience. But no—we didn't lock it up and save it for a later date." Hannah stays close, leaning against me as she opens the bag. The thing on top is a journal. She sets it aside without flicking through it, so I don't ask.

Desperately, I wonder if it was Liam's, and if it held some secret—I fear it might've even held the words he said to her tonight, a replication of his feelings before he was brave enough to speak them aloud. An unfortunate truth, that he was never brave enough when he was flesh and blood and boy, when he was more than a ghost.

He appears then, as if he sensed my discomfort. Liam materializes in the space on my other side, and it's only because I am so used to him that I don't even flinch.

But Liam looks wild and scared, and he grabs my arm. "*Drew*," he says. "We have to go."

I nod over to Hannah, and he only spares her half a look before he's tugging my arm again. "Come on," he says, babbling, "if we start moving now, we might have time."

I can't ask him what's wrong, not with Hannah here. Things are going so well—I can't act like I'm talking to myself, and there's no way to whisper something inconspicuous when she's so close, reaching for another notebook.

His hand is still on mine, pulling—and then Liam freezes. The lights buzz and flicker. Hannah looks up . . . and I follow Liam's gaze.

There are pale, ghostly fingers wrapped around the square that opens to the outside. Liam and I both watch, frozen, as a husk pulls itself through the hatch.

It has lank hair falling around its shoulders, and an open mouth that stretches far too wide. There's a sound coming from it, somewhere between a creak and a moan. Black sludge drips from the corners of its mouth. I don't know if it's blood, some sort of manifestation of the decaying body, or if it's something else. Something worse, like a manifestation of the decaying *soul*.

I do my best to breathe. I've faced them before—in this very forest. I can do this. If I can get Liam and Hannah to safety without being a fucking weirdo, I can fix it.

It's only halfway through, tatters of flesh clinging to a rib cage, when I notice a second pair of hands, and a third.

"Drew?" Hannah asks. I realize I'm staring at the hatch, a look of horror on my face, and I clamp my mouth shut. My heart races in my chest.

I grab Liam's hand and tug him behind me.

"Are you okay?" Hannah asks.

Here's the conundrum: If I don't do anything, the husks will get Liam. They will drain him right here, right in front of me, until there's nothing left.

They're blocking the exit. I can't get Liam past them without fighting them, and I don't know what would happen if I try to drag Hannah through. I've never really understood what husks do with the living—I have always managed to stay far enough away from them that I haven't seen. Reece only wrote about what husks do to the dead in their journals, and Mom's accounts of ghosts didn't include descriptions of husks at all. Just the shadows.

Liam could disappear, but I don't actually know if he can

with the husks in such close proximity, or where he would go, and even if he did, there's still the question of what they could or would do to Hannah.

I don't know. I don't know, I don't know, I don't *know*.

Softer, Hannah says, "Drew?"

I promised Liam I would save him.

"Hannah," I say, forcing my voice to keep steady. "I'm about to say something, and you're going to think I'm mad."

"Drew—"

"Icanseeghosts." I do it all in one rush, as if that makes it easier.

Liam says, "Drew, what are you—"

"And we're in danger. Just. Please. Get behind me."

"Drew, what—"

"Please," I snap, and it quiets both of them. Hannah scrabbles over the bench, on the other side—if she feels the cold when Liam drops my wrist and wraps an arm around her shoulders, she doesn't do anything to indicate it.

The first husk is almost through, dragging its body up onto the floor. I can see the top of the head of the second, and the hands of the third. Three husks—it's not too many, but it's not *nothing*.

Reece taught me, when we were little, what to do. The most important thing about husks is to not let them touch you. If they can touch you, they can hurt you.

And I'm not just talking about the bruises and broken bones, that ugly remnant of the bite wound I still have from my last run-in—a husk is looking to feed on energy. It can sap the happiness out of you. Side effects are bouts of depression and a thick mental fog, but that can lead to a thousand other things; Reece's big theory is that letting a husk drain you takes off years of your life, but obviously there's no way to prove that.

Last week, I didn't get close enough for them to drain me. I managed just fine with my stick. But now, I have Liam and Hannah, and I'm severely outnumbered—and I really, *really* hope Reece is wrong that a husk draining you takes time off your life. Because I am pretty sure I'm about to get drained.

"Stay behind me," I say to Hannah. I need to force the husks away, because if I can do that, I can give us room to escape. I grab the only thing I can: the photo album. It's weighty in my hands.

Across the treehouse, the husk hisses at me, dragging itself closer. The other husk gets its bony arms through and starts to come up too.

"Drew, what are you doing?" Liam asks, his voice panicky. Hannah is saying something, too, but I can't focus on either of them right now—

The third husk makes a loud noise. Abruptly, its hands are gone, as if it fell—or as if something had yanked it down. The second husk looks over its shoulder, chittering, making a sound like bones clacking together.

I take the opportunity of the distraction to whack the first husk with the album. It screeches in pain, going for my ankles, but I step away before it can. I'm wearing shoes—before I can think better of it, I stomp down on the back of the husk's neck. It howls in pain.

"Drew!" Hannah shouts. "What the fuck are you *doing*?"

"Just hang on! Liam—"

But she's distracted me. I feel cold fingers wrapping around my ankle, clawed talons digging into my flesh. I recoil, nearly falling backwards, but it's too late.

What was the worst day of your life? The worst moment of your life? I probably haven't had mine, but there are moments that come to mind, like watching the Watcher consume that husk at the edge of the wood.

But really, if I peel back the years, there's a moment that comes to me; it's a moment that I consciously forgot. It's late at night, and I'm on my side in my bed. I'm little. Mom is gone. But then, even though the door doesn't open, even though there are no footsteps, her hand is on my forehead. She just rests it there. She's cold—it's winter—and I'm cold, and then she says, very quietly, "I love you, baby girl."

I close my eyes tighter, like if I open them and turn to look at her, she'll disappear.

There's another moment, and it sounds like she's crying. She gets up. Her hand disappears. There are voices in the next room, Mom and Reece, and then Reece is crying.

And all I can feel is that dark, endless dread, that sadness. Waking up the next morning and finding Reece in my bed, curled around me, and knowing that Mom was still gone. That I'd dreamed it or made it up in my head or tried to pull her back into reality.

The husk's hand is around my ankle, and I feel that horror growing—Mom is gone forever, Reece wants nothing to do with me, I'm going to fail school, Dad thinks I'm a disappointment, I've been lying to Hannah, everything is crashing down and there's not a single thing I can do about it. Every time I've tried to make things better, I've only succeeded in fucking them up more and more.

"Drew!" Liam shouts behind me, his voice rough, like he's been shouting it for a *while*.

I try to pull back, fighting out of the pit. That's when I look up and notice the shadow creeping through the hatch.

The shadow wraps around the second husk, pulling it down just as sharply. The first husk, the one holding my ankle, turns and hisses.

"Shit, shit, *shit*." I jerk my foot back, and this time the husk releases me. More shadows spill through the hatch, solidifying into . . . something. Vines, or tentacles, growing more and more dense and real by the second as they wrap around the first husk's legs and slither over its body.

"Drew!" Hannah shouts. "What the hell is that?"

She can see it. She can't see the husk or Liam's ghost, but whatever is happening here, she can see it.

I try to keep my wits about me and stomp down again on the husk's hand with my other foot. As I do that, the tentacles of smoke slither over the husk, pulling it back out the hatch. It withers away, crumbling even as I watch, becoming even more desiccated. It only takes a second before it's gone, leaving us with one last echoing screech.

"Drew," Liam says while I'm still frozen. "It's the Watcher—if it's still here, still occupied, we have to go. We have to *run*. We have to—"

But it's too late. He cuts off sharply as we hear one of the steps below us rattle. The treehouse shakes, just the briefest tremor, as if something large and heavy is climbing the tree below. Liam stumbles forward, turning, and I suck in a breath as a shadow-like leg slithers through the hatch of the treehouse.

"Oh fucking shit," I hiss, grabbing for Hannah. She starts to protest, but then follows my gaze to the leg, and her grip on me tightens. She makes a noise as the tentacle-like leg winds higher, deeper in, but I clap a hand to her mouth. I drag her back with me against the wall, bringing her to my chest.

"You need to calm down," I hiss to Liam. "If it senses you . . ."

I don't need to finish that sentence. We both just watched it consume the other husks.

He looks at us, aghast, and then the seething limbs of the Watcher slip through the open hatch. Liam skitters back, too, back to the corner where Hannah and I are crouched. She's breathing too hard, hyperventilating against my hand, her eyes locked on the black shadows spilling into the treehouse, blotting out the light.

"Don't scream," I whisper in her ear. "Breathe with me, okay? You can keep watching it, just breathe with me." I focus on getting her steady, on calming her racing breath against my palm. When she's a bit more stable, I take my hand away from her mouth, holding her more securely against me. Liam is pressed to my other side, energy rolling off him like static. I taste his memories on my tongue.

"Drew," Hannah whispers, hysterical. "What the fuck *is* that?"

I shake my head. There's no point explaining now, while it's in front of us. "Be quiet," I plead, but I know it's unconvincing. My heart is hammering against my chest as the black tentacles move like a shadow over the floor. Liam leans even closer next to me; when he reaches a hand out, I don't even think twice before tangling my fingers with his.

"I didn't mean to," he says.

"I know."

"What?" Hannah asks.

My heart pounds faster. The game is up, and I don't know what it means for any of us—but I know that we have to hold it together as long as the Watcher is here.

The tentacle wraps around the light. The treehouse goes pitch-black, and I feel Hannah's breathing speed up again, bordering on hyperventilating.

"Liam," I say, because we're going to have a really fucking awkward conversation after this anyways. My priority now just has to be getting through this moment to the other side, to a time when we're not threatened by this and can move on to the truth. "Are you feeling calmer?"

"Yes," he says.

"*Drew*," Hannah half-sobs. "What are you even saying?"

"Hannah," I say, my lips moving in her hair. "You have to keep breathing, okay? It senses panic. If you just keep breathing, it will be okay. Liam, you too—breathe with me."

"*Why do you keep talking to Liam?*" she half-shrieks, which really, I should've seen coming. A moment of stillness, and I feel the tentacle at the bottom of my leg, wrapping around my ankle. I gasp in horror—but I have to be the sensible one, the calm one, even as I feel it creeping up my calf.

If I don't keep my head on straight, I don't know if we're going to make it to the other side of this. I don't know what the Watcher is capable of, what it could do to me or Hannah or Liam, and there *are* actually fates worse than death.

My ankle is already sore, burning cold from the touch of the husk. I don't know why, but even with my terror, the Watcher's touch is like a balm. Aloe on a sunburn. Where the tentacle touches, the pain dissipates.

I can't process this through my terror, if it's trying to lull me into a false sense of security.

"I will explain it to you," I say, trying to keep my voice measured, even. "I will explain it, but you have to calm down, or else it won't go away. It feeds on—" My breath hitches, a half-cry tearing from my lips as the tentacle moves up to caress the back of my knee, the back of my thigh.

Breathe.

I fight to make myself still, to maintain control. "It feeds on bad energy," I say, my voice a bit sharper than I want it to be, but all I can focus on is the slithering black against my skin. "We have to *focus*, okay?"

"What are you even saying," she babbles.

In Reece's notes, they talked about how the darkest of spirits can be fought with good energy. After all, bad energy, like fear and terror and despair, is what calls husks in the first place.

And maybe there's something that can combat the grief. Maybe it's because she's pushing it so hard, keeping it at bay.

"Tell me about him," I blurt out. "Tell me about Liam."

For a half-second, she is utterly silent, and I worry that she's not going to. That she's going to think this is some trick, some mental break (I don't think I'd blame her for that, at this point; I'm really damn close to a mental break myself). But there must be something in my voice, because she says, "He was . . . my best friend."

"Right," I say. I know it's risky, asking her about him when he's the very reason the Watcher is here. But Liam's bad feelings are so tied up in the unresolved emotions he has for Hannah, and Hannah's feelings are . . . well, jury's out on that right now. But I think confronting it directly, talking *about* one another even if they can't talk *to* one another, might level them out to send the Watcher away. "Tell me your favorite memory of him."

"I don't know!"

"The river," Liam says quickly. "Ask her about Ohiopyle last year."

"Ohiopyle last year," I tell her, my voice creeping up an octave as the Watcher's grip on my leg tightens further.

"How do you even know—"

"Tell me about it."

Another moment of silence. Then, "We did a, uh, a pedal paddle, it's called. Like, a bike trail, then white water rafting? The whole group went. And on the way back, Liam got the idea to attempt a bit of river piracy."

I draw a breath as the tentacle's grip on my leg loosens, ever so slightly. "Yeah?"

Hannah, too, takes a breath, and her voice sounds steadier when she continues. "Yeah. He would hang back, then turn his boat over. Creep up on someone—usually Adam or Caleb, because they're the most competitive. Then he'd spring out of the water and steal their oars."

The tentacle slips further, down by my calf, loosening. I let my eyes close, let some of the tension leave my body. I'm pretty sure we're not going to die, but it's not gone yet. I feel Hannah relaxing slightly, too, the tension in her back softening against my chest. I rest my chin on her shoulder. There's a headache growing behind my eyes.

"Then we had ice cream," Liam says.

"And then ice cream?" I prompt Hannah.

"Yeah," she says, her voice thin. "We had ice cream, and the place had chess and checkers—we didn't mean to stay, but they're so damn competitive. I hate chess, but we played pairs. And Liam and I went against Rin and Sophia, and the game took *so* long, because Liam and Sophia have always been good at it."

There's a moment of quiet. We both watch the tentacles as they retreat from the light, then back across the floor, then down the hatch. The treehouse trembles again. I am wire-tense for a moment longer—but the crackling of leaves recedes, and I let myself relax, muscles aching like I just ran miles.

Hannah takes a shuddering breath. Sags forward, head in her hands. "Drew, what the *hell* was that?"

But I'm not looking at her. Liam is next to me, knees to his chest, arms wrapped around himself. He's looking down, probably so he doesn't have to look at me.

"I thought you were cool with this," I say.

He only shrugs.

"*Drew?*" Hannah prods.

I look at Liam a moment longer. Sigh. Roll my shoulders. It was good while it lasted, but I have the feeling that this is going to crash and burn faster than I ever thought possible.

"I am too freaked out to stay here," I say, which is vulnerable, but I can't afford anything else right now, "but we need to talk. Would you rather sit in your car or go inside? I won't ask you to come anywhere you're not comfortable, but there are a few things we need to discuss."

Hannah must sense the change—her gaze hardens too. "My car, then."

I nod, letting out a breath. "Okay," I say. "After you."

CHAPTER 19

Hannah turns the heater on, but the mood inside her car is absolutely frigid. Liam is with us, in the back, still looking miserable.

I really can't blame him for that. There's a lot to be miserable about right now; the Watcher is still out there somewhere, and I don't think there's much we can do to keep it at bay. I don't know why exactly it's following us, and I can't tell both Liam and Hannah to keep themselves forever in check, because unfortunately, that's not how feelings or grief work.

There's also the problem of the scope of this. That I have been lying to Hannah, and in some ways, Liam has been lying to me—but I can't be mad about that, either, because if I were in his shoes, I would probably make the same shitty choices.

"We can drive or sit," I say, sitting in her passenger seat, worrying at a loose thread in my jumpsuit. It must've snagged while climbing down from the treehouse.

"Let's drive," she says, her tone short. She's probably thinking the same thing I am—neither of us want to be anywhere close to the Watcher, and if we're in motion, in a car, there's less chance of it catching up to us. Unless I think about it running alongside us the other night, which is not a conducive thought right now. So I only nod, and Hannah turns the car on.

"I'm sorry," Liam says from the back seat. I can only sigh at that.

Because truth be told—no matter what I tell Hannah, no matter what she says, the reality of what happened, what we *did*, is sinking in. The feelings I told her I had, caught in the haze of Liam's persuasion; the way I convinced her to trust me. None of it was really me, was it?

There's dishonesty in all of this. I have been awful, using him this way, to get to Hannah. And no amount of mental gymnastics can absolve me from the truth: Whatever Liam felt for Hannah during his life was more than just friendship. I can taste it in his memories when he lets me too close. I could feel it earlier, as his words rushed out of me. It's obvious, and if I'm being totally honest with myself, I knew this from the beginning. I knew what advantages I was taking, and how shitty it was, and I did it anyways.

I don't know how Hannah felt about Liam when he was alive, but does it really matter? He's dead now. Whatever was between them lingers, but only in the cast of memory and what-ifs. He is not coming back.

The things I just did, they all add up to the type of person I am not. The kind of person who is deceptive and manipulative, who doesn't care about other people or their feelings. It's not me. Or worse: Maybe it is me, and I really, really don't want it to be.

"Okay," I say. "I am going to say some things, and you are probably not going to believe me. But I just want you to hear me out, if you can."

"Okay." Her voice is flat—sepulchral, really. Hannah turns onto the main road that goes through town. We're the only two people on the road. It's long past midnight now, and the stillness adds another layer of uncanniness. I wish it were daylight, or that we could hold off until the night isn't so dark, the shadows aren't so long. But I don't think I could ask that of her—I owe her answers, and I don't think Hannah will settle for me procrastinating on them.

Just an hour ago, her mouth was on mine. An hour ago, I probably would've said this was one of the best nights of my life.

There's no way to sugarcoat it, no beating around the bush, and so I take a deep breath, and: "I'm just going to come out and say it: I can see ghosts. And talk to them, if I try."

Hannah is silent for a long stretch of time, just driving. I hold my breath at first, but she's quiet for so long that it's all moot, and there's nothing I can do but watch her and hope. I wait for some surprise, some change in her, but if anything, she just looks more exhausted, the shadows under her eyes deepening. I brace for whatever comes next, but—

"Okay," again, is all she says.

I swallow, searching for words. Liam must realize that I need to do this myself, because he's silent in the back seat.

She takes over, though. "So when you moved in," Hannah says, her voice still flat, "Liam was there."

"Yeah." The word barely makes a sound when it comes through my lips. "Liam was there."

"His ghost, you mean."

"Yes."

She is silent for a moment, processing this. I don't know what I expect—not the silence, probably, but something else. Any sort of reaction. But there's just quiet, and her white knuckles on the wheel, and then a weariness in her voice when she says, "Is he here now?"

I glance to the back seat. Hannah's hands tighten even more on the wheel. Liam meets my eye and grimaces. Sometimes, when I look at him in the pits of despair, it's like I can see the layers beyond the ghost he is now, to the rot and decay, to the remains of the real boy. I hate it when I get any glimpse of that, any reminder.

"Yes," I say.

Hannah draws a breath, and it comes out as a sob—I look back at her and realize that there are tears streaking down her face. She sniffles, then angrily wipes the tears away with one hand.

"Are you ever going to stop haunting me?" she asks, whisper soft. "Are you ever going to let me go?"

Another one of those heavy silences surrounds us.

I don't know if there are answers. It's all chance, all circumstance. There's no reason why Liam is in the back of the car, dead, instead of me or Hannah; no reason why he's the one who isn't flesh and blood and dreams and hopes.

"I don't mean to," Liam says, his voice as ragged as I feel. I hate that we've hurt her, that we've made her cry, and I know Liam feels just as terrible. "Tell her, Drew. Tell her I don't want to hurt her."

"He doesn't want to hurt you," I parrot, but even I know it's not enough.

"You can hear him still?"

"Yeah."

"And he can hear you?"

I bite my lip, weighing what to say next—but I owe her the truth. "He can hear you too. You just can't hear him."

When Hannah speaks next, her voice is wet with tears. "I thought you were better than this," she says, half sobbing. "I thought you would let me go."

"What are you *talking* about?" he asks, and I echo.

"Are you still here because I broke your heart? Because there's some unresolved bullshit, because you can't leave until I love you? Because I *can't*, Liam, and that's not how it works. Are you trying to keep me close, keep me holding on?"

I hate that I'm here for this, witnessing the worst of both of them. Liam isn't looking at her, but rather out the window, at the trees whipping by. "I wouldn't do that to you," he says, just as weary as she is. "I am not sticking around of my own volition. If it were up to me, I'd go right now."

I relay his message.

"Then what does Drew have to gain from this?" Hannah says, like she's actually talking to Liam, like she doesn't have to ask *me*.

I hesitate—because, at the end of it all, I don't know. What do

I have to gain from this? A lot of heartache. Regret. That feeling like I've fundamentally changed who I am as a person, and not for the better.

"Nothing," I say. "It was a mistake."

She doesn't answer. Just nods, her lips pressed together.

Hannah doesn't say anything else after she turns the car around. Drives it back to my house. She does not say anything as I get out, at my drive. She backs out, leaving Liam and me behind in the glow of the headlights.

He sighs. I hate him, I think, but that's not quite true—it's not fair to hate Liam. Right now, the only person I have to hate is myself.

CHAPTER 20

Any comfort I found in my new friends dissolves in a matter of hours. I have to remind myself that they were never really my friends for *me*—after all, they were around because of Hannah, or because Liam told me what to say. They liked a version of me that never really existed.

Which sucks. I think they might like me, if they tried. But honestly, right now, I'm not even sure if *I* like me.

That feeling sticks with me all the way to Wednesday. The one person I haven't lost is Rin, but that might be more because of Bee's cinnamon rolls than anything else. They bring me apas and Filipino hot chocolate after run club, and we sit together in the empty bleachers after everyone else has gone.

"She just said it didn't work out," Rin tells me, sipping their chocolate. "But she said it in such a way that made you sound . . ." Rin winces.

"Yeah," I say. "I, uh, kind of said some things I regret."

"I think she did too," Rin guesses.

I shrug. Whatever she said to Rin, she was probably justified. I remember the feel of her, terrified in my arms, as the Watcher cornered us—and maybe that's the truth of it. Whatever vengeance the monster was going to dole out, we deserve it,

Liam and I. What we did to Hannah wasn't fair. Wasn't right.

"After the whole Liam situation," Rin says carefully, "we're all a bit protective of her."

I run my thumbs over the ridges of the cup, feeling that now-familiar guilt—but also a spark of something else. Curiosity. "Can I, um, ask about that?"

"About what?"

"Liam."

Rin sighs through their teeth. "What do you want to know?"

Oddly, I wish he were here—he hasn't spoken to me since the other night, since the showdown with Hannah. I wonder if he feels just as guilty as I do—or worse, if he feels like I've wronged him somehow. Like I haven't held up my end of the bargain.

And he'd be right. I promised I'd help him move on. Everything I said I would do, everything I said I would look into . . . well, it all took a back seat the second Hannah looked at me, the second I had something I wanted.

But I can make this right, I think—for Liam, if not for Hannah. I can figure out why he's still here. I can help him move on.

I run my finger along the edge of the hot chocolate cup. I wish there were more apas—Rin's mom is a great baker, which explains a lot of her affection for Bee's cinnamon rolls. Talent recognizing talent, or something.

"I know Hannah was there, when he died," I say. "I think that, um, had something to do with our fight."

"Ah," Rin says tightly. "Yeah. She, uh, said you read his journal."

I wince, but it's the closest we can come to the truth. "I really didn't mean anything by it," I say. "I just wasn't thinking."

That, too, is a truth, if you spin it some way.

"I know," Rin says, a touch softer. "I doubt you were trying to be shitty. But . . . yeah. Liam. He's the one thing that Hannah will never be over, and I'm not sure I blame her. I don't know if *I'll* ever be over him. If you move on from something like that. He was just . . . well. He was here one second, and then he wasn't. That's how it felt."

"Car accident, right?"

"Yeah," Rin says. They chew on their lip, seeming to come to some decision. "Caleb's brother always used to throw these big parties, and now Caleb's taken them on since Derek—his brother—graduated. They live out in the woods, in the middle of nowhere. Everyone drives up and leaves their keys in a bowl and goes wild, and then there's a huge crash-in-the-basement or campout kind of vibe, you know?"

"I get the idea," I say. It sounds like some of the things Andie and I went to back at my old school, neither of us brave enough to really enjoy them. We'd usually go for like an hour, get freaked out, and then take ourselves to the closest town's all-night diner, where we would make a pact that we'd definitely talk to the girls we liked . . . *next* time.

"Yeah. None of us were going to go, and Liam never went to those things. He knew himself, and parties were never his thing—I respect it, really. He never did a thing that was against his personal code, even though he and Han were pretty much inseparable."

"But she went," I say.

"Yeah. Last-minute thing. Caleb really wanted her to, and he'd been having a hard time, so she went. She texted us to come, but we were all either doing other stuff or just didn't want to." Rin peels away the edge of their coffee cup. "I think about it, all the time . . . what would've happened if I'd just gone."

"Probably nothing," I say, because if a lifetime of talking to the dead has taught me anything, it's that death is an inevitability.

"Right. Well. The rest is hazy. Caleb says he was with her while she was sick, and he called Liam to come get her. Next thing we know, we're all getting calls the next morning that they were in an accident. Liam died on impact. Someone found the car—no one saw it go into the tree—and Hannah was there, covered in her own blood and vomit, lying on the forest floor on Liam's side of the car. Like, she'd pulled herself out and crawled around. Reached through the window to grab his hand as he died."

It's awful. It's awful, and there are tears in my eyes, because—

fuck, neither of them remember it, and I can't fight the feeling that there's something else here that we just don't *know*. Something else that isn't making sense.

But also because it's brutal, and Liam is still dead.

And yet, it has me thinking again about the hoodie in Liam's attic, the one he was sure was Caleb's. Could it be possible, if Hannah was drunk and sick, that he put it on her? That he wanted her to be warm, before he handed her off to Liam?

Maybe it wasn't covered in Liam's blood, but Hannah's. But that doesn't explain anything of how it ended up in Liam's attic.

"That is . . ."

"I know," Rin says. "It's fucked. And she doesn't remember anything until the hospital the next morning. And when they told her—god. My aunt is a nurse, and she was working on the ward at the time—"

"Whatever you're about to tell me," I say gravely, "is probably a HIPAA violation."

"They had to sedate her," Rin says.

"Oh, one thousand percent violation," I mutter.

They shrug. "So, yeah. It's rough. And I miss him. Fuck, I miss him so much."

I don't know what else to do. I drape my arm around Rin and pretend not to notice the tears that roll down their cheeks.

"It'll be a year next week," they say after a moment. "He should be applying to colleges, and going to football games, and showing off in his AP classes. He shouldn't be gone. He shouldn't be buried."

"I know," I murmur, and that's when I see him, scuffing his shoe along one of the bleachers. It's incongruous, now that October's here with its teeth out, to see him standing there in his short-sleeved shirt. I wonder why he's not wearing a coat. I wonder if he took it off to drive, or if he left in such a hurry he didn't put one on in the first place.

The corner of my mouth turns up. Guilt, apology. He nods, offering his own half smile.

"God, I hate crying," Rin says. They sigh, wiping their eyes one last time.

"What would you say to him?" I ask, my gaze not leaving Liam's face. Because maybe this is it, the secret to it all: Maybe Liam just needs to know that everyone cared.

"That's hard," Rin says. They bite their lip, thinking for a moment. Liam scales the bleacher and sits on their other side, leaning his head against Rin's shoulder. Rin shudders, probably feeling the cold. "I would probably say . . . you *suck*, Liam," they say, their throat thick. But when they laugh, they really laugh. "When we were little, we used to ride our bikes up and down the road. This one time, Liam went over a pothole, and I shit you not—he went *flying*. Broke his arm. And I cried so much that he was the one comforting *me*." Rin sighs, dropping their head back, eyes closed. It's drizzling now, and the rain mists their face. "You would've liked him," they say.

"I'm sure," I agree, meeting Liam's eyes past Rin.

"I would say that I hope he's happy," Rin says. "I hope his granddad is there. I hope he can see us, and that he knows we still think of him all the time. I hope he wants us to be happy. I hope he's okay. I hope there are mandatory exams wherever he is, and he gets to study a lot, because he loves that shit. I hope there's chess. I hope there are dogs. I hope it's all a bit nicer, and I hope it doesn't hurt."

Liam looks away, biting his lip. If he were alive, I think he'd be crying too. I know I am.

LATER, he's still there when I'm back, alone in my room.

"I am so, so sorry," Liam says when I come in with my school bag.

I shrug. Yeah, it fucking sucks. Yeah, I have lost whatever social capital I've earned. But it was never really mine to begin with.

"I can't blame you for my shitty plans," I say, grabbing my Stats book.

Liam comes over, leaning against my desk. "Drew," he says.

"Yeah?"

"I think we need to figure out how to make me move on," he says slowly. "Because I think . . . I think by being here, I'm making everyone else's life worse."

I set my pencil down. "I wouldn't say *everyone's*."

His smile is wooden, barely there. He ignores what I said. "Will you help me?" he asks, crouching so we're eye level. "Will you forgive me for blowing everything up and help me move on?"

I sigh. "Depends." I nod down to my Stats book. "Care to assist?"

He smiles, and it's like the sun coming out from behind the clouds. I know Rin's right—I know I would've liked him.

Wherever he's going next, I hope it's nicer. I hope there's chess, and I hope there are dogs, and I hope, when he moves on, it doesn't hurt so much.

Dear Liam Orville,

Congratulations on your acceptance to the *Class of [redacted]!* Let me be the first to welcome you to a family of accomplished, reliable, hard-working people who

~~Liam you're still dead you're never going anywhere again~~

make up our complex, varied network of students and alumni. Though I am sure it can be difficult to accept your untimely end,

~~college? Not happening. You used to lie in bed at night and dream about the future you would have. About the choices you'd get to make. The things you'd study and the places you'd see~~

everything happens for a reason, and we are delighted to welcome you to the afterlife. In our program, you will find peace and happiness

~~do you remember the taste of your mother's coffee? The smell of petrichor in the spring, rain and damp clinging to the treehouse? Do you remember the sound of your father's voice? Ella's laugh? Do you remember how much you loved going to school early, the smell of cleaner in the air, the squeak of the library chairs under you? Do you remember the cold snap of grass underfoot in the morning? The leather of your steering wheel under your palms? Ella's smile on Christmas morning? The sound of your mom's laugh? Your breath fogging in the cold? The feeling of Hannah's arms wrapping around you? Do you remember what it was to be flesh and blood, a boy, a person, a living thing?~~

by moving on. We know it is an adjustment, but there is joy to find in moving on from this life. We hope to see you joining us as soon as possible on our campus.

~~do you remember the dreams you left behind? The things you'll never do? The person you'll never be? Do you? Do you?~~

CHAPTER 21

That night, after I'm showered, Liam and I are going over my Stats homework when there are two quick knocks at my door.

"What's up?"

Bee comes in, her mouth in a frown. "Can I talk to you?" she asks, her voice a tone quieter.

Clearly, there's something bothering her. Whatever it is, she didn't bring it up at dinner. Dad's at the gym, so it's just the two of us home.

Liam and I exchange a glance. I turn my chair around. "If this is about Stats," I say, already too quick, "then I'm sorry I didn't tell Dad about that bad test, but I've been studying a lot since then, and I'm really getting better and scoring higher so I don't think it's the end of the world that—"

"It's not about Stats," Bee says. She closes the door and leans against it. I realize she's holding something, and then she pulls it around to show me.

Two journals. One Moleskine, one black-and-white composition book.

Dread blooms in my stomach. "Where did you get those?"

"They were at the bakery," Bee says. "Tucked between boxes.

I just thought someone left them, and you stowed them, but—" Bee draws a breath. Shakes her head. "One of them is Reece's. And the other one . . ."

She doesn't finish the sentence. *And the other one belongs to your mother.*

I swallow hard. Liam lays a hand on my shoulder. "Want me to knock out the power?" he asks. "Cause a distraction?"

I shake my head as subtly as I can. "Bee," I say slowly. "I can explain."

"I read them, honey. I know I shouldn't have, but I thought the other one was Reece's, too, and then . . ." She breaks off, drawing a sharp breath. "Drew, when I asked you about your friends, you talked about a boy called Liam."

Dread pools in my stomach. "Yeah, he, uh, he lives—"

"Please don't lie to me," Bee says quietly. She never yells at me or Reece. She doesn't really discipline us in any big way and never has. So hearing her speak like that, cool and low, makes my palms feel sticky.

I've already fucked things up with Hannah. Ruined any chance I could have friends here. I can't bear to hurt Bee too. What's the end of that? Will I lose Reece? Become someone Dad doesn't recognize?

What if everyone leaves you?
What if you leave everyone else first?

Maybe there's a reason I've been ignoring Andie's calls. Not returning her texts. Pushing Reece away. Packing away friendships and getting ready for my next adventure—alone.

Maybe if I leave everyone else first, they don't have the chance to leave *me*.

Years of therapy pounded that question out of my brain until it wasn't worth asking, but now there it is again, rearing its ugly head.

I don't know if Bee sees it in my face, because her expression changes. She comes close, drops to her knees in front of me, and gently touches my face. I must look like I'm panicking.

"I'm sorry, peanut," she says. Her thumb brushes over my cheek, and I realize my face is wet. I sniffle, rubbing away the tears. Bee drops her hand to hold mine. "I just . . . sorry. I did some snooping, and there *isn't* another Liam at the high school."

Dammit, Bee.

"Your friend. It's the ghost of Liam Orville, isn't it? You can see them too. Like Reece. Like . . . like your mom."

There's nothing else I can say to defend myself, no protection against the truth. I can only nod. "How did you know?" I ask. It comes out weird and creaky.

Bee opens her mouth to answer, then hesitates. "Reece," she says finally. "They've always been . . . well. Weird about old things, and certain places. And then I found that journal you left at the shop the other day and . . . I can't say I already *knew*, but I had a hunch."

"Oh." It comes out like a squeak. I guess I can't be surprised, all things considered, but I am a bit taken aback by how well she's taken it, especially since it has always felt like such a big, unspeakable secret to me.

"Is this bad?" Liam asks, pinched.

"Is he here now?" Bee asks.

I can only nod. And then it's like some dam within me breaks, and I find myself crying. Wracked with sobs.

"I need to help him move on," I tell Bee, crying too hard, "and I just can't figure it out. Reece has always been better at it, and I've barely even tried, and I've made such a mess of things."

She shushes me gently, throwing her arms around me, pulling me down into her shoulder. Bee holds me until I stop crying, and then she makes me wait while she goes downstairs to make a pot of tea and warm up a cinnamon roll. There's no telling when Dad will be home from the gym, so I wait, sniffling and miserable, until she comes back in.

"Okay," Bee says after she's poured me a cup from the pot. "Tell me everything."

I chew my lip. Liam says, "Is this a good idea?"

"I don't know," I say to him, or maybe to both of them.

But then Bee reaches out and squeezes my hand, her dark brown eyes open and forgiving, and there's nothing more I can do. I cry as I tell her about Reece and me and what we can see, as I tell her about Liam's ghost and our deal. She chews her lip when I start on what I did to Hannah, and I can't meet her eyes.

"That wasn't very nice of you," she says finally. "To use what you found out about her like that."

"I know," I say, and I wish I could take it back. I wish I could start over. I chew my cinnamon roll and take a sip of tea. "But I can't undo it, and I've ruined everything."

"We can un-ruin things, sometimes," Bee says contemplatively.

"And then it got worse," I say. Bee's frown deepens when I tell her about the husks, and the Watcher, and the other night in the treehouse. She gets up and goes to look through my window, as if it's still there, as if she could see it.

I know it's not, because I've been checking every hour.

"We could burn the treehouse down," Bee says dubiously.

"I'd rather you didn't," Liam says.

"I just don't know what to do," I lament. "If Liam's still here because of his family, there's not much I can do. I can't just call them and search for things he's left unfinished."

"No," Bee agrees. "What does Reece usually do when there's a particularly difficult spirit to work with?"

"I wouldn't say I'm difficult to work with," Liam argues.

"I don't know," I admit.

Bee sighs. "Oh, peanut," she says. "Then why don't you just *call* them?"

Because it means admitting defeat. Because they're right that I have no idea what I'm doing. Because they finally got away from all of this, from having to protect me, and I shouldn't need them to constantly fix my problems.

It's as if Bee sees all of this playing out on my face. "They love you," she says softly. "And I can only help so much. Call Reece. I can sit here and hold your hand."

I wince. "I don't think Reece will like you knowing."

To Bee's credit, she doesn't look like this hurts her feelings. She looks out the window again, thoughtful. "Then we won't tell them I know," Bee says. "And I can leave you if you want to call without me here. But, love—I'm here if you need me. Even if you just want to talk it out. This is too big for you to do alone, okay?"

I nod. Hesitate. I look at Liam—he looks as tired as he ever has been. "I'll tell you if it goes awry," I promise Bee. "But I think . . . I think this is something I have to fix on my own."

She nods, then touches my cheek as she gets up to go. "I'm here if you need me," she says. "I'm not going anywhere."

I don't know how anyone can promise that, ever.

After Bee leaves, I open up my contacts. My thumb hovers over Reece's name in my recent call log—a graveyard of missed and cancelled calls from all the people I promised to keep in touch with, from everyone I've left behind.

I flip over to my texts with Reece. *Miss you,* I type.

The response is instantaneous: *Miss you too.*

I lie back, the phone on my chest, and wait for the moment to feel right—but it doesn't. It never does. I know the truth: I can't call Reece, no matter how much Bee wants me to, no matter how much *I* want to. If I call Reece, I'll ask about those notebooks, and our mom, and there will be truths there as dark as the Watcher's inky shadows.

I don't call. I'm not ready to know what Reece has protected me from.

CHAPTER 22

When I wake up a few days later on Saturday morning, there's no smell of coffee or baked goods. I'm not sure, for a minute, why I woke up when I did at all, because it's before my alarm—and then I hear the front door open and close, and a familiar voice chattering in the front entry.

I'm up before I can think, then I'm running down the hall. Reece stands in the entryway, unwrapping their scarf. I freeze halfway down the stairs and just look at them.

"What are you doing here?" I ask, my voice caught in my throat.

Reece looks exhausted, with dark shadows under their eyes. Their copper curls stick up in all directions. But the smile they give me—

It's warm. Familiar. Mine. I sit down hard on the step, and that's when I notice Bee in the entry to the family room, setting down Reece's duffel bag.

"Bee called," Reece tells me. They open their arms.

I slide down the rest of the stairs and collapse into them. I can't even be mad that Bee tried to fix it for me, because it's been days and I still haven't called Reece myself, and I'm still avoiding everyone at school, and I still can't find my way out of this.

Their arms wrap around me, fierce and close. I breathe in the familiar scent of Reece's coconut shampoo and force myself not to cry.

"You dumbass," Reece says into my hair. "What did you do? Why didn't you just *call*?"

"You told me to fix it myself," I say against them. It's a simplification, but it's all I can manage right now without getting into everything else.

Reece snorts. "*Drew*." They hold me tighter. "Not if it meant putting yourself in danger."

"I'll put the coffee on," Bee says. "Your dad should be asleep for another hour or so."

Reece drags me up to my room—they're still wearing their coat, but they throw it on the end of my bed and curl up in the tangle of unmade sheets.

"Right," Reece says. "Tell me everything."

I hesitate. I have the feeling they're going to point out everything I've done so wrong, and they would be absolutely right. But I need help, and I need to be just as honest with Reece as I can afford to be with myself.

"Reece, I messed up."

They raise an eyebrow. "Go on," they say.

I can't help pacing, and when the admission comes, it comes out all in a rush. "We keep attracting husks, but there's something worse following them and maybe eating them, and it has black tentacles and looks like a giant alien spider, and I can't help Liam move on, and I don't know why you left me Mom's journals or how you got them in the first place, and Liam is dying in his afterlife too, and I keep making things worse, and I imploded my social circle, and the girl I like hates me—"

"Dree. Slow down and start over."

I throw up my hands. "I don't know what to say!" I tell them.

"Say it all," Reece says, leaning back so their head rests against the wall. "I've messed up before too. If you start from the beginning and tell me what we're dealing with, I can help you."

I go back to pacing. It comes a little easier, now that I've told Bee everything—but it's worse, too, because Reece understands a lot more than Bee did. They stop me every so often to ask clarifying questions, first about the husk, and then about the Watcher. When I explain what happened the other night at the treehouse, the odd sensations when the Watcher touched me, their face goes stony and cold.

"And that's it," I tell them. "I have no idea what to do, because I don't know what I've done, or what I'm dealing with."

Reece drops their head to their hands, massaging their scalp. "I think I need to think this through a bit," they admit. "Do some research, and—"

"I'll help with the research," I say. "I'll help with all of it. I just need someone else who has some idea of what they're doing."

Reece nods. "Let me shower," they say, "and think. And then we'll reconvene."

It's a fair enough plan. I just—well. It's been years and years of me sticking my head in the sand, of letting Reece deal with anything ghostly that occurs. I took this on on my own, and I've only made it worse—I need to be here for the solution too.

Reece recovers their duffel and goes for a shower. I can hear Dad stirring in his room; he'll want to go running soon. I head downstairs. Bee is in the kitchen, pouring Reece's and my lattes into travel mugs. She's already dressed for work—she probably did all the bakery prep even before she went to pick Reece up from the airport.

I don't know when she sleeps.

Bee turns, sees me. "I'm sorry," she says, all in a rush. Her lower lip is darker, like she's been chewing it; the creases around her eyes are more pronounced. "I didn't mean to overstep, but I just thought, if you hadn't called Reece yet, you might not know how—"

I throw myself into her arms before she can say more. Hug her as tight as I can. "Thank you," I mumble into her shoulder.

Her fingers tangle in my hair, holding me close, like she did when I was a little kid. "I love you, peanut," she says.

"I know." And I hold her back tighter, tighter, tighter. Maybe not every mistake is an ending.

I go on my run with Dad, to keep up appearances. He's surprised to see Reece, but they make up some excuse about a surprise birthday party for a friend tomorrow at Pine Hollow, and he lets it go easily enough. Of course he does. I'm not saying Reece is Dad's favorite, but I also don't ask him thrilling, multi-level questions about contract law.

When I'm back, after Liam finally shows up and I make introductions, Reece, Liam, and I go to the competing coffee shop across town (sorry, Bee) with a few more of Reece's notebooks and a folder they brought back with them from Boston.

I know I have a million things to ask them, like how they got ahold of Mom's notebooks, and what they read into them—but I don't want to talk about that with Liam, and I'm also not really sure what to say.

"Okay," Reece says, when we're at one of the bigger tables at this coffee shop with the papers spread out in front of us. They look at Liam. "I want to hear it from you, now. Everything you remember about the Watcher, and what it makes you feel, and if it's ever touched you—every interaction with it you've ever had."

Liam fidgets as much as a ghost can. He's still a bit frosty with me—can't blame him for that, really—but he answers all of Reece's questions. His answers are pretty much the same as mine, with a few additions: He noticed the Watcher before we moved in, but only as a shadow in the woods. Nothing like what we've seen recently or experienced the other night.

Reece nods, taking careful notes. I sip my coffee and try not to think of Hannah, or the shame. The least I can do is solve this without hurting her more.

"Okay," Reece says when Liam is finished. "So, I don't know how much Drew explained about ghost energy?"

"I can attract bad things," Liam says. "My existence brings on the husks, and they try to feed on me."

"Yeah," Reece says. "So, basically, I think this might be a greater predator. Something that feeds on the husks—that explains what you saw the other night, if it was knocking those out. And you can repel most bad things with good memories, so good thinking on that front, Dree. I imagine it feeds on bad energy. So we return to: The best way to make it go away . . . is to make *you* go away."

Liam sighs. I lay my hand over his. "Don't take it too personally," I say.

"Thanks," he says dryly, but at least he sounds a bit more like himself. When he looks at me, he offers this pathetic little smile, like he doesn't fully hate me anymore either.

Reece goes back to my scant pages of notes that I've been keeping throughout all of this. I thought about tearing out the sections on Mom's notebooks, but there's not really a point: Reece has read those too. Nothing here is a revelation for them.

"There's a tactic Drew hasn't tried yet, and I get why. Sometimes, it helps for us to revisit the scene of what happened, with everyone who was present. If we do that, we can kind of . . . well, not reenact it, exactly. But we can model the thing that happened in a way that allows for closure. Your friend—"

"Hannah," Liam says, and I can hear the despair there too.

"Yeah," Reece says. "Hannah probably has a lot of guilt attached to this. Unfinished feelings."

"She does," I say quietly. Admitting to it feels like a betrayal of her confidence, and I remember that day she came into my house like a storm cloud.

God. How many ways I've betrayed her. It's monumentally fucked up, the things I've put her through without even realizing.

But Reece only nods. "Yeah. So, if we can recruit Hannah into it, go to the place where you died at the time you died, and come to terms with it all . . . that could make things easier, and that could be the push you need to move on."

Liam and I exchange a look. "I don't know if she'd be a willing participant," I admit. "I really, *really* messed things up."

Reece leans back, arms crossed over their chest. "Look, Drew," they say. "You did. You did a lot of really ethically shady things that I would not recommend—"

"You *dated* a *ghost*!" I exclaim. A girl at a nearby table looks at me oddly, so I lean in, lowering my voice. "You've done some ethically shady shit too."

"Sure," Reece agrees. "But you know what happens when you mess up?"

My stomach sinks. I look at my hands. "She hates me."

"She has the right to," Reece says, a little softer.

"Hannah will . . . well, maybe not understand," Liam says after a moment. "But if working with us is the only way to lay me to rest, to help me move on and save me from misery, Hannah will do it."

And then, when Liam's gone, I can leave her alone forever. There will be no reason for her to talk to me ever again—and I can accept that.

Reece gives me a long, level look, like they can read my mind.

"It's going to hurt," Reece says, like I don't already know, "but it's what we've gotta do."

I nod. "But first," I say, "we have to get her on board."

CHAPTER 23

I think it's fair to say, at this point, that I don't always make the greatest decisions. I don't think things through half the time, and sometimes I choose stuff based on selfish motivations, or because I really just have not been thinking. Take the easy way out.

So, let's be clear: If Liam weren't involved, I would've left the Hannah situation alone. Let her ice me out in the hallways. Avoid her during lunch, and before school, and try not to catch her eye at the football games (if I ever went again, considering everything that happened).

What I'm saying is I am both a coward and a pacifist.

Liam, unfortunately, is neither of those things—he can't leave well enough alone, and I can't blame him for pushing, considering the fact that he's still hanging around and no longer wants to be.

And Reece always fixes their mistakes.

Together, it's not too hard to work out a plan. Reece finds out as much more as they can about Liam's death and constructs a timeline. They drive us over to Bakerbee, where we pick up supplies.

After that, we head to Hannah's.

I've never been before, so Liam gives Reece directions. It starts pouring when we're halfway there, like the sky is preparing for a meltdown of epic proportions. I lean my head against the window, watching the drips roll down the glass with the chatter of Liam and Reece fading into the background.

For all my thoughts that Liam and I maybe could've been friends, there's no doubt about Liam and Reece. They get on like a house on fire.

Hannah lives in a house that belongs in a storybook: one of those Victorian farmhouses near the woods, cheerfully and lovingly maintained. There are two cars out front, and I recognize one as hers.

"I'll wait for you," Reece says as they park down the street. "Call me if things are okay and you want me to come explain. But you don't need to rush to get me involved—do what you need to do first."

"Thanks," I say. It doesn't take a genius to see Reece has already pulled up AO3 on their phone. They'll be occupied for a *while*.

I get out, and Liam follows. I think about asking him to stay behind, but there's really nothing about this that I'd hide from him anyways—plus, he has his own apologies to make.

It's pouring, so I hold the box close to my chest and dash through the rain. I'm not actually sure about the structural integrity of a lemon tart, and my stomach is heavy with anxiety, and there's no way to know if this plan will work.

I stand on the front porch for a long, long time, hand poised to knock. Beside me, Liam sighs. "You going to do it, or . . . ?"

"Or," I squeak.

But he rolls his eyes, puts his hand over mine, and together, we knock.

There's a moment of silence, then shuffling, then the sound of either someone throwing a hamper down the stairs or running down them at high speed. The door swings open and—

And Hannah is smiling for a moment before she realizes it's me. Her face falls, her shoulders sag. She's wearing a hoodie and leggings, her hair piled up in a messy bun on top of her head, and all the words leave my mouth.

Silent, I thrust the bakery box out to her. It's a little limp, done in by the rain, and she assesses it for a moment without taking it before she looks at me.

"What is this?" Hannah asks.

I look at Liam for help, but he only shakes his head. He was clear: My apology has to be *mine*. No stolen words. He had me write his own letter to apologize to Hannah, and though I can't un-know what's in it, I can't use it for my own.

I take a breath. Steel myself.

"I'm sorry," I say.

Hannah raises an eyebrow.

"I'm sorry for all of it," I say, searching for words. "For not being honest when I should've been. For not telling you about . . . him. And what he told me. And how I used it. For being really fucking weird and manipulative? For making you think I'm someone I'm not. For *pretending* to be someone I'm not. For all the little, stupid things that didn't matter at the time but all added up to this clusterfuck—for *hurting* you."

I stop, biting my lip.

Hannah reaches out. Takes the box. She pulls the twine of the bow on top, then lifts the lid. The corner of her mouth quirks up when she takes in the double-slice of tart.

She looks up at me, her eyes dark and sad. "Was any of it real?"

"All of it was real," I say before I can stop myself. Liam coughs.

Her eyes narrow. "Was any of it *you*?"

I—stop. Open my mouth, then close it. Take a breath. "I think you're wonderful," I say. It's not fanciful, nor poetic, but it's true. "I think you're beautiful. I like being around you. I like who I am when I'm around you, without, erm, outside influence." I fold my hands. "I just . . . am not good at expressing myself. Never have been. So, all this stuff I feel, I don't really know how to say it."

"I will . . . accept that," Hannah says.

"And I would give anything to start over." I hold out a hand. "I'm Drew Tarpin. New in town."

She looks down at my hand, then up at my face, and I know I've lost her in some ways—but won her back in others. I can only hope it's enough to save Liam.

"No need for that," she says, so I drop my hand. She sighs. "Come in—you're drenched."

"I'm fine," I say primly, even though my teeth are chattering.

Hannah rolls her eyes, grabs my arm, and drags me over the threshold. "I'm sure you have more to say about other things," she sighs. "And I would rather do it behind a closed door."

I nod, because she's right. "Hannah."

She glances up, halfway to the kitchen, possibly to get a plate for the lemon tart. "What?"

"Even though they weren't my words . . . I meant every one of them."

Hannah bites her lip. "I'll keep that in mind," she says, which isn't much of a reply at all—but it's a start.

WE decide to get through the most emotional stuff before bringing Reece into it for the technical.

In Hannah's room, I sit in a chair while she perches cross-legged on the bed, eating her lemon tart as she regards me.

"He's here, isn't he?"

"Yes," I say, because we're not lying anymore. "But he isn't, um, contributing."

"Hey, Liam," Hannah says, her voice softer.

"Think it's time for the note?" he asks. I nod, going in my pocket, hoping it's not as sodden as the rest of me.

"He wanted to apologize too," I say.

Hannah's hand shakes when she reaches to take the note from me. We sit in silence while she reads, Liam's hands clenching into fists and relaxing. Halfway through, there are tears rolling down her cheeks.

"You know," she said, "I thought I would've given everything, just to talk to him one more time. Just to say goodbye to him."

"Just not like this," I say, finishing the sentence.

"I'm sorry," Liam says next to me. I repeat it for Hannah, and she only nods.

"Drew," she says. "Can you give Liam and me a second?"

"You won't be able to hear him," I hedge.

"I know," she says. "I think he needs to listen to me for a change."

I nod. Get up. I don't know why I feel like this, so odd, so tired, but I go downstairs and shut the door behind me. Hannah's here alone, so there's no one watching me as I go down to the kitchen and pour a glass of water from the tap. I look out over the backyard as I drink it, into the forest.

There's nothing there. Just trees, and mist, and that murkiness of the autumnal wood. And if there are shadows—well. If there are shadows, and if they do look like tentacles, they do nothing to cross the yard. If my own foolish heart is pounding in my ears, beating in overdrive, it has nothing to do with what I do or don't see outside.

When Hannah comes down, her eyes are red and puffy. Liam also looks like he'd be crying if he had the ability to.

"So," she says, pouring water into a kettle, then setting it on the stove. "Liam's letter said you need me to help him move on."

"We think so, yeah," I say. Behind her back, I shoot him a look that I hope says, *you okay?* He offers me a half-hearted thumbs-up. "We think, if we can figure out what happened that night, we may be able to figure out why he's still here."

"Right," Hannah says tightly. Her hands are clenching the edge of the countertop.

I force my tone softer. "And you don't remember."

"No," Hannah says.

Neither does Liam. I chew on the hangnail on my left thumb, an old nervous tic.

"I've told you about my sibling before," I say. "Reece. They've come down from Boston to help with this. If it's okay with you, they know more about what to do than I do—do you mind if we get them involved?"

Hannah looks at me shrewdly. She doesn't trust me—of course she doesn't. But Reece is a third party.

"If it helps," I say, folding and unfolding my hands, "they also think I'm an asshole."

Hannah's face softens. "I don't think you're an asshole, Drew," she says. Then she seems to rethink this. "Well. Not totally. Bring Reece in, and we'll see what they have to say."

It's a correction that I probably don't deserve. But I text Reece—it takes them a couple of minutes, during which we stand in awkward silence and sniffling, all three of us a little hurt. I'm about to text Reece again (*please stop reading Hannibal fanfic and help me*) when there's a knock at the door. Hannah goes to get it, leaving Liam and me alone.

"You okay?" I ask softly. I don't know if we'll have any more time alone after this.

He shrugs. Sighs. Nods. "Yeah. It was rough; I'm not going to sugarcoat it. But everything she said was correct." He smiles sadly. It doesn't reach his eyes. "And I'm sorry, too, Drew. I might've pushed in my own self-interest. . . ."

I shake my head. "No. Don't you dare. It was me driving, and you know it. You never would've agreed to this if I hadn't asked, and I didn't uphold my end of the bargain."

He sighs again. "We both kind of suck, don't we?"

I chew my lip. "Yeah," I say, and my voice comes out a little foggy—because yeah, I suck, and yeah, Liam sucks, but at least now, for the last time, we share that suckiness. We're shitheads *together*.

My best friend—
Hannah
Han
Hannah.

It's funny—there's actually not a lot left unsaid between us. In fact, I would hazard a guess that there's been too much said between us. I don't think this is going to fix anything, but if this is the last thing you have of me... I have to try.

Do you remember, after my cousin's funeral, when you asked me if I was afraid of dying? And I said that it didn't matter, because I was too busy?

I'm sorry I didn't give you a straight answer. I'm terrified of dying, even now, when it's already over. Not of the process of it: I don't think it hurt, and I don't think that was a consequence of how it happened.

But the worst thing that ever happened to me, the worst thing I ever did, was not dying. It was hurting you the way I did. I defiled my own memory, didn't I? This isn't some elaborate guilt trip, or some way to get you to love me back from the afterlife, or even to let me move on in peace.

What I did to you, Han, it's not forgivable. Don't forgive me. But I hope you remember who I was before the loneliness set in, before the chill of death made me desperate for any scrap I could cling to of you. Of who you are, and what I wanted us to be.

I love you, Hannah. Nothing changes that. And you loved me on your own terms, in your own way. I should've respected that more. I should've appreciated it for the gift that it was.

I'm sorry. I'm yours. Now and forever, as long as you'll remember me.

  Love,
   Liam

CHAPTER 24

"Right," Reece says when we're all gathered in Hannah's living room, after the introductions are all done and we're able to move on to the plan. "We're in the right time of year, so I think our best bet is to relive the events of Liam's death, basically, but to do the things we would've done differently. He'll still be dead, at the end—sorry, Liam—but that gives us the opportunity to confront every guilt the assembled would feel."

"But what if it's not us?" I ask. "What if the reason Liam's still here has nothing to do with Hannah, and it's his family after all?"

Reece only sighs. "Then we'll start down that path tomorrow, if we need to."

I don't think there's a good way to point out that the only two people who remember what happened that night have significant memory damage, so I just nod along.

Reece turns to the notebook they've co-opted. It's probably better this way: Their notes are much tidier than mine.

"So let's start from that evening," they say, all business. "Hannah, what do you remember?"

She chews her lip. "There was a party that evening. At Caleb's."

I'm not eager to involve him in this, but maybe we can just

go sit on the street by his house and . . . not do anything that actually involves him.

Reece crushes those hopes in seconds. "Okay, are you still friends? Would he let us access his house?"

Hannah and I exchange a look—that brief flash of camaraderie surprises me, but at least we can bond a bit over how much neither of us want to do this.

"Do we have to actually go inside?" I ask.

"Well, no, but it makes it . . . more real. And we're trying to trick fate, here. So even if it's for a few minutes . . ."

"Yeah," Hannah says. "I think we can swing it."

Reece nods, making a note. "Okay. So here's the plan: Drew, you go with Hannah, and retrace her steps. I'll stay with Liam and run through what he was doing. Hannah, if Drew knows your friend, too, you can take her with you. If you decide to leave Drew in the car, just make sure you keep your phone on you so we all meet up again on time."

If I didn't know better, I would think that Reece was trying to fix this mistake I've made, perhaps put in a chance for me to fix this. But I *do* know Reece, and though I don't think they're actively trying to torment me, they're also not going to change their plan just because I've acted like a dick.

But it's not *im*possible that they're punishing me, just a little bit.

Reece checks their watch. It's late afternoon, and Liam didn't die until almost midnight, so we have a few hours.

"Right," Reece says. "I don't know what things we're going to attract, and if that Watcher of yours is already following you . . . we should go over some defenses."

CHAPTER 25

It doesn't take me long to remember why I hated going hunting with Reece, and sometimes, that had nothing to do with ghosts at all. For them, everything is by the book; there are solutions to every problem, yes, but it all involves rules and complex processes and the kind of automatic reactivity that I've never been good at.

It's almost eight by the time they finally deem Hannah and me ready enough to be released—it should bother me that Hannah picks up as many protective processes in a few hours as I have in over a decade, but then again, it's *Hannah*. Reece and Liam head back to our house in my car, pretending to be studying like Liam was that night. That leaves Hannah and me alone in her living room.

"I like Reece," Hannah says after a moment of awkward silence, when the stillness becomes too much. She starts to gather up our empty coffee and tea mugs from the table; I hurry to help.

"I do too," I say. It's a nice reminder that, actually, I suck at talking to Hannah Sullivan.

We fall back into tense silence, because really, what is there to say? She washes the mugs, and I dry, and I cycle through all the things I could say in my head:

I'm sorry things went this way.

I'm sorry I didn't tell you about Liam.
I'm sorry I'm a coward.
I'm sorry I don't know what to say now.

There are a million things I need to express, both explanations and apologies. But as soon as I get up the courage to open my mouth, she glances at the clock and says, "I should change. Are you okay to wait here?"

"Yeah, of course," I say, leaning against the counter, folding my arms in front of me. "Have. Um, have you already texted Caleb?"

"Yeah," she says quietly. "I said we just need to pick up a couple of things I left there a few weeks back. I figure doing that and then sitting in the driveway or something should be sufficient."

I nod. That sounds close enough, based on what Reece told us.

She goes upstairs, and I tip my head back, blowing the air out of my lungs in one *pfft*, thinking of everything I could've said to even *try* to make it better.

I wait for five minutes, then ten. She can take as long as she likes. I decide to run to the bathroom, just in case we're doing this for the next six hours. I'm at the top of the stairs when I hear her, the quiet sniffling and choked breaths, like she's crying hard and trying to keep the sound down.

I freeze in the hall. Part of me wants to tiptoe back downstairs, to pretend I heard nothing and play it cool . . . but.

But Hannah is upset, and it might not all be my fault, but part of it is. I know what we're doing tonight: We're going to relive the night her best friend died, the night that left scars on her body and her heart. And whether I like it or not, I've definitely tainted her memories of Liam—now, when she looks back at him, she won't just remember who they were when they were living, but also what we did after his death.

I can't ignore it. I can't push it under the rug.

I walk down the hall to her door and knock softly. "Hey. Can I come in?"

There's a pause, a moment when I think she's trying to pretend she isn't crying, or maybe she's trying to get it together—but then the door opens, and she appears, her face blotchy and red.

"Sorry," she said. "I'm almost ready."

I crack a smile at that. "I can tell."

She goes back to her desk, where her makeup and mirror are all set up, but she doesn't pick any of it up. She just sits in the desk chair, facing me. She's changed into a black T-shirt dress and tights, her hair split into two French braids.

I come in cautiously and sit on the edge of her bed. "I'm sorry," I say. "I know it . . . well. I know I've apologized already, and there's not really a good way to make it up to you."

Hannah wipes at her eyes. "I just don't get *why*. Why did you lie to me? Why did you both pretend?"

She's not meeting my eye. "I mean, I can't really defend my actions," I say quietly. "They're indefensible."

"But probably not without reason," she says. "Definitely not, if Liam was involved."

"I can't speak for him," I say, searching for words—for my *own* words. "It wasn't like this, at first. I mean—Hannah, I've liked you since the moment I first saw you." God, I sound like such a creeper.

"You don't *know* me, Drew," she says.

"No," I agree. "But I'd like to."

A beat passes between us. She draws a quick breath, but she doesn't fill the silence between us. Hannah looks up and meets my gaze.

"The whole thing . . . it's not like we set out to hurt you," I say, trying to make it sound as much like a promise as I can. "If anything, it was like an avalanche. It was that moment, in the hall, with you and Caleb, and all I could think was that I wanted to get you out of there—and so did Liam. That's all it was. Then, when I told him I liked you . . . well. Wanting you comes with its own vocabulary of desire, Hannah. Turns out Liam and I are both fluent."

She closes her eyes. Turns her face. There are tears streaking down her cheeks. "When I started talking to you . . . it was like I could be known again. And that betrayal, of finding out that none of it was *actually* you . . ."

"A lot of it was me," I say quietly. "That day, at the river, was all me. Homecoming was mostly me."

"When you told me you dreamed of me? Before Homecoming?" She's not looking at me, like she can't bear the answer.

I wince. "That was Liam," I say.

Hannah nods slowly. "But this is my point. My understanding of you and what you feel, it's like a patchwork. It's this weird mix of things you've said and things you haven't, but all of it has come from you. And I can't *see* Liam, not like you do, so there's no real way for me to put the pieces together."

"Yeah," I say. My mouth is dry. "I get it."

Hannah nods. She turns away, back to her mirror, and goes back to her makeup. I sit quietly, searching for anything else I can say that will make it better.

"Tell me something," Hannah says. "Something that's just you."

I glance up. She's still doing her makeup.

"I'm . . . I'm afraid of heights," I say. "It's a cliché, but I can't get over it. They make my palms sweaty. My heart race."

"Good to know," Hannah says dryly. "What else?"

I shrug, looking out the window. I know I need to do better than that.

"I let go of things too easily. Reece . . . they're always clinging on to everything. Holding on as tightly as they can. And I just can't do that. Like, all my friendships at my last school. I've just let them go."

Hannah's quiet for a moment. "I think I hold on to things too tightly too," she says finally.

I nod. It makes sense with her personality, but there's another part to this confession that I need to make. "I . . . I don't think I want to ever see my mom again. And I think Reece does, and I need to talk to them about it, but I don't know how to bring it up, or if I should."

Hannah's hand stills halfway through blending her blush. "Why?"

I shrug. "I don't think it's . . . helpful? Productive? Healthy? I don't know. Maybe I'm bitter because she left, because we weren't enough, in the end. Maybe I know no good would come of it. But I think, when there are choices to make, and one very clearly leads to pain—I think I tend to go for the easy road."

Hannah turns to me. "You didn't, when it came to me."

I shrug. She has a point, but I don't really know how to explain it fully. "No," I agree. "I didn't."

She doesn't say much more after that. But when we get into the car, when she's ready and it's time to head to Caleb's, she turns the music up and smiles just a little as she sings along.

"So," I say, trying to pretend like I'm not nervous as all hell when we pull up in front of Caleb's. "What kind of stuff did you leave here?"

"Not much," she says. "A hoodie, a notebook, a water bottle."

"Did you hang out a lot?"

Hannah sighs. "Enough," she says. She pauses, glances at me. We're still on the street, sitting in the idling car. There are trees between Caleb's house and the road, so I'm not super concerned about him seeing us.

"Sometimes," she says, running her fingers along the wheel, "it's just . . . nice to be on equal footing with someone. To know exactly what they want from you. So yeah, I knew Caleb was only interested in hanging out because he wanted to hook up with me, but the simple fact that anyone wanted me after everything . . . well. That was enough, then. And I just thought, my friendship with Liam ended so badly. I couldn't really stand for things to go to hell with Caleb too."

I nod. I get it, in a way. People are confusing. Sometimes it's nice to know what they want, at a base level.

"So no, I didn't want to give him any of those things, but at least it didn't come as a surprise when he asked. Like, it didn't feel like a betrayal, to know that there were deeper feelings on his end. I knew about them, so I could avoid them—it didn't feel like every step was a bomb that I could set off."

I suck in a breath. "Is that how it felt, at the end? With Liam?"

Hannah chooses her words carefully. "If I could have him back in any way, I would, in a heartbeat," she tells me. "But I wish . . . I wish he didn't care about me like he did. I wish there was a way around that, to have him as my friend and that alone. And I feel so fucking shitty every time I think about that, because I'd much rather he be here.

"So maybe I put myself through Caleb because I understood what he wanted, and I could handle it."

"You don't have to explain it to me," I say. "I'm not judging you for whatever you did or didn't do with Caleb or why. I actually have no moral high ground to take here."

She laughs, quick and sharp, surprising me. "God," she mutters, looking out the window. "Maybe we both suck."

"Or we're dealing with things the best we can," I say. "Survival and whatnot."

Hannah sighs. She nods, then turns off the car. We sit a moment longer, in silence, Hannah chewing on her lip and looking up at the house.

"Before you go," I say. "I have . . . a question."

Hannah glances over at me. If there's any way to know if Caleb is involved . . . "I found a hoodie, in the attic at my—Liam's house. It had blood on it. Liam was sure it was Caleb's."

"Ah," Hannah said, looking down at her hands. "That was . . . me. I was wearing it. And I gave it to Ella, after the crash. None of Liam's clothes . . . well. I don't know why I did it, but I needed her to have something that was there with him, at the end."

I nod. It makes a lot more sense than I expect. "And she must've forgotten it."

"Please," Hannah says softly, "do not mail Ella a bloodstained sweatshirt. It's my own—well. She needs to move on too. I was probably misguided leaving it."

"You were doing your best," I say. But at least it explains things—and at least Caleb isn't a murderer. "Want me to come? I don't have to, if you'd rather do it alone, but I can, if you want."

She shakes her head. "I think I need to apologize too," she says. "I don't think some of what I did was fair, to be honest."

I nod. There's no point reading into that statement. If I poke it like a bruise, it will only ache.

Hannah gets out. I text Reece that we're here, and I settle in to wait.

Hannah has a point. Sometimes we don't try to hurt people when we're all here, just trying our best to stay alive. I certainly didn't set out to hurt her when Liam and I started talking to her, and I'm sure she wasn't trying to hurt Caleb with whatever happened between them.

But it's like treading water; sometimes we're flailing so hard to stay above water that we end up taking others down with us, causing bruises that mirror our own. Sometimes it's easier to be around people we understand, even if being around them is worse for everyone. Falling into those patterns is easier than doing the hard thing and getting out.

I hate that I get it. I hate that it makes me think of my mom.

I wish I'd asked Reece for the other notebooks, to have some sort of better understanding of what she was going through, if there's clarity to be gained there at all. If Reece is still here tomorrow, I think it might be worth talking to them about her—they might know if she's still in Pennsylvania. Maybe they are meeting with her after all.

I'm still thinking about that when Hannah gets back in, sniffling less, wearing a hoodie over her dress.

"It wasn't as horrible as it could've been," she says when she catches my look.

"Well, that's good," I say.

Reece responds, *We can come now and wait with you?*

They explained the timelines don't have to be exact for when everyone reconvenes as long as we get to the accident at about the right time. Besides, if we're righting wrongs, it's very possible Hannah would've called for Liam earlier.

"You ready for them?" I ask her.

She sighs. I wonder if the fragile peace between us will be ruptured when Reece and Liam are back. "Yeah," she says. "Let's do this."

It doesn't take long until we see Reece's headlights. There's a small dirt parking lot a little ways down from Caleb's house, so we all head there. Hannah and I switch to Reece's car. Hannah gets in the back seat, where Liam already is, and I slide into the passenger seat.

"We've got some time," Reece says, "but we shouldn't really go anywhere else. So, make yourselves comfortable, I guess."

Hannah snorts. I wonder if she feels like she's in enemy territory right now, and I feel a little bit bad for her.

I grab Reece's phone, already connected to the Bluetooth, and search for some music that Hannah will like. Then I crank it up so it's just slightly too loud for anyone to talk—and in the mirror, I catch the edge of her smile, and the sight of her shoulders sagging with something like relief.

THERE are only about twenty minutes before we have to go, and my stomach is in knots. I have the feeling that we're going to meet our friend again tonight, and I really, *really* am not looking forward to it.

I turn to Reece, in case Hannah still wants her space. "Do you have any more theories on what the Watcher could be? What kind of demon or whatever?"

Reece chews on their lip. "I have theories, yes," is all they say.

I raise an eyebrow. "Care to share with the class?"

Hannah leans over—she does want to be involved, apparently—and Liam too. I turn the volume down a little bit.

"You've seen it before?" Liam asks.

"No," Reece says, shooting both of us looks. "No, I've never seen one. But I do wonder if . . ."

Reece trails off in a way that sometimes means their wheels are turning, and sometimes means they're keeping something from me. I can read my sibling well enough to know that it's the latter.

"What do you wonder?" I ask, pushing.

Reece fiddles with the controls on the dash. "How much did you read of those journals?"

"All of them," I say. "I thought they would be important." I can't say they necessarily *were* important. . . . "Where did you get Mom's? Are there more?"

Reece swallows hard. "She left them," they say. They're not looking at me as they speak, which is not a good sign. "You read the whole thing?"

"Yeah," I say. The realization dawns on me, cold and clear.

There's something in the woods.

"You think she saw one. At the end of the second journal," I realize. "You think that's where she ended the journal."

Reece nods slowly. "I think whatever Liam has attracted is similar to what Mom dealt with when she was handling Grandpa's ghost."

Reality comes screeching to a halt. "Hold on," I say. "What are you talking about?"

Reece looks at me now, a little oddly. "Mom had to deal with Grandpa's ghost," they say. "He died, and there were things he couldn't . . . well. My impression is that Grandpa's ghost came back, and she waited too long to deal with him, but there was something else there that either made things worse or protected him from becoming a husk. It's not really clear, and she never explained what it was, in those journals. We were so little when she left, and I never got to ask. But I think there are too many similarities between them."

Reece's timer goes off—it's time to start driving the path Liam and Hannah drove. Their theory is that if we can stop and pull over safely, we can create an environment where Hannah can say goodbye to Liam, and we can hopefully send him on his way.

But I'm afraid of the Watcher, and I'm chewing over this revelation as Reece follows Liam's instructions and traces the curves of the road.

"Is there any way we can call and ask?" I question. "Like, if Mom has dealt with this before—"

The car jolts—Reece nearly missed a stop sign, and they slam the brakes. They turn to me, pale even in the darkness of the car.

"What?"

"If we just ask—"

"Dree," Reece says, very quietly. They don't move from the stop sign. "Where do you think Mom is?"

I don't know why they're asking me this. Frustrated, I say, "I don't know! She left. I assume she can be anywhere, but if you're right and she's dealt with a Watcher before, it might be worth—"

"Drew." Reece's voice cuts through my spiraling panic. "Mom is dead."

There's a small noise from the back, a sharp breath from Hannah. I stare at Reece, uncomprehending. "No," I say.

"What do you think happened?"

I'm shaking my head, and I know my hands are clenched too tight, but I can't make sense of this. There's no way—there's no way I wouldn't know. No way I wouldn't have discovered it.

"What do you remember?" Reece presses. There's a car behind us, and it honks, so Reece pulls up and then pulls over at the next spot they can. They shouldn't—we have to get to the accident site at the right time, but—

"She put us to bed," I say, my voice barely audible. "She came back to put us to bed. She kissed my forehead. She went to talk to you."

Reece is looking at me sadly, and I *hate* that expression on their face. I hate it, even as I look out the window and see the curling black tendrils moving through the woods.

"That wasn't Mom," Reece says, very quietly. "It was only her ghost."

I suck in a breath. It feels like there's something tightening in my chest—but it also feels like a confirmation of what I've always known. I shake my head. "You're wrong."

"I'm not," Reece says, level, measured. "I'm the one who helped her move on. And in the end—she told me it was better that way. Better to leave, because the alternative was worse."

But it can't be real. "She's not dead," I say, a little stronger. "Dad would—Dad would—"

"Dad doesn't know," Reece says. "And I don't know how she died, or where, or when, really. All I know is she came to say goodbye to us."

I stare at Reece, open-mouthed.

"When her father died," Reece says cautiously, "she grieved so much—she couldn't deal with the ghost. That shadow reminded her every day of what she couldn't handle. So she let him degrade into a husk, and then the shadow ate him, and it was so horrible that she never recovered from it."

I look at Reece, aghast. "That wasn't in the journal."

"I know," they say. "I ripped the pages out before I gave them to you. It gets bad. Really bad. And I couldn't bear you reading it."

From the back, Hannah says quietly, "So she grieved that demon into existence?"

Reece takes a breath. Tears their gaze from mine, and pulls back onto the road. It feels like my entire world is imploding.

"It looks that way," Reece says. "But I don't really know the technicalities."

"Would it be possible for someone not like you to do the same?" Hannah asks.

Reece and I exchange a glance, but I'm not sure how much help I'll be. I could, possibly, be hyperventilating.

"Maybe," Reece allows.

"It was me," Hannah says, the words barely passing through her lips.

I look at Liam, and Liam looks at her, and Reece says, "What do you mean?"

"It has to be me," Hannah says. I glance out the window—and my heart clenches, because the shadows are there, and they are *close*. The Watcher moves through the woods, keeping pace with us, like it's no effort at all. "Whatever happened to your mom—what if I did that to Liam? What if I brought this thing to him?"

Reece and I exchange a glance. I taste bile in my throat—we need to talk about Mom, what they kept from me, but we need to finish this first.

"It's possible," Reece says, following the curves of the road. "I don't know enough to say it's wrong."

I don't recognize where we are; then again, I've never been out here, by Caleb's house, in the space between his house and Hannah's. But this is Hannah's hometown. I wish we'd let her drive, and I hope it's not a disruption to Liam moving on that she isn't. Because she knows this place like the back of her hand, and I'm sure Liam does too. I glance back at him, and he's watching her, his mouth tightening into a thinning line.

At Hannah's direction, Reece turns onto another road, this one narrower and more remote. I'm about to ask where we're going when I see it, up ahead: Just to the side of the road, there's a white cross. Flowers rest at its base.

Hannah takes a breath behind me.

I've never been to the places that hold Liam's death. One of Reece's solutions in their notebook talked about this, about visiting the places where the ghost's death occurred and where their body is contained, but I could never bring myself to do it. For whatever reason, going to the graveyard where part of Liam's ashes were buried or to this place, the place where he died, filled me with a deep sort of dread that I could never move past.

Reece eases on the brakes and pulls to the side of the road. There's a break in the guardrail, like they couldn't bear to fix it, to erase the last moments of a boy who existed here and who died here. It's a sharp bend in the road, and I can see it: If he was going too fast, eager to get Hannah home or somewhere else, worried about her well-being; if they were arguing and she was drunk and he just wanted to move past it; if it was raining all evening and cold that night; if it was the first frost of the year—

I can see it all, in my mind. Him trying to recover. The car going through the guardrail, flipping. Both of them screaming—or maybe he was dead before he could open his mouth. Maybe the car flipped and that was the end and he never even got to rage against the unfairness of it all.

Hannah is out of the car before it's even fully stopped, lurching through that break in the guardrail, and I can't even warn her about the Watcher. I see it lurking through the woods, the tendrils of smoke coagulating into something real, and though there is a husk creeping towards us, the shadows spill over and consume it.

"Go go go," Reece shouts, like I'm not already moving.

Hannah's running, and she *has* to see the tendrils of the Watcher as its body moves through the forest, a shadow as dark as an oil spill. I feel a hand on mine as I lurch out of the car after her, and Liam practically drags me as we race after her into the woods.

Hannah doesn't go far.

She falls to her knees at the base of a tree, new growth green around us, even in the autumn. She's sobbing, shoulders shaking, but I'm not sure what there is for us to do—and there's not much we *can* do.

Because Hannah is not alone for long.

Reece comes up behind me, and we both draw a breath as we watch. The Watcher slithers over the ground, an unsightly spider of tentacles and smoke. Hannah doesn't flinch as one leg races up her spine, then another. She doesn't move as it wraps her in its embrace.

When she turns back to us, enveloped in it, she is more monster than girl.

"It was me," she says again, her voice duplicate, triplicate. "I was the one who called it. Who made it. Right?"

I stare at her, mouth open. I want to warn her away—I'm so afraid that the Watcher will consume her like it did all those husks. But next to me, Reece says, "Yeah." Their voice breaks a little, so they clear their throat. "I think it was you."

Liam doesn't seem to have the same fear we do, even though he's seen this thing consume husks right before our very eyes. He frowns, obviously wary of the Watcher, but he crosses the space between us and Hannah without recoiling.

Her gaze follows him.

And then I realize: *Her gaze follows him.*

Liam lowers himself to the ground in front of her. Reaches up to cup her face. "It wasn't you," he says.

"You don't understand," Hannah says, her voice fracturing, shattering. "I needed you. They called you for me. This road—it doesn't go to your house. It goes to *mine*. You were speeding in the rain, because you thought something was going to happen to *me*."

Liam sweeps the tears away with his thumbs, and I—

I have to watch it, don't I? I have to bear witness, because he witnessed the worst of me. Because she let me inside, she let me see this moment of vulnerability.

So I stand, and I suffer it.

I can barely see Hannah past the murk of the Watcher. It's begun to rain, the drizzle pattering through the trees. Mud seeps through the knees of Hannah's leggings; Liam is unchanged. He will always, forever, be unchanged.

"It is not you," Liam murmurs. "It was never you."

"You are not here right now because of decisions *I made*—"

"I am not here because I'm a terrible driver and the odds were against me," Liam says. He brushes the hair back from her face. "It's not always logical, Hannah. Not everything is causality."

She shudders, another sob racking through her. "It's me now, isn't it?" she asks through tears. "Keeping you?"

Liam closes his eyes. I can read his face—I know him too well now, and something inside of me aches. "Yeah," he says, ragged. "It's you. It's always been you."

Hannah throws her arms around him. Hugs him as tight as she can. "I might've loved you," she says, her voice cracking. "If we had time. Maybe I would've—"

"It's okay," Liam says, just as ragged, "if you never did. If we were only ever this."

"You deserved so much more from me," Hannah says. "You deserved so much more *than* me."

"That's not how it works," Liam murmurs. "I wanted every bit of you I got, and I loved all the pieces I couldn't have." He leans forward, kisses her forehead. It's not romantic—if anything, it's reassurance. "You have to let me go, Han. You can't keep me."

Hannah looks up at him, and I see all the scars that made her into this. The Watcher is fading, second by second—

And so is Liam.

"I know," Hannah says.

"Will you hold my hand?" Liam asks. "For the end?"

She nods, her lip trembling. She reaches down, takes his hands in both of hers. As we watch, Liam flickers again.

"Drew?" Liam asks, not looking at me. "Is this it?"

"Yeah," I say, surprised to find my own voice is rough. I don't try to clear it. "This is it."

He glances over his shoulder, then, and I see him for a flash of who he was instead of this worn-through, sepia version, the remnants of a soul left behind.

"It was good, wasn't it?" he asks me, or Hannah, or both of us.

"Yeah," I say again. Before I can think better of it, I'm there with them, kneeling in the mud. "It was good."

I blink, and Liam is gone.

CHAPTER 26

We're all quiet as we drive back to the place where we left Hannah's car. I don't know, really, what there is to say.

When we pull in behind her car, Hannah gets out. Reece says, "Drew, you should go with her."

"We have things to talk about," I say to Reece. *You didn't tell me Mom was dead.*

They nod. "I know," Reece says. "But I think you need to go with Hannah for right now."

I swallow hard. Nod too. "I'll follow you," Reece says, "and pick you up. Just get her home, okay?"

It's not difficult to convince Hannah that I should drive. As soon as the car door closes behind her, no matter how she tries to hide it, it's obvious she's crying. Obvious she isn't fully in control.

I hate driving, but I'll do it for her.

She doesn't say anything as I pull out, following the road back to her house. She only says directions, for a couple of minutes. I turn on the radio to a low murmur so at least there's background noise.

Finally, Hannah sighs, burying her face in her hands. "I just so desperately wanted there to be a reason," she tells me. "Some other cause, some nefarious thing. I was so desperate for it not to be . . . random. Tragic."

"It's shitty," I agree. "Life is shitty sometimes."

"Life fucking sucks sometimes," Hannah agrees. She drops her head back against the headrest. She's not trying to hide her tears anymore, so they slip down her cheeks, unrestrained. Hannah sighs. "I'm sorry, you know."

"You have literally nothing to apologize for."

She shakes her head. "No. The way I acted when it all went down—that wasn't like me."

I blink at her. "Hannah, the ghost of your dead best friend and I were conspiring to get you to like us."

She laughs, tears coming through in it, but then she sighs. "Yeah," she says finally. "That is pretty shitty."

"It's super shitty, actually," I agree. I turn onto the main road, and I know we're nearly at Hannah's, that this moment is nearly over.

Honestly? I don't know where we go from here.

"And—I *am* sorry, and I do have things to apologize for. I'm sorry any of it went down the way it did."

Hannah bites her lip. "I get it."

"Possibly not, but I appreciate the effort."

She rolls her eyes. "Rin was hard on me, you know. For the way I treated you, when things went downhill."

I wince. "If Rin knew the full story, I think they'd be more judgmental about it too."

"Possibly."

The silence settles between us, but it's not awkward. I look over at her, red-eyed and blotchy-nosed. Her hair is damp, straggly wet clumps of it hanging around her face, and her sweatshirt still has spots of mud on it. She's not wearing makeup, and she looks like she hasn't slept in days.

She's more beautiful than ever. Because this is who Hannah really is, who she always has been. Someone who cares so fiercely, she would rebel against death itself.

I turn down her street. It's quiet, suburbia after midnight, the kind of place it would be nice to raise a family. It's the kind of town where these tragic things aren't supposed to happen.

I park in Hannah's drive. Reece pulls over on the side of the road, waiting for me. Hannah clasps her hands in her lap.

We're quiet for a long time. I turn the car off and let the silence press between us. I'll get out when she does, but I don't want to rush her if she wants to say something.

"Will it be weird, without him?" Hannah asks, surprising me.

I shrug. "It's better this way."

In truth? Yeah. It'll be really weird without him. I know I'm going to miss Liam, and though it doesn't compare to those who loved him, those who actually knew him—it's still going to suck. And a lot of it is my fault, suckiness caused by things that I could've done differently or better, but I guess that doesn't much matter.

Hannah nods. She undoes her seatbelt, the click overloud in the silence of the night. "Thanks for telling me, in the end," she says, her voice shaking. "I wouldn't want to keep him suffering."

He wasn't suffering, I almost say, but it's not quite true. He would've if we'd kept him.

Hannah gets out of the car. I do, too, then hand her keys back after I lock the car. She looks at me for a long moment, studying me as I've never been studied before.

I don't know what I'm waiting for, nor why I'm frozen in place.

"I'll see you around," she says finally, nodding with a weak smile.

"See you later," I tell her. I watch as she goes down the path to her porch, then up the stairs. As she disappears into the house. I watch until the light upstairs turns on, just to know she's safe, and then I turn back to Reece's car.

They ruffle my hair when I lower myself into the passenger seat and cross my arms. "That wasn't your finest work," they say.

"You didn't tell me about Mom."

Reece winces as they turn around at the end of the drive and start back home. "I thought you knew," they say finally. "And I didn't . . . I didn't know how to say it. It's not really something that rolls off the tongue easily. I just thought you had put the pieces together yourself, and there was no way to talk about it with Dr. Tams because she'd report it back to Dad, and if I said, 'Hey I know my mom is dead because I saw her ghost—'"

"I get it," I say, probably too sharply. Maybe I should be mad at myself, because the way Reece says it, it was obvious. It should've been obvious.

But I've never been good at the ghost thing like Reece has. I've never been the most intuitive. I like things to be straightforward, clear-cut. I wish they had done more than hint; I wish they'd just *told* me. I wish we could've gotten through it together.

And there's this new, raw wound in my heart. I'm not sure if it's because I know now that Mom isn't coming back, that there will never be another cycle of terribleness that would at least mean she's alive. It could be guilt, because now I know the reason she never came back—and I know it's not because I wasn't good enough. All those years, and I didn't even look for her. I didn't even *question* it.

I wish, with a heinous twist of irony, that Liam were here to talk about this.

For some reason, that's what does it. I drop my head to my hands, and Reece rubs my back as I ugly cry. They offer soothing noises, but none of it really touches the pain.

When we get home, Dad and Bee are already asleep. Reece lets me take the first shower, and I stand in the spray, waiting for it to stop hurting.

After I'm clean, I crawl into bed and face the wall. When the ache doesn't stop, there's not much else to say. I don't protest when Reece comes into my room after their shower, when they crawl into my bed and turn the light off and curl into my back, like we used to do when we were kids. And they don't protest when I turn into them, bury my head in their shoulder, and cry.

CHAPTER 27

The world does not stop because Liam is gone, because my mom is dead.

When I wake up Sunday, Reece is still there, snoring next to me. I crawl over them and get dressed. I run until my lungs burn, until my legs are numb with cold and exertion. I shower again.

There are no new texts. This is not the kind of loss where someone can send condolences or patch up the bruises. No one would even know to check on me, mourning Liam, and my mom has been dead for years.

The truth is: Life keeps going. And so do I.

Reece and Dad and I have breakfast when I'm back, and I try to smile as Reece and Dad talk about their classes, all the things they are doing to make him proud. He doesn't comment on my quietness; he's so happy to have Reece here, even for a few hours, that it's like he doesn't notice I'm distressed at all, and I can't even find it in myself to be upset about that.

After breakfast, I call Andie. I ask about the camping trip, and listen as she recounts all the things they did, the stuff they saw. I lean into the ache of missing her—and I try to figure out a way to exist in this space of loneliness that doesn't require me to cut everyone out the second they start drifting.

Reece and Dad have plans to spend the afternoon together before they go back to the airport, so I head to Bakerbee. When I get there, Bee is working the register, laughing with a woman as she hands over a to-go cup of coffee.

I go to the side and put on an apron, then start folding boxes. There are never enough boxes, and it's nice to have my hands busy. If Bee wants to stay on and work the register, I'll be happy to stand here and fold boxes for the rest of the shift.

I don't have that luxury. Before long, she leans against the counter next to me, her dark green apron smeared with chocolate ganache and speckled with flour.

"Did you and Reece work things out?" Bee asks quietly. I know what she's really asking: *Did you help Liam move on?*

"Yeah," I say. My voice must not quite sound like me, because Bee frowns. I swallow hard, and then the words are leaving before I can stop them: "Did you know my mom is dead?"

Bee's expression drops. "Oh my god, Drew—baby, no. What happened?"

I shake my head. I can't stop my hands from folding boxes, the repetitive motion the only thing keeping me from crying. "I don't know," I admit. I swallow hard, trying to push the lump away. "It was a long time ago. Reece helped her ghost."

It takes two seconds for Bee to wrestle the boxes out of my hands, and another for her to sweep me into her arms. It doesn't matter that there are people in the café, or if they're looking, or if anyone is waiting for service, because right now, Bee is only focused on me.

"My baby girl," she murmurs into my hair. "I'm so sorry."

I squeeze my eyes shut and fold into her. I won't cry. I refuse. But I let her hold me, and ever so slightly, I feel that ache ebb for the briefest of moments.

AFTER asking a thousand times if I'm okay, Bee lets me stay on shift. She disappears into the back after a while to get a start on the dough for tomorrow, and I drown my sorrows in cleaning. I scrub down the milk fridges and the counters. I'm taking apart the back-up coffee machine for a thorough scrub when someone at the counter says, "Drew?"

I turn—and freeze. Hannah Sullivan is here.

Her eyes are still a bit splotchy, and so is her nose. She wears an oversized hoodie over leggings, her hair pulled up into a messy bun on top of her head. Everyone else has left, so it's just her and me here, and I'm staring at her like a fool.

I set my rag down. "What are you doing here?"

"Would you believe me if I said I came for a coffee and some lemon tart to make myself feel better?"

"Maybe," I hedge. "But that doesn't feel like the whole story."

The corner of her mouth lifts in a smile. "I have an idea," she says.

"What's that?" I ask. My mouth is dry.

She holds out her hand between us. Her fingers are short, hands small. She's got nail polish on, burgundy, chipped from Homecoming. "Hannah Sullivan," she says.

"Hannah, you don't—"

"I hear you're new in town."

I look at her for a long, long moment, but she doesn't shift. Doesn't drop her hand. Doesn't change at all. I'm smiling when I put my hand in hers, and I can't even help it.

"Drew Tarpin," I say. "Nice to meet you."

"Drew," she says. When she wraps her fingers around mine, shaking my hand properly, a chill goes down my spine.

I don't think I made any right decisions. In fact, I think, at every turn, I made the worst decisions possible.

I miss Liam. I wish he were here. I wish, with all my heart, that he weren't dead.

I wish I knew what happened to my mom, and that it didn't hurt so much to know that she's gone—I don't know how to process any of it, and I think I will probably need to talk to Dad and get working on even more years of therapy.

"I want to start over," she says. She doesn't drop my hand. "I'm sorry if we got off on the wrong foot—my best friend died, you see, and it's been difficult for me."

"I understand completely," I say, sinking back into it. "And I have a tendency to pretend to be someone I'm not. But I'd like to show you who I am—the real me, if you're up for it."

Hannah grins, but even that doesn't fully cover the grief. I know that this is who she is, scars and all, grief and all. "I'm up for it," she says.

ACKNOWLEDGEMENTS

Dear reader, this one was a doozy to get through. It's a messy book with messy people, and to make it coherent, I needed quite a lot of people to ensure *I* wasn't messy.

Lauren, my fearless editor: Thank you for everything you did to make this book exist. The number of existential crises I had over it hit a new high, and I am so grateful to you for dealing with every single one.

To my team at Page Street: Thank you so much for what you've done for this book (and all others). I wouldn't be here without you. Thank you to Emma Hardy and Rosie Stewart for the cover design and direction, and to Sarah Rain for the gorgeous artwork. Thank you, also, to Kumari Pacheco, Jane Horovitz, and Shannon Dolley.

To the agents who worked on this project: Uwe and Amelia, I appreciate you so much for taking this pitch and proposal and helping me to shape it into a coherent idea. Maddy, thanks for helping to take it over the line (and for talking me off the ledge during the final week of deadline, when everything was hard). To Valentina, thank you for bringing this book to new readers around the world. To the entire team at Madeleine Milburn, thank you for your support for this project.

To my publishing teams around the world: Leo, I'm so grateful for the support you and the team at Umbriel have shown this book.

To my beloved friends: Tasha, Georgia, Karin, Alice, and Nadia—this book would not have been completed without the group chat. Love you all, and thanks for dragging me, kicking and screaming, over the line. Thanks to all of my other insightful and wonderful friends who were open to discussing this project and helping me work through the snarls in the plot. Thanks, always, to Becca, for getting me through.

To my students: This book was incredibly hard to write, partially because the emotions were so deeply tied up in the loss of one of you. I hope you continue working on the difficult projects, even when they hurt.

To my family, related by blood and marriage and wherever I found you on the streets: I love you. Thank you for your support. There is so much of you in this one—your love, your support, and the trials we went through as a family. It was a relief, for once, to write a book with a super supportive family that mirrored the love I have for my own. Parents, thank you for being here as I fought my way through another book. Lex, you're the best sister anyone could ask for, even when we're stubborn and evil to one another.

This book deals with topics like addiction, grief, and trauma. I wish I could say this wasn't firsthand experience—I wish my cousins were still around, and that they could watch their kids grow up. Robert and Justin, I miss you, and I'm sorry. I wish things were different, and I wish it didn't still hurt so much.

To Sir Gordon (feline, loud, indignant) and Wynne (canine, larger than Gilly in size but not spirit): Thanks for (occasionally) sitting on or in proximity to me while I was working on this, when everyone else was asleep.

To Matt: Thank you for supporting this book, even when it made me stay up way, *way* too late, or question my own sanity.

And finally, to my readers: Thank you for following me here. I appreciate you, every step of the way.

ABOUT THE AUTHOR

TORI BOVALINO (she/her) is the author of multiple horror novels, including *My Throat an Open Grave*, and the editor of the Indie-bestselling anthology *The Gathering Dark*. Tori also writes adult fantasy as V.L. Bovalino. She is originally from Pittsburgh, Pennsylvania and now lives in the UK with her partner, their very loud cat, and their puppy. She holds a PhD in English and splits her non-writing time between publishing and academia. Tori loves scary stories, obscure academic book facts, and impractical, oversized sweaters. She can be found on Instagram as @toribovalino.

For more fantastic fiction, author events,
exclusive excerpts, competitions, limited editions and more

VISIT OUR WEBSITE
titanbooks.com

LIKE US ON FACEBOOK
facebook.com/titanbooks

FOLLOW US ON TWITTER AND INSTAGRAM
@TitanBooks

EMAIL US
readerfeedback@titanemail.com